DOUBLE OR NOTHING

DOUBLE OR NOTHING

a
real fictitious
discourse

b
y

Raymond   Federman

THE SWALLOW PRESS INC.

CHICAGO

First Edition

Published by
The Swallow Press Incorporated
1139 South Wabash Avenue
Chicago, Illinois   60605

ISBN 0-8040-0543-5
LIBRARY OF CONGRESS CATALOG CARD NUMBER 71-171875

Ce qui est dit n'est jamais dit puisqu'on peut le dire autrement

Robert Pinget

for   S
           T
           E
        R V
S I M O N E
        B
     J I M
        N

THIS IS NOT THE BEGINNING

Once upon a time (two or three weeks ago), a rather stubborn and determined middle-aged man decided to record (for posterity), exactly as it
happened, word by word and step by step, the story of another man (for indeed what is GREAT in man is that he is a bridge and not a goal), a somewhat paranoiac fellow (unmarried, unattached, and quite irresponsible), who
had decided to lock himself in a room (a furnished room with a private bath,
cooking facilities, a bed, a table, and at least one chair), in New York City, for a year (365 days to be precise), to write the story of another person -- a shy young man about 19 years old -- who, after the war (the Second
World War), had come to America (the land of opportunities) from France under
the sponsorship of his uncle -- a journalist, fluent in five languages -- who
himself had come to America from Europe (Poland it seems, though this was not
clearly established) sometime during the war after a series of rather gruesome
adventures, and who, at the end of the war, wrote to the father (his cousin by
marriage) of the young man whom he considered as a nephew, curious to know if
he (the father) and his family had survived the German occupation, and indeed
was deeply saddened to learn, in a letter from the young man -- a long and touching letter written in English, not by the young man, however, who did not
know a damn word of English, but by a good friend of his who had studied English
in school -- that his parents (both his father and mother) and his two sisters
(one older and the other younger than he) had been deported (they were Jewish)
to a German concentration camp (Auschwitz probably) and never returned, no doubt
having been exterminated deliberately (X * X * X * X), and that, therefore, the
young man who was now an orphan, a displaced person, who, during the war, had
managed to escape deportation by working (VERY HARD) on a farm in Southern France,
would be happy and grateful to be given the opportunity to come to America (that
GREAT country he had heard so much about and yet knew so little about) to start
a new life, possibly go to school, learn a trade, and become a good, loyal citizen.

Now the first person (the stubborn and determined middle-aged man) simply wanted to record, to the best of his ability and as objectively as possible, but for reasons that were never clearly stated (man is indeed inexplicable), the activities of the second person (the irresponsible paranoiac fellow who, incidentally, was also an inveterate gambler) as he planned -- the day before he was to enter the room (this is important) -- projected, calculated, and determined what he would need in the room (for 365 days) such as food, toilet articles, writing material, and so on, in order to survive and write the story of the young man who had come to America from France (by boat) and who had had such a ROUGH time during the war and was now an orphan. Basically, this did not present any major problems for the first person since he was merely to be the recorder, the designer, the scribbler as it were of the second person's story, though it should be pointed out immediately that this first person had very little experience in such matters, and that, in fact, he was a poor recorder, a lousy designer, a weak scribbler, and that on top of that he was a very bad typist, but, and that is the essential in matters such as these, he was stubborn and determined. For him, therefore, it was simply a matter of keeping track of, and keeping up with the activities, thoughts, decisions, and indecisions of the second person (however incoherent these might be) as HE (the second person) noodled around (if one may use such an expression) -- the day before he was to enter the room, this should be emphasized -- in order to ascertain what he would need in the room (besides the bed, the table, and the one chair) to survive, while at the same time organizing (conditionally of course) in his mind (and eventually on paper) the elements of the story he wanted to write (about the shy young man who was so inexperienced in the American-way-of-life), and decide also how he was going to compose and write that story in some coherent and artistic form. In other words, for the first person, it was just a matter of patience and determination, a matter, so to speak, of being able to keep up with the second person, and of course, this

is understood, of trying to be as faithful and as precise as possible in
his recording of the second person's activities, however messed up, screwed
up, chaotic these might be, for indeed, as it was once said: "One must have
chaos in one to give birth to a dancing star." Or better still: "What but
an imperfect sense of humor could have made such a mess of chaos."

As for the second person, the one who suffers paranoia, the gambler,
the one who has decided <u>to lock</u> himself in the room for 365 days, his task
is much more difficult than that of the first person. First of all, he has
to establish some sort of schedule for his creative activities, and then he
has to plan (carefully) the details of his survival in the room, and this
with rather limited means (the sum of approximately 1200 dollars and some
change which -- and this is never to be clarified -- he has won gambling in
Los Angeles or Las Vegas, he has possibly stolen, borrowed, or perhaps even
saved -- penny by penny -- though the last is quite unlikely), and furthermore, he has to invent (and tell of course) the story of the young man, word
by word and step by step, describing, for instance, in details and obviously
realistically, the journey across the Atlantic Ocean, the love affair the
young man had on the boat with a girl from Milwaukee, the arrival of the boat
in New York, the encounter of the young man with his uncle on the pier (he had
never met his uncle before), the subway ride with his suitcase and his uncle
in what can be called THE BELLY OF AMERICA as they went from the pier to the
Bronx to visit a Jewish family (possibly relatives of the uncle) who then
asked them to stay for dinner, and beyond that everything else that will or
may happen to the young man during his first year in America. Originally,
the second person thought he would cover the first five years of the young
man's life in America, but eventually, for obvious reasons (man is indeed
unpredictable), he decided to limit himself to the first year only so as to
have "the time of the story" correspond "to his 365 days in the room" (why
this should be so will probably never be clarified), particularly the period

in Detroit where the uncle took his nephew after a few days sightseeing in
New York City. His problems (the second person, the inventor, the noodler)
are, in a sense, double because he has to work out (mentally and physically)
all the details of what he needs in the room (within the limits of his rather
limited means), and at the same time invent, or at least organize in one way
or another, the details of what he is going to write once he has locked himself in the room -- assuming of course he can find the kind of room he needs
on the basis of his limited budget. Moreover, what makes his situation more
difficult, more critical, is that he plans the whole thing, the whole under-
taking, on the 30th of September, that is to say the day before he is to enter
the room (he has decided that he will enter the room on October 1st, and that
nothing -- yes NOTHING -- will interfere with his plans, for indeed there are
too many men who scatter words in advance of their deeds, and always do less
than they promise, but not him). The only way then he can possibly solve this
complex double problem is to start at the beginning, deal with the question of
the room first, and then keep going, as best and as fast as he can, with all
the other details of his survival: food, toilet articles, writing material,
and so on, and the elements of the story he wants to write; but most important, in order for him to succeed, is to avoid (at all cost) talking about his
own life, or better yet to forget about himself completely (at least until he
and his invention converge and merge), so as to better concentrate on the life
of the young man who, certainly, has had a much more interesting life than the
second person. In other words, for the second person, the unattached, paranoiac,
irresponsible gambler, it is a matter of coping (in spite of his paranoia) with
the difficult and critical task he has undertaken, for he knows that he loses
nothing (NOTHING!) when he loses his time (or his life).

Now the third person, the young man who is going to come to America (from
France) and who is very SHY and Jewish and naive, he does not have anything to do

(at first) except wait for the second person to get started with HIS story,
wait and see how he is going to be invented, told, composed, and eventually
written as he and his story unfold during his first year in America. All he
has to do, in fact, is submit to the second person's imagination and sense
of organization as he (the inventor) invents, projects, organizes, composes,
and (eventually) writes everything that will happen to him. His only concern,
therefore, is to be created (artistically), or better yet to be granted a role
(a meaningful role) in this intramural setup, to be described (coherently) by
the second person, and to some extent to be scribbled (precisely), recorded
(faithfully), and so on, by the first person, though it should be pointed out
here that this first person had no intention of interfering (orally, physically,
manually) with the activities of the second person. However, if eventually, for
personal reasons (man is indeed free to choose his own destiny, free to propose
and dispose), the third person (the shy young man) is not satisfied with the way
the second person is writing him, or what he is saying about him (and by simple
extension how the first person is recording him), then he might (quite possibly)
disagree with him, argue with him, and even try to convince him to change the
way his story is being told, shaped, written (and beyond that scribbled, designed,
and recorded). For indeed the speed of thought is not superior to that of speech!
But all this is, of course, strictly hypothetical since the young man (very unsure
of himself) has really no voice, at least initially -- ultimately he may have a
partial voice -- in the activities of the second person (but none, that's quite
obvious, in the recording of the first person). In other words, he is NOTHING
in the double setup, the interplay between the first and second person; as a
matter of fact, unless the second person invents him, and the first person records him, he will never become anything, he will always remain non-existent
(a BLOB in somebody's imagination), and of course neither the girl from Milwaukee,
nor the uncle, nor the girl in the subway, nor the Jewish family in the Bronx,

nor any of the other people who might have entered into the story, nor
anything else that would have happened to him (the poor young man) during his first year in America will ever be told

scribbled
written
and

recorded.

Therefore.

It is essential indeed that the second person allows nothing to interfere with his plans (however irresponsible these might be), and that
the first person persists in his stubborn and determined recording,
and that finally the third person do nothing, nothing but wait to
see what will happen to him and to the others who are involved
with him.

Meanwhile.

A short (double) poetic statement might be in order at this point:

    REFLECTION

    Forging
    with my (his) hands
    from the experiences
    of my (his) skin
    a mask for reality
    Carving
    in my (his) bones
    a meaning for life
    I (he) heard something whispered
    and my (his) fingers burned
    at the touch of flesh
    Quickly
    I (he) denied the dreams
    of my (his) father
    reshaped my (his) memories
    to convenient usage
    and stood
    almost a winner
    Slowly
    settling into lethargy
    when a clumsy gesture
    destroyed the illusion.

Now some people might say that this situation is not very encouraging...

but one must reply that it is not meant to encourage those who say that.

                                                                    t
                                                                    e
                                                                    v
And this is why the FIRST PERSON -- the recorder   o
                                  the scribbler   b
                                  the middleaged man, as established a

simply sat down one day (two or three weeks ago) and started recording

-- as best he could -- the activities of the SECOND PERSON and kept at

it full speed, scribbling faithfully
                          stubbornly and exactly as it happened   step
                                                                    by
                                                                   step

everything that person was doing, saying, thinking, planning, calculating, organizing, inventing, composing, anticipating, projecting, writing, ETC, even though much of it appeared totally incoherent, illogical, gratuitous, fragmented, all loused up, messed up, zero, irrational, unreadable, irresponsible, unpublishable, full of errors, bad, ETC

Nevertheless
the FIRST PERSON recorded it all, as it was, as it were, as it happened.

                                                                    t
                                                                    e
                                                                    v
                                                                    o
                                                                    b
While   a
the SECOND PERSON struggled, day after day, to solve
                                      to resolve, as pointed out

this double problem simultaneously and with very limited means on hand

since (and this will be clarified eventually) before locking himself i

n the room to write the story of the not-yet-invented THIRD PERSON who

was to come soon to America from France he had to cope with the prepar

ation -- if one may use that term -- of his survival in the room while

at the same T I M E think   ahead
                           plan
                        calculate
                        anticipate - and so on - what he was going t
                        WOULD UP SET WHOLE THE ELSE OR ABOUT WRITE O
                        fall a--part   ←
                        be use--less
                        & hope--less
                        & make him even more paranoiac
                        t h a n   b e f o r e   &
                        f o r e v e r   &   e v e r

THEREFORE the best thing for him to do was to start
at the beginning wherever that might be allow nothi
ng to interfere with his plans and keep going howev
er incoherent irrational all screwed up and so on w
hat he was doing became for indeed as an inveterate
gambler that he was why should he be ashamed when t
he dice or the cards fall in his favor and why shou
ld he ask himself AM I A DISHONEST PLAYER since fro
m the beginning he is willing to succumb if not imm
ediately at least eventually for indeed having deci
ded on the 30th of September the day after he arriv
ed in New York City by bus from Los Angeles or some
other place with what was left of his original 1200
dollars or so to lock himself in a room the next da
y October 1st he had very little time indeed to get
the room and all the things he needed in the room t
o survive and compose the damn story he wanted to w
rite ready on time and at the same time decide what
he was going to write how he was going to write and
finish eventually the story of the young man and wh
at that story would be all about while obviously th
e young man whose story was going to be written and
recorded though not yet written and recorded or for
that matter not even yet invented had nothing to do
but wait and see what would happen to him and to hi
s life when he arrived in AMERICA screwed the beaut
iful girl from Milwaukee on the boat met his old un
cle on the pier went with him by subway to the Bron
x and on the way sat across from a beautiful tall a
nd slim negro girl whose legs were widely spread ap

art so that he got all excited and by the time he arrived with his uncle at

the apartment of the Jewish people he and his uncle were visiting in the Br

onx he locked himself in the bathroom down the corridor a few minutes after

they had arrived to jerk off a good one feeling sorry for himself wondering

sadly what would happen to him as he waited to see how he and his story wer

e going to develop be handled by the SECOND PERSON his creator his maker an

d finally how the FIRST PERSON would record them artistically for POSTERITY

----

this is then how it all started at the beginning just like that once upon a
time two or three weeks ago with the first person recording what the second
person was doing as he planned the way he was going to lock himself for one
year in a room to write the story of the third person all of them ready anx
ious to be to go to exist to invent to write to record to survive to become

----

It all began at the beginning: stubbornly and determinedly on the part
of the first person   (number one)

paranoiacally and confusedly on the part
of the second person   (number two)

shyly and with some reservations on the
part of the third person (number three)

It all started just before number two entered the room (the day before to be

exact) when he said to himself: JUST THINK ... FOR INSTANCE ...

just like that!

A very simple straight forward statement

which was immediately recorded by number one while number three awaited his

fate in the hollow of his fate not thinking or saying anything at all. From

that point on number two was on his own: JUST THINK ... FOR INSTANCE ...

That's exactly what was   thought
    exactly   said
    exactly   written
    exactly   recorded For indeed the three of them agreed:

Here all is clear ... No all is not clear ... But the discourse
must go on ... So one invents obscurities ... R H E T O R I C .

FOOTNOTE: It should be noted here that overlooking the whole intramural
set up described in the preceding pages obviously there has t
o be a fourth person Someone to control organize supervise if
you wish the activities and relations of the other three pers
ons Someone who can keep things going in an orderly manner wh
o can resolve arguments smooth out difficulties Someone who l
ike a father or like a supervisor but not necessarily like an
inventor The second person is the inventor nor like a recorde
r That function belongs to the first person And of course not
like a protagonist The third person will fit into that role e
ventually But someone who can be called an overall looker who
has no creative power of his own but who is simply here and n
ot here above aside beside and of course underneath the whole
set up and who is to a great extent responsible and not respo
nsible for what is going on and what is going to go on And th
erefore even though he may or may not be real and may never b
e heard and his presence never felt nonetheless is implied an
d implicit in the discourse Or else the question can be asked
how is unity created between the three persons involved in th
is story which is about to begin if someone is not hidden som
ewhere in the background omnipresent omnipotent and omniscien
t to control direct dictate a behavior to the three other unf
ortunate beings And of course to write and present the preced
ing pages which obviously cannot possibly have been written b
y any of the three persons involved in what will follow short
ly that is to say the REAL FICTITIOUS DISCOURSE now to begin.

```
noodlesnoodlesnoodlesnoodlesnoodlesnoodlesnoodlesnoodlesnoodlesnoodlesnoodles
noodlesnoodlesnoodlesnoodlesnoodlesnoodlesnoodlesnoodlesnoodlesnoodlesnoodles
noodlesnoodlesnoodlesnoodlesnoodlesnoodlesnoodlesnoodlesnoodlesnoodlesnoodles
noodlesnoodlesnoodlesnoodlesnoodles          noodlesnoodlesnoodlesnoodlesnoodles
noodlesnoodlesnoodlesnoodlesnoodles          noodlesnoodlesnoodlesnoodlesnoodles
noodlesnoodlesnoodlesnoodlesnoodles          noodlesnoodlesnoodlesnoodlesnoodles
noodlesnoodlesnoodlesnoodlesnoodles          noodlesnoodlesnoodlesnoodlesnoodles
noodlesnoodlesnoodlesnoodles                      noodlesnoodlesnoodlesnoodles
noodlesnoodlesnoodlesnoodles                      noodlesnoodlesnoodlesnoodles
noodlesnoodlesnoodlesnoodles                      noodlesnoodlesnoodlesnoodles
noodlesnoodlesnoodlesnoodlesnoodles          noodlesnoodlesnoodlesnoodlesnoodles
noodlesnoodlesnoodlesnoodlesnoodles          noodlesnoodlesnoodlesnoodlesnoodles
noodlesnoodlesnoodlesnoodlesnoodles          noodlesnoodlesnoodlesnoodlesnoodles
noodlesnoodlesnoodlesnoodlesnoodles          noodlesnoodlesnoodlesnoodlesnoodles
noodlesnoodlesnoodlesnoodlesnoodlesnoodlesnoodlesnoodlesnoodlesnoodlesnoodlesnoodles
noodlesnoodlesnoodlesnoodlesnoodlesnoodlesnoodlesnoodlesnoodlesnoodlesnoodlesnoodles
noodlesnoodlesnoodlesnoodlesnoodlesnoodlesnoodlesnoodlesnoodlesnoodlesnoodlesnoodles
noodlesnoodlesnoodlesnoodles              noodlesnoodlesnoodlesnoodles
noodlesnoodlesnoodlesnoodlesn            snoodlesnoodlesnoodlesnoodles
noodlesnoodlesnoodlesnoodlesno          esnoodlesnoodlesnoodlesnoodles
noodlesnoodlesnoodlesnoodlesnoo        lesnoodlesnoodlesnoodlesnoodles
noodlesnoodlesnoodlesnoodlesnood      dlesnoodlesnoodlesnoodlesnoodles
noodlesnoodlesnoodlesnoodlesnoodl    odlesnoodlesnoodlesnoodlesnoodles
noodlesnoodlesnoodlesnoodlesnoodle  oodlesnoodlesnoodlesnoodlesnoodles
noodlesnoodlesnoodlesnoodlesnoodles  noodlesnoodlesnoodlesnoodlesnoodles
noodlesnoodlesnoodlesnoodlesnoodlesn  snoodlesnoodlesnoodlesnoodlesnoodles
noodlesnoodlesnoodlesnoodlesnoodlesno  esnoodlesnoodlesnoodlesnoodlesnoodles
noodlesnoodlesnoodlesnoodlesnoodlesnoo lesnoodlesnoodlesnoodlesnoodlesnoodles
noodlesnoodlesnoodlesnoodlesnoodlesnoodlesnoodlesnoodlesnoodlesnoodlesnoodlesnoodles
noodlesnoodlesnoodlesnoodlesnoodlesnoo lesnoodlesnoodlesnoodlesnoodlesnoodles
noodlesnoodlesnoodlesnoodlesnoodlesno  esnoodlesnoodlesnoodlesnoodlesnoodles
noodlesnoodlesnoodlesnoodlesnoodlesn  snoodlesnoodlesnoodlesnoodlesnoodles
noodlesnoodlesnoodlesnoodlesnoodles  noodlesnoodlesnoodlesnoodlesnoodles
noodlesnoodlesnoodlesnoodlesnoodle  oodlesnoodlesnoodlesnoodlesnoodles
noodlesnoodlesnoodlesnoodlesnoodl    odlesnoodlesnoodlesnoodlesnoodles
noodlesnoodlesnoodlesnoodlesnood      dlesnoodlesnoodlesnoodlesnoodles
noodlesnoodlesnoodlesnoodlesnoo        lesnoodlesnoodlesnoodlesnoodles
noodlesnoodlesnoodlesnoodlesno          esnoodlesnoodlesnoodlesnoodles
noodlesnoodlesnoodlesnoodlesn            snoodlesnoodlesnoodlesnoodles
noodlesnoodlesnoodlesnoodles              noodlesnoodlesnoodlesnoodles
noodlesnoodlesnoodlesnoodlesnoodlesnoodlesnoodlesnoodlesnoodlesnoodlesnoodlesnoodles
noodlesnoodlesnoodlesnoodlesnoodlesnoodlesnoodlesnoodlesnoodlesnoodlesnoodlesnoodles
noodlesnoodlesnoodlesnoodlesnoodlesnoodlesnoodlesnoodlesnoodlesnoodlesnoodlesnoodles
noodlesnoodlesnoodlesnoodlesnoodlesnoodlesnoodlesnoodlesnoodlesnoodlesnoodlesnoodles
noodlesnoodlesnoodlesnoodlesnoodlesnoodlesnoodlesnoodlesnoodlesnoodlesnoodlesnoodles
noodlesnoodlesnoodlesnoodlesnoodlesnoodlesnoodlesnoodlesnoodlesnoodlesnoodlesnoodles
noodlesnoodlesnoodlesnoodlesnoodlesnoodlesnoodlesnoodlesnoodlesnoodlesnoodlesnoodles
noodlesnoodlesnoodlesnoodles                      noodlesnoodlesnoodlesnoodles
noodlesnoodlesnoodlesnoodles                      noodlesnoodlesnoodlesnoodles
noodlesnoodlesnoodlesnoodles                      noodlesnoodlesnoodlesnoodles
noodlesnoodlesnoodlesnoodlesnoodlesnoodlesnoodlesnoodlesnoodlesnoodlesnoodlesnoodles
noodlesnoodlesnoodlesnoodlesnoodlesnoodlesnoodlesnoodlesnoodlesnoodlesnoodlesnoodles
noodlesnoodlesnoodlesnoodlesnoodlesnoodlesnoodlesnoodlesnoodlesnoodlesnoodlesnoodles
noodlesnoodlesnoodlesnoodlesnoodlesnoodlesnoodlesnoodlesnoodlesnoodlesnoodlesnoodles
noodlesnoodlesnoodlesnoodlesnoodlesnoodlesnoodlesnoodlesnoodlesnoodlesnoodlesnoodles
noodlesnoodlesnoodlesnoodlesnoodlesnoodlesnoodlesnoodlesnoodlesnoodlesnoodlesnoodles
noodlesnoodlesnoodlesnoodlesnoodlesnoodlesnoodlesnoodlesnoodlesnoodlesnoodlesnoodles
```

B E G I N N I N G

Just think

for instance

      if the room costs 8 dollars
             8 dollars a week

      then it'll have to be noodles
            noodles then it is

Imagine that!

In matters such as these there's much food for thought
                 undoubtedly

Another guy would say there's little food.............

That's his business!

      If the room costs 8 bucks it'll have to be

    (for 6 bucks   could eat better
         7 even   survive

           on the edge of the white p
                         r
                         e
                         i
                         p
                         i
                         c
                         e

    feet first).

Just think

      a little piece of meat PERHAPS here and there
      - canned meat -- it's better than NOTHING.
      So many guys starving in the world!

      But 8 dollars a week   that's 52 times 8
                    52 times 8 makes 416

Imagine that   416
        dollars just for a room
            but the room is important
              extremely IMPORTANT

Left margin (bottom to top): IS HIS BUSINESS BUT IF THE ROOM COSTS 8 DOLLARS THEN UNDOUBTEDLY IT WILL HAVE TO BE NOODLES NOODLES

Right margin (top to bottom): IT WILL HAVE TO BE NOODLES NOODLES THEN IT IS IMAGINE THAT IN MATTERS SUCH AS THESE THERE IS MUCH FOOD

Noodles too
Noodles   by themselves: a complete food -- contains all sorts of good things --

But the room of course is more important though a room
                                     a room without food is useless
                                     with   a large window
                                     with   a view

that's essential.

Who gives a damn about the garbage (cans) in the yard and the grey sky. NO!
                                                             RIDICULOUS!

A view on the street   HUGE white HOLE and you fall (in) d
                                                              o
                                                              w
                                                              n

that's better.

So many rooms all over many without views but this time it's different:

        8 bucks a week for a room
        6   that's what it should be
                  that's what it was last time   (NO!   9)

        52 times 6 makes only 312
                            312 for a room that's almost half (almost human)
                                             not quite

A ROOM not just a room to sleep (in) to take craps (in) jerk off (in) hide (in)
feel sorry for yourself (in) A ROOM with a meaning to sleep (in) only when you'
re tired......
                 Eventually a symbol: | R |

                 A working room and a piece of blue sky perhaps   without the room
                                                           it's useless
                                                             hopeless
            particularly at times like these.

So many words ---- A N   E N O R M O U S   G A P ---- A   H O L E ----

So many joints in one's life. Just hope there's no bugs in this one
                                          rats even worse scares
the shit out of me   rats with long trailing tails
at night you dream they come to nibble your ears
                              your nose   gives me the creeps.

Who cares
Who cares about the furniture as long as there's a chair and a table
                                       a working table
                                          a table to work on
of course   the wall paper is important _too_.
                 So many crummy wall papers in one's life:

uninteresting shitty unexciting unimaginative even plain white wall paper...

This time it'll be tremendous: HORSES ALL OVER -- yes! flying horses (⅄ ⅄ ⅄).

Brown on white.   Could help through the rough days
                                    moments of panic.   The horses brown the
                                                           background white   -

Bet by the time you're out of there will know exactly how many of them there
are flying all over the walls in some places of course will have to put some
of the pieces together - in corners at the bottom and at the top of the wall
- Horses all over - near the ceiling - but as long as you've got four legs -
four legs and a tail make a horse - you'll have a horse - one must work that
out of course - slowly.

What a stroke of luck after all these years. Here it goes: DOUBLE OR NOTHING!

Could have lost your pants did you think of that?
It's obvious
Surely one thinks of that (quickly) anybody would.   And living it up now
                                                               living
                                                          the time of noodles.

Could call it that: A TIME OF NOODLES

                              A TIME OF MACARONI   (!)

Noodles is better simply noodles that's not bad better in French though
(when they translate it) LE TEMPS DES NOUILLES (wouldn't do it myself).

Tremendous   Could have him do the same eventually locks himself in a room
for 365 days or if you prefer 52 weeks (but days are better) locks himself UP
with his life -
              it's
                   the
                      only
                         way
                            to
                              do
                                it - all that crap about doing

it at night staying up all night it never works you fall asleep night after night
and then you're forty (41-42-43) and it's too late and nobody believes you any mo
re and your hair is falling and your hands are trembling and you're all fucked up
day after day night after night sliding down the white precipice   of
course everything has to be planned in advance to the last detail
                                        to the last penny

                              goes hand in hand.

It's going to be TOUGH
              tomorrow
              tomorrow morning   October 1st
and that's it   let's say you begin on   October 1st
                 put the date on the first page one never knows that's for sure:

-- How long did you work on it?   (They'll ask for sure).
-- One year.
-- Only a year!
-- Just about. 365 days to be exact (got to be precise).
-- Remarkable! Unbelievable! Only a year! (That's the way to go).
-- Yes...

Yes.   You see only 365 boxes...It's not unusual...You see Stendhal wrote
LA CHARTREUSE DE PARME in 63 days (that's something)...Think it was 63 or
maybe it was 66...At least that's what they claim...

— Who?

   WHO CARES‼

October 1st and goodby world goodby people society and the little guy in

the street and the big guy in the big room and all the rest goodby fresh

air in the street in the parks in the country in we GO
                                        GO ahead.

              Could call it   A STATE OF SIEGE

                                         SIEGE IN A ROOM (‼)

You start just like that: Yesterday he arrived in New York. Sounds like
                              Yesterday my mother died......Or was it today?

                              Almost the same. No got to start before that.

On the boat with New York somewhere in the background
                                        out   there————————————→

        It's morning in New York it's always morning in New York when
        you arrive when you come back never fails you always come bac
        k to New York by train by boat by plane on foot bicycle autom
        obile bus of course he doesn't know that the first time it is
        not possible
        It's morning in New York people are awakening slowly and gett
        ing up and getting dressed and so on intheircrummylittlerooms
        and cursing the new day and feeling sorry for themselves most
        of the time
        He's got to think ahead be afraid a little anticipate with ap
        prehension the worse but hope for the best
        It's foggy in New York that morning you know the kind of grey
        fog that gets you after a while the kind that drips from ever
        ything like soapy water from everywhere the kind that makes y
        ou say whatafuckingweather
        He's got to be really scared in the beginning it's very impor
        tant it's a damn important moment in his life he doesn't know
        that but he thinks about it (but no sentimentality) in his ow
        n shy way he's about 19

Tomorrow morning that's it you enter into the nights of your skull (somebody

has to do it) into the chambers of the mind (just like that) (NO KIDDING) it

has to be told straight though without tears THE TRUTH because one can never

expose only that which at a certain moment can become present can manifest i

tself that which can show itself present itself as a present a being-present

in its truth the truth of a present or the presence of the present (correct)
                                        therefore
                                        GOODBY WORLD !

gggooooooodddbbbyyy   I SHALL NOT SERVE THAT IN WHICH I NO LONGER BELIEVE

whether it calls itself myself my race my country A
                                                  M
                                                  E
                                                  R
                                                  I
                                                  C
(you can bet on that even if it doesn't work)!   A

correct.   416 dollars.   imagine!

Should make a list (quick) before I forget And the wall paper Nice wall paper
Horses all over And the sixth floor nothing less Won't take anything less NO
reasons It's higher than the fifth floor That's for sure Gives you the sense
of being way up at the top before falling into the stinking white nothing Feet
first without speech SPEECHLESS Dammit!
                         Dammit is right That extra 2 bucks (even one
could have made a difference) could have helped Didn't think of that NO didn't
think of anything Didn't even give a damn at first Nor figure on that   (Even
during the trip on the bus And what a trip) Figured on 6 all the time
                                        6 never 8   not even
                                        7 or 6.50   nothing

SOME GUYS ARE DREAMERS
SOME GUYS ARE REALISTS

But 6 bucks for a room TODAY who gets that kind of a room   :

queersshitheadsliarscommunistsbumsdumbbastardsfakersmaniacsanarchistsjewsqueers

        Like that filthy stinking room in Detroit (in the beginning)
        must use that when he arrives in Detroit with the same furni
        ture the bed in the right corner one chair and a table in fr
        ont of the window only one window exactly the way it was and
        the crummy wall paper plain white without anything on it shi
        tty ugly wall paper uninteresting boring lonely sick looking
        WALL PAPER

That one cost even less: 5 bucks if you remember correctly
                         REMEMBER   the smell
                                             the stairs
                                             the old lady
                                             the bed bugs
(who can work in these conditions?)

8 times 52
work from that   What a blow!

Noodles next   (got to be)!   N O O D L E S   :

macaronispaghettielbowsmanicottishellsspearsspiralsflatroundcurlysquaremacaroni

        Variety that's the spice of life Though after a while it ge
        ts repetitious A guy must vary if he wants to survive Must
        invent Let it happen by itself Let the damn thing shape it
        self by itself Create new forms New noodles Improvise any
        thing Improvise on a puff of smoke QUICKLY And keep going

DO SOME RESEARCH :   copy add multiply cut quote steal invent transform
manipulate reduce turn type note lie write rewrite
cite smoke a cigarette cut your nails blow your no
se watch the flies keep going reshape remake throw
it away step on it eat it up chew it down crap out

---

each one hundred grams of that stuff contains approximately
5.1021 milligrams of sodium imagine that the average serving of this product no kidding when cooked contains approximately 1.52 milligrams without exaggerating of sodium there
fore each 4 ounces of this enriched product will provide th
e following percentages of minimum daily adult requirements
of these essential food substances how can a guy go wrong :

    Vitamin B$_1$ (Thiamin).......................... 50%
    Vitamin B$_2$ (Riboflavin)...................... 25%
    Iron... 32%
    No Salt Added.. 00%
    Niacin... 40%

(doesn't come out even - but what a discourse - incredible)

A pound a day (one pound daily) of that enriched product should be plenty enough
at least enough to survive on top of the wall before falling into the huge white
hole (feet first) with the bugs and the flying horses and the chair by the window

365 pounds -- then

365 one pound boxes .   Incredible !

Get BOXES (of course)   it's better
                      it's easier
                      it's safer
                            safer to stack
                                    than those damn cellophane bags they use

too clumsy
too slippery   those damn cellophane bags they use

Get BOXES
    BOXES keep better too   that's for sure (surely -- at my age).

    Would be funny as hell (though) if the whole damn thing
                                    the whole damn batch
                                    the whole damn stock
                                    the whole damn pile went bad after a
couple of weeks a few months   let's say two or three months and you have to
quit.
        Everything spoils.

        A disgusting smell in the room everything gets green moldy with all
sorts of little bugs flying crawling sneaking in and out of the boxes all over
the room (with the flying horses) and you can't stand it anymore and you have to give
UP !   That would be a JOKE !   WOW!

not NOODLES though
that stuff that en
riched stuff keeps
for years could us
e something else t
hough just in case
POTATOES for insta
nce NO you have to
tell it straight e
xactly how it happ
ened there is enou
gh to tell without
inventing 39 cents
a BOX that's too m
uch 25 that's clo
ser check of cours
e but can one surv
ive on NOODLES cou
ld take a quick su
rvival course just
in case perhaps eg
g NOODLES might be
safer richer in ca
lories egg NOODLES
for a more complet
e diet tastier too
just a few pennies
more for a BOX let
us say 29 cents fo
r a BOX sounds rig
ht could vary a ma
n's got to vary sh
ells one day macar
oni the next spagh
etti elbows spears
manicotti flat one
s round curly then
back to shells all
kinds all the same
price 29 cents for
a BOX 365 times 29
careful now 365 mu
ltiplied by 29 ma
kes $105.85 just t
hink $105.85 for N
OODLES alone defin
itely POTATOES wou
ld be cheaper of c
ourse but would th
ey keep NO eventua
lly they get those
long grey rat tail
s and after a whil
e they're like spo
nges gives you the
creeps NOODLES you
said NOODLES it is

Yes but the POTATOES   the raw
         POTATOES on the train (remember?) what a story: A
             on the way to the CAMP   N
                  the CAMP (X * X * X * X)   D

                                            I

                                          F
                                          O
                                          L
                                          L
                                          O
                                          W
                                          E
                                          D

                                          M
                                          Y

                                          S
                                          H
                                          A
                                          D
                                          O
                                          W

Can't come into this one...Nothing before the boat...

(Damn good story!) Could sneak the potatoes ih...Next time.

The train
The rats
The old man
The farm
The camps
The potatoes... Wow!

                  A TIME OF POTATOES

could have a whole series   like that 20 or 30 volumes
could have a whole series   a kind of Balzacian comedy

               THE VEGETABLE COMEDY

no even better than that

               THE HUNGER COMEDY

                         no even worse than that

              THE STARVATION COMEDY

                    20 or 30 volumes in folio.

So many guys starving (dying) in the world!

But there are so many ways
to cook potatoes a guy can
really get confused go mad
mashed French fried boiled
potato salad yes but then
you need oil and vinegar
doesn't matter much and
anyway can't waste too
much time peeling the
damn things and could
never decide how to cook them agreed on noodles N O O D L E S it is Love noodles
adore noodles have a passion for noodles and they keep well too easily a year if
not more also you cook the whole
box in the morning for the whole
day one cooking per day and you
have breakfast lunch and dinner
in one POT over and done and UP

even cold they're not bad   takes only a minute to warm UP

Every moment
Every minute will count   can't waste a moment
                              a minute

Should be able to work at least 12 hours a day (even more: 15 or 17)
at times like these one must push a little:
                              12 hours a day minimum
                               7 days a week maximum

                              No Sundays
                                Sundays are for proletarians.

12 times 7 (minimum) that's 84 hours a week

                              and those bastards who complain
                              with a 40 hour week:
                                            THEY
                                            DONT
                                            KNOW
                                            WHAT
                                            WORK
                                            -IS-

Definitely.   The period in Detroit is important. Describe how he worked
                -(48 hours a week in those days)- in the factory: CHRYSLER
                that's the place (what a joint!)- Hands literally bleeding
                even with gloves on (canvas gloves).   Every detail counts:
                got to think about every detail
                              NO BUTTER though too expensive
                              and anyway it wouldn't keep no
                              even if there is a refrigerator
                              in the room not all places have
                              one
Doesn't matter. Only one chair. In time the table will move by the window.
That's where the work will be done. 10 pages a day? That's a little less
than a page an hour if you work 12 hours a day (minimum) that's already a lot.

Would be easier and simpler and more logical to do one page an hour

if only to keep track.   12 pages a day.   365 days.

                            12 times   365 (doesn't make sense
                                                       at this time   )

Some days will be better than others
Some days will be blank
Some days will be tremendous

But most important you've got to keep going

                                    the whole thing depends on that
                                    the whole thing is settled then

        NO BUTTER (right) just a few cans of tomato sauce (perhaps)
                                          tomato sauce (to add flavor)
                                          tomato sauce (on Sundays)

        that stuff is cheap   10 cents?
                                 15 cents?
                                    a
                                    can
                                     ?

        Separate problem   See how you come out at the end

                                     Let's say once a week on Sunday

I
D
I
O
T   obviously there'll be no Sundays!

Then just a can of tomato sauce once a week (anytime) for extra flavor
(a little flavor) (a little favor) once in a while when you can't take
it anymore when you can't stand it anymore just like that (anytime) on
the spur of the moment in moments of panic tomato sauce HEINZ all over

C
R
E
T
I
N

evidently no weeks either after a while you won't even know which week
which day which month it is (for sure) won't even know if it's night o
r day particularly if you decide to work with the curtains closed in t
he chambers of night I didn't consider that yet but it's a possibility

all alone
    alone with my 365 boxes
    alone with my 365 days   RUN OUT OF BOXES
                                            RUN OUT OF   DAYS

It's like a guy in jail or on an island carving the days on the wall or on a piece of wood with a knife with anything a fork with his teeth ROBINSON CRUSOE OF THE NOODLES but in t his case it's different it's backwards diminishing rather t han augmenting the boxes that is not the days when there'll be no more boxes then you'll know it's the end END of the y ear The guy in jail he's stuck unless of course he knows wh en he's coming out but if he's serving for life if he's a m urderer or a sex maniac then in his case it's hopeless Don' t understand why he goes on carving the days on the wall un less he's just faking it Didn't think of that But if he's a thief a petty thief serving only for a few months then he h as a right to go on carving on the wall unless of course he doesn't have anything with which to carve except his finger nails or else unless he doesn't want to carve That's his bu siness Nobody is forcing him But the other guy on the islan d he can't give up For him it's a different matter than for the guy in jail There's always a boat in the back of his ca rving or something like a boat a submarine a seaplane a des troyer unless That's quite possible he decides instinctivel y to carve a boat a canoe in a tree instead of carving days

on a crummy piece of wood ell decide to do both The OTS who always do everyth his decision Nobody is te is deserted island unless bals after his ass then t e purpose on the one hand ther to escape alive It m ntually it pays IT'S DOUB permits him to keep track s been on the island as w it takes him to carve sin boat Of course the number e but at least it gives a t if the cannibals are af ly it might be better for Though the guy may very w re are guys like that IDI ing the hard way But it's lling him what to do on h of course there are canni he carving serves a doubl to save his life on the o ay be double work but eve LE OR NOTHING and also it of the number of days he' ell as the number of days gle-handed his lifesaving of days may never coincid meaning to the carving Bu ter his ass then definite the poor guy to forget ab

out counting the days he's been on the island and concentra te on his boat in order to get the hell out of there or els e instead of ending in the BOAT he ends up in the POT it al l works out only if he has marked the day he began the carv ing of the boat because a guy on an island never begins car ving a boat the first day First he waits a few days a few w eeks before starting hoping that something like a boat will show up to get him out of there But after a while depending on the guy's temperament and how fed up he is with the scen ery he gives up hoping and starts carving the boat But he m ay have already started carving the days unless of course t he cannibals got to him before that then things don't reall y work out or else they do depending how much the guy value s his life But carving for carving's sake the guy on an isl and is better off than the guy in jail That's for sure He h as more wood and more room too But in either case the trick is never to give up and never count the days That would sol ve the whole thing But can they do it Can anybody with a co mmon sense of time do it The trick is to swear in advance n ever to count the days though it's always possible to count something else The pages for instance when a guy is writing

Swear (cross your heart and spit on the floor) never to count the boxes:

                                                    that
                                                    would be
                                                    cheating
                                                        ..

Only towards the end
it'll be inevitable when there is only one box left
then you can't avoid counting one box
                          or even two or seven
it's self-evident.

              For sure then you'll know how many days are left
                                          UNAVOIDABLY

              But definitely in the beginning and most of the
              time   AVOID AT ALL COST COUNTING THE BOXES

Indeed can already see myself

    365      of them

that's a fucking lot of boxes when you think of it
(and the tomato sauce - one can a week - 52 cans)!

              ! H-O-L-Y C-O-W !

won't be able to see my horses... Oh well... only way is to leave a passage
behind the boxes to be able to count my horses even if the room'll be small
                                                              er

Didn't think of that!

The tomato sauce won't take much room (52 cans) but the noodles sort of juD
ge for the time being a can here and there now and then after a while you G
et a kind of inner sense of time an inner mental clock that tells you the E
nd of the week has come   e
nd of a period   an inner cycle some guys call it   of course girls
have less of a problem   they have their periods once a month to help them
keep track   never thought of that   TOO BAD YOU'RE NOT A GIRL

And suppose you get sick
              never thought of that   who gets sick?

              Not me NO
                    nobody to call   refuse even if there is a
                    NO
public phone downstairs
usually there is a public phone downstairs in places like these -- but who
needs it?   PUBLIC MY ASS
                          Been lucky so far that's good enough for me

              What a stroke of luck!

              And nobody there to see it
                 nobody
              That's the way to go: DOUBLE OR NOTHING

Agreed for the tomato sauce

              52 cans at about 15 cents a can

                    That's $7.80

              I should be able to afford that
              I'll squeeze   somewhere

                O-----------K

Noodles and tomato sauce once in a while

              NOODLES every day TOMATO SAUCE
              for extra flavor hereandthere
              •••••••••••••••••••••••••••

COFFEE next: I'll need lots of coffee: Nescafé Maxwell House Yuban or
                                 xxxxxxxxxxxxxxxxxxxxxxxxxxxxxx
                                 instant xxxxxxxxxxxx of course

        98 cents a jar! That's about right.   79 on sale?
•••

        Now the crucial question: How many spoons in a jar   ?

        That's a tricky one   Should measure to make sure .

        (Would be stupid to overstock)   Let's assume

        for now a jar a week (NO) a jar for two weeks   That's

        more logical even with a little extra cup hereandthere   :

        during the nights p a r t i c u l a r l y during the
                 nights   if things are
                 not going well getting all screwed up.

                           26 jars

        then   that should do   but that too should be decided:
DO   I   WORK   DURING   THE   DAY   OR   DURING   THE   NIGHT   ?
Can't tell now - can't be both though (One could overlap
                               it happens all the time)

But the way to solve this problem would be to keep the curtains closed all
the time (night and day) this way you wouldn't know if it's night or day .

                          26 jars

        That's a lot of COFFEE!   I wonder

if it wouldn't be better to work at night or during the day when you are
nice and fresh (can't tell now) Depends when you begin and also when it
happens and also when you decide to sleep and how you feel and how disgusted you are

(running vertically in the right margin): if you are tired during the night then you sleep during the night BUT AND if you are tired during the day then you sleep during the day

Makes sense!   With the curtains closed one might easily overlap   Sleep

partly during the night and sleep the rest partly during the day   Also

you might feel bad one day but tremendous another and again it might   be

the reverse: yad eht gnirud yltrap tser eht peels dna thgin eht
                gnirud yltrap peels in either case comes out even.

                                                              Let's

say I work after I sleep   That simplifies matter:

        The first day however should establish some sort of rou-
        tine I won't do much the first day I'll be too nervous (
        October) tomorrow (October 1st) I begin Let's assume I g
        et into the room early in the morning around nine I just
        can't go to sleep immediately that wouldn't make sense s
        ince I slept (supposedly) the night before no reason for
        not sleeping the night before unless I'm too nervous OK
        first I look around I start counting a few horses just t
        o see how it goes line up my boxes my cans (no all of th
        at is already set up in advance) then I don't start coun
        ting anything I just go into the room even if I waste pa
        rt of the first day some sort of cycle should be establi
        shed set in motion (doesn't have to be an inner cycle) I
        just can't walk into the room tomorrow morning around ni
        ne and go to sleep immediately that wouldn't be fair tha
        t wouldn't be logical who knows I might even write a few
        pages the first day the first scene down the precipice c
        limbing up the wall hanging on by my fingernails carving
        the days on the wall bleeding like hell anythinganything
        YESTERDAY HE ARRIVED IN NEW YORK BY BOAT IT WAS A SUNDAY

        anything...That's it

        No it was foggy.............................anything.

        Describe the boat
                New York
                the girl   on the boat
                the uncle   waiting for him on the pier.........
                                        That's it

But suppose (yes suppose) the whole thing is not finished at the end of the
year?   365 boxes?   At the end of my 365 boxes?   I didn't think of that.

what
    do
      I
    do
then   It's ridiculous. If you put in 12 hours a day
                        minimum for 365 days maximum that makes 4380 h
                                                                     o
                                                                     u
                                                                     r
                                                                     s
(do you realize how many hours that makes: four thousand three hundred
                                        and eighty hours! ! ! !)

Anyway toward the end if you see you're running behind running out of boxes you can always put in a few extra hours -- double time -- though by then it might be getting TOUGH or EASY who know?   Some guys say that the more
                                                        you do it the easier it gets but
                                                        other guys say that the more you
                                                        do it the harder it gets comes o
                                                        ut the same at the end most impo
                                                        rtant however is to get going an
                                                        d keep going quickly stubbornly
                                                                        regularly
                                                                        steadily
                                                        and no fucking around   .
                                                        I'll start on the boat.   Just
Before he arrives in New York.
                            Would be nice to have the Statue of Liberty
in the background (very symbolic).   He meets a girl on the boat (the first
day).   An American girl from Milwaukee (Mary.   That's a good name).   She
spent the summer in Europe.

Typical American girl: blondish
                                cute
                                sexy
                                enormous ass (but not too much.   Just right).

They have an affair/ a love affair/ that's easy on a boat/ he screws her

once or twice in her cabin/ no/ he doesn't screw her/ he is too shy/ and

also she won't let him/ just a romance/ nothing more/ the sort of things

that always happen on boats/ yes/ she is willing but she is afraid to do

it/ and besides she shares her cabin with another girl/ and he has no ca

bin/ he's in the big HOLE/ you know where they shove 20 or 30 guys/ toge

ther/ and it stinks like hell/ and anyway she shares her cabin with anot

her girl/ a fat American girl from Chicago/ so they can't get in/ that's

not unusual/ one often sees things like that on a boat/ but on deck/ the

upper deck/ at night they bring a blanket and mess around/ of course/ he

thinks he is in love with her/ the two of them are so young/ he is 19 or

so/ she hasn't told him her age but it's obvious she's about 19 too/ and

it's really the first time he gets involved/ temporarily/ with such a fi

ne girl/ before that only pigs/ in Paris/ and she seems to like him too/

at least that's what she tells him/ naive the two of them/ naive like he

ll/ and it's only the beginning/ wait till you see what happens to them/

Should be able to write at least a dozen pages on that even more if you go into
all sorts of details: description of the boat - the clothes both of them wear -
the mood they are in - the messing around on the deck - the color of the blanket

and of the sky - and all the crap she tells him about America - and all the crap he tells her about himself. TREMENDOUS. Easily 12 pages. FORMIDABLE

She tells him all about America: What a great place
                                        How he's going to like it
                                        How lucky he is
                                        How rich he's going to be
                                        How famous he's going to be
                                        How tremendous things will be
                                        What a great place
                                        ETC.   ETC.   ETC.

He believes every word she says: He's so scared   It's natural   And

she's such a nice girl (and she has a bit of college French   that helps   a bit)   She thinks she understands him and tries to reassure him   (typically American)   and she tells him

                       : You'll see everything will be fine . . . . .

Meanwhile

his uncle is waiting on the pier   (almost forgot the uncle)
-- the boat should dock soon -- in spite of the weather -- --

Meanwhile

she goes on and on   (What a girl!):

                  Your uncle will meet you at the boat (with his car - even threw that in). I can see the whole scene already and maybe you'll cry a little and your uncle too and me too and we'll keep in touch and I promise to come and see you in Detroit and we'll write to each other you regularly and you'll see what a great place and you'll forget the past I am sure (that's a good one). You are so lucky. Everything will be nice everything will be for the future and so on (WHAT A GIRL!)
<u>12 more pages on that</u>

YES.   But....(he squeezes in a few words here and there).... I never met my uncle (doesn't matter).... I don't even know how he loo ks.... He never sent his picture.... I sent him one of mine in color (that's the way to go - IT'S OBVIOUS - <u>3 more pages</u>)....

YES.   He just wrote after the war not to me but to my father you see he's not really my uncle he's my father's cousin No! I mean he's a cousin by marriage He married a cousin of my father I think   that's why he wrote to him after the war to my father just to see what had happened   but   but since he was not there any more my father I mean you know since he was dead I read the letter I mean I didn't really read it it was in English I had someone who studied English (a good friend) read it to me   (that's important he doesn't speak a damn word of English. Therefore all that in French. I'll translate later)

YES.   (While Mary is shaking her head approvingly and affectionately -- too bad he didn't screw her she needed it. Typical America n girl. <u>Easily 12 pages</u>). Then after a while my uncle starte d sending me packages: food (canned food) candies cigarettes.

YES.   he sent me a lot of cigarettes (American cigarettes: Luckies

Camels -

Chesterfields -

but I didn't smoke in those days so I sold them on the black)
market)


```
I                                                           I
  A                                                       U
  M                                                       N
    S                                                     D
    O                                                     E
    R                                                     R
    R                                                   dnats
    Y  -    -    -    -    -    -    -    -    -
```

YES.   and soap too and coffee (but no noodles though) and clothes -
socks a tie and a beautiful green sweater -   and beautiful
stamps on the packages (in those days I collected stamps)   *

```
    *                                                       *

        *                                                   *

            *                                               *

                *                                           *

                    *                                       *

                        *                                   *

                            *                               *

                                *   *   *   *   *   *   *   *
```

Definitely.   Describe the clothes they are wearing. It'll make a nice contrast.

Absolutely.   YES. This tie I've got on and the socks and also a beautiful green
               sweater in my suitcase they are from America. American clothes. My
               uncle sent them to me. Also I used to collect the stamps, from all
               the letters and packages (that's a nice cultural touch), and then I
               would sell them at the stamp market on the Champs Elysées (yes what
               a memory).

               YES.

I've got it. All you have to do once you're in the room is keep going
at full speed. Anything just as long as you keep going and never give   UP

                                            if you f   b
                                                  a   m
                                                  l   i
                                                  l   DOWN   l
                                            into the hole you   c
                                                          you
                                            h a n g   o n
                                            YOU'VE GOT TO
                                            ‾‾‾‾‾‾‾‾‾‾‾‾

and   after a while
                   he asked if I wanted to come to America: What would you have done?
                                                             What could I do?
                                                             What would you have done?
                                                             What could I do?

These are the kinds of questions he asks all the time
                   so many questions and no answers!

But once you get him started he goes on and on getting everything all mixed up:

               You know it was not easy to decide (all that in French of course)
               -- he doesn't speak a word of English except for a few words here
               and there he picked up on the boat words like YES NO GOOD MORNING
               SORRY GOODBY SONOFABITCH but u-n-b-e-l-i-e-v-a-b-l-e the way he p
               ronounces them (lucky Mary speaks French she studied in college a
               year or so and after a whole summer in France she has improved tr
               emendously -- must be a rich girl to be able to afford a whole su
               mmer in France -- a bit older than he is too and more intelligent
               but no complex no mother complex that is). You know it was not e
               asy at all you see I have an aunt (that's on his mother's side) w
               ho lives in Africa (that's right in Dakar) and she wanted me to c
               ome there and live with her she has some kind of big business yes
               A BIG HOTEL and she wanted me to come and work after the war with
               her in her BIG HOTEL or something like that and she wrote after I
               knew I was an orphan (not to his father therefore but to him this
               time) a long letter addressed to me personally in French but
                                                                    But your
               uncle will take good care of you (she cuts right in). You'll see
               he'll send you to school (unbelievable that girl) to learn Englis
               h (that's essential in America). In America everybody goes to sc
               hool (everybody speaks English too). You'll be happy. You'll se
               e life in América is quite different than
                                                  Than   ALL THAT CRAP!

If I start on the boat like that should be able to move fast (with Mary).

Three boxes of noodles and I'll have the whole scene.... A dozen cups of

coffee.

COFFEE: let's get that going --   26 jars
                                          79 cents a jar (on sale)
                                          that's a lot of jars MAN   --

          But everything has to be ready in advance. One never
          knows. Suppose those bastards decide to raise the pr
          ice of things in the middle of the year just like tha
          t for no reason at all. Inflation and all that crap.
          What a society! Doesn't matter of course since you'l
          l have the whole stock ready in advance but another g
          uy would really be fucked if he didn't have his whole
          stock ready in advance and right in the middle of the
          year they decide to raise the prices of everything ju
          st like that. Even a penny here and there can fuck u
          p the whole system. That's the advantage of planning
          ahead.

          One has to: 26 times 79 makes 20.04
                                                   20.04
                              just for COFFEE
                                       COFFEE
                                       COFFEE

          Expensive that shit when you think of it BUT essential.

          Could round it off to 20 (even) - 20 bucks - ridiculous
          that extra 4 cents that zero four that little decimal 4

          If I start like that (on the boat) and keep going thing
          s begin to add up.   Should make a list perhaps A LIST:

          Noodles
          Tomato Sauce
          Coffee
          ....
          Toothpaste
SURE   ....
          Toothpaste   A guy's got to brush (everyday)
                                if not you get a lousy taste in
                                the   mouth!

Here we go then: HOW MANY SQUEEZES IN A TUBE OF TOOTHPASTE?

A great deal depends on the number of squeezes in a tube - regular size -
who ever thought of that - I refuse to buy family size - they look bigger
the tubes but it's a fake in fact it's an illusion the family size - fina
lly they leave too much space - empty space - at the top and at the botto
m too - those bastards - you think you get more for your money a bigger t
ube a better buy for only a buck 19 or something but in the end you don't
even have more squeezes - you squeeze air - an illusion - same thing with
all the other junk they sell family size - hair lotion shampoo hand lotio
n talcum powder after shaving lotion - all that shit you rub on yourself-
Same crummy deal - an ILLUSION a stinking
          ILLUSION.

But you've got to brush: I knew a guy who refused to brush everyday. What a mess twenty years later. It's useless if you want my real opinion. Doesn't even pay to talk about it.

Minimum once a day: Family size! A joke! You're damn right. Anyway I'm not a family. I refuse to be taken in. They see you coming and immediately they assume you're a father and there you are helpless here they go shoving the family size at you.

60 squeezes in a tube: Regular size. Right! No! More than that! 80! Give or take a bigger squeeze here and there (a bigger squeeze one morning out of despair on the edge of the cliff going over in and out down the white hole). But you've got to brush. Damn right!

75 cents for a regular tube: Cannot do without (seriously). Once in the morning that's enough. Some guys are fanatics they do it twice a day or even after each meal (3 meals a day minimum). That's pushing a bit. Deodorant fine. Never use the stuff and anyway deodorant that's for other people that's part of human relations human contacts. Alone in my room (surrounded by my noodles) there won't be much (indeed) human relations. But toothpaste that's indispensable.

Colgate! Taste better: 75 cents for a regular tube. Those motherfuckers! And then they have king size - extra long size - giant size. They push the damn sizes on you and after a while you're like a midget in the midst of all that gigantic stuff. Gives you a complex. It's as if they wanted to crush you kill you exterminate you with all their sizes. And quick too.

75 cents: No! They always make it 79 - 89 - 98 - 199 always just a penny or two under the next Zero. That's another one of their tricks. You think you're paying less closer to 70 or 80 or 90 or 180 but in fact you're closer to 80 - 90 - a buck - 200. Same with noodles cars bicycles televisions overcoats shoes refrigerators. You see the prices in big NUMBERS: $2.98 - $49.99 - $228.98 - $2498.99 and BANG it costs you 3 bucks or 50 bucks or 230 bucks or 2500 bucks. Never fails.

80 squeezes: Like that suit I bought at Kleins's. His first American suit. $48.98. With the 50 bucks I had he didn't even have enough for a tie. Kept wearing the one his uncle sent him from America. But the socks they had big holes in them. That's ironical. And the green sweater. He never wore the damn thing. Too green.

I'll have to waste a whole tube counting squeezes.   It's safer.

Can't afford to overstock. What would I do with an extra dozen tubes

                    Regular size   COLGATE?

At least the first three or four squeezes won't be wasted   I'll

make them big ones   (the first day).   But that doesn'

t solve the problem: How many times can you brush in one day? R**I
                                                                 D**I
One tube shot to hell.   That stuff doesn't keep once   C**U
                                                                 L**O
you take it out.   That raises an enormous question: U**S

How the hell do they get it in?   They must shove the stuff in with

a spoon or something.   A shoving machine no doubt.   Just

imagine a guy spending his life (8 hours a day) shoving toothpaste in

a tube.   What a disgusting business.   I could have him work in

a factory   (in the beginning) where they   make

tubes (it's not unusual). Did it myself. What a system!   Nobody

would believe it.   No.   I'll find something better for

him to do.   I'll make a list of jobs he gets during that time (firs

t five years. That's the story. First five years in America.   No

that's too much. One year that's enough. Got to limit yourself   a

little.   365 days to be exact.   12

pages a day. I'll start on the boat).   Forget the factory for n

ow.   So many other things to think   about

: A NAME for instance.   Can't use his real name.   No

rush though the name can wait.   First the toothpaste   80

squeezes in a tube that makes 80 days (once a day of course)   365

divided by 80 (doesn't come out even) (but a bigger squeeze here and

there)   that's 4 point 56 and something tubes for the year. Ma

ke it an even FIVE.   Can't take a chance   Or

maybe   FOUR.   Should be enough. Let's say five tu

bes for safety's sake. If I run short I'll cut down on the size of t

he squeezes towards the end. A guy's got to be practical. 79 cents?

NO!   79 that's the price of coffee.
       69   ?   Then
       69 times 5 (sorry) that's $3.45 for toothpaste alone.

Maybe I should start my list (here and now) or else it gets all confused.

But   Toothpaste   implies also
       Toothbrush   obviously   I have one now (everybody does)

       and not in bad condition BUT what's the life span of a toothbrush ?

       HAS-ANYONE-EVER-CONSIDERED-THE-LIFE-SPAN-OF-A-TOOTHBRUSH-HAS-ANYONE?

       Good question. They say "replace after three months". But have they
       really been checked? Have they really and truly been examined? Have
       they really examined the question?   The question of the toothbrush?

Bought this one (let's see?) (when was it?) (no!) (before) before (exac

tly before) LOS ANGELES (must have been) (unless it was?) in DETROIT (yes)

(no!) or before CHICAGO?

Detroit!   Last March (the way I ran out of that place who can remember) ?

Detroit!   Hell he'll find out quick. Won't take him long. Those damn fac
           tories. You get caught up with those damn factories and you can
           not escape any more even when they lay you off you go on looking
           for another job. It's a vicious circle (they must shove the stu
           ff into the tubes with a spoon). A pile of lousy shit that's it
           that's what it is (with a spoon or something like a spoon) YES!
           the factory.   YES!
           I'll have an important scene in Detroit   YES!
           He works in a factory -- CHRYSLER -- on the line   YES!
           Cutting springs for car seats (that's a good one)   YES!
           The night shift (that's more dramatic)   No the late afternoon!
           YES the late afternoon (that's more logical)   From four in the
           afternoon to midnight   No it's the other way
           around from *8:00* A.M. to *12:00* Noon.   Impossible! Can't
           be because in the morning he goes to school.   Definitely!
           Then it'll have to be the late afternoon shift: Definitely!
           (I'll have him go to school in the morning)   from four to
           twelve (midnight) and school in the morning: from eight to
           twelve (noon) -- N O R T H E R N   H I G H   S C H O O L -- YES!

           Courses in: American History
                                    Government and Social Sciences
                                    Physical Education (Swimming)
                                    English (for Foreign Students)
                                    Music (eventually saxophonist)

           Then he has to work the afternoon shift (4 to 12) fingers bleedi
           ng like hell even with gloves on (canvas gloves) particularly th
           e first few days even with gloves on it starts bleeding right of
           the bat. It's a mistake. It's a joke those canvas gloves becau
           se first of all the damn things never last and then they get all
           greasy and you can't even get them on after that. They should m
           ake leather gloves or even metal gloves for guys like us but eve
           n that would not help. Could write a whole book about gloves or

bleeding fingers: MYFINGERSHISFINGERSOURFINGERSTHEIRFINGERS

After he gets off the boat in New York he spends a few days in New York
with his uncle. Uncle George? Uncle Sam? Too obvious. Uncle Arthur?
Theodore? Ted? Erskine? No good. Something more real... more human.
.. more unclish. DAVID? That's it! DAVID! It's a real good credible
believable human name. And then... then after that they move on... to
Detroit. That's where the uncle (David!) lives and a few days later...
just like that... he begins to work in the factory (Chrysler!)... About
a week or ten days after he arrives he starts working... That's about

right.   No it's not

right! It won't work. He's got to learn some English first. Takes at
least a whole month before you can even put a sentence together .... At
least in his case. For a guy who does not speak a word of English what
else can he do? It's the only thing he can do .... THE FACTORY .... In

the beginning it should be tough for him... real tough to get a job....
to get anything... a piece of ass... a friend... a recommendation... at

least a week. A few weeks a month or even two or even three... and....
then of course there is loneliness despair homesickness and so on...but

no suicidal tendencies. Not in the beginning... that's too phony...too

dramatic. A guy's got to be careful. No sentimentality either. Got to

tell it straight ---------------- $3.45 for toothpaste ---------- Right!

AND-WHAT-ABOUT-THE-TOOTHBRUSH-DO-I-GET-ONE-OR-DO-I-NOT-GET-ONE-AND-WHAT
?   ?

The most difficult will be to find the right tone... In French it would
be easier of course (le ton juste)... Have him talk the whole time...as
if he were telling his own story to somebody else (to me for instance).
Or simply remembering it... (yes!) That's one way of doing it... even
though it's a bit restricting. No descriptions then. Just talk. Talk
all the time. I only ... no HE ... And of course in English. Hastobe!
No accent... that's too contrived... we skip the accent... Just let him
talk... talk... for himself even if what he says does not make sense...

: BLAblaBLAblaBLAblaBLAblaBLAblaBLAblaBLAblaBLAblaBLAblaBLAblaBLAbla :
- QUAquaQUAquaQUAquaQUAquaQUAquaQUAquaQUAquaQUAquaQUAquaQUAquaQUAqua -

But first he has to go to school (NORTHERN HIGH SCHOOL). In the evening
maybe at first (adult education even though he's only 19 or so). No he
can't or else he'll have to work the morning shift. You can't work and
go to school at the same time. It's not practical. I'll have to work I
.out t

WORK! Don't talk to me about work.

      It's that stupid girl on the boat who got him all confused
      about school -- and happiness -- and all that jazz -- :

      -- And you'll see your uncle will take good care of you.
      He'll send you to school. Everybody goes to school
      in America.

      -- That's for sure. I did enough jobs in my life. The
      number of crappy jobs I did in my life. Oh happiness!

      UNBELIEVABLE the number of crappy jobs in one's life.

      Should make a list just for kick.

So many problems

So many unexpected problems.   A smart guy would simply give up
                             give up
                  the whole thing before starting
                        before starting
                  to get involved with such a story
                        before falling   into
                                    the
                                    hole
                        (feet first)

You could keep the room though.   Then it'll just be another room
                                  a room
to sleep (in) to feel sorry for yourself (in) to waste time (in) to . . .
                        JUST ANOTHER ROOM - a room.
without a meaning. just a wasted room   and
                        all
                          the rest.

8 bucks a week for a room   that's a lot of money when you think of it.

Especially for a room where you do nothing in it. I mean nothing serious YES

nothing constructive.

DEFINITELY then   YOU DON'T GIVE UP   and besides
             YOU CAN'T GIVE UP before starting.

Then you start all over: first the room
                      then the noodles
                      then the coffee
                      then the toothpaste.   ETC.
                                              YES.

That's the way to go

Make a list
Make a list

before you
      get
      all
screwed up   And then the toothbrush: I have one now but who the hell
remembers how long a toothbrush lasts   When you bought it and
how much it costs   It happens one day just like that
      You decide you need a new one but of course you just don't
rush out to buy it immediately on the spot   First you consider
      You contemplate   You think about it   Hesitate   The pri-
ce   The color   The texture   Do you really need a new one?
   The old one still has quite a few good brushings in it   39
cents   59 cents   They even make some for 69
                              even some that cost more than a buck
All kinds   Red ones Black Green Yellow Pink for girls   Even
bought one once with that little rubber prick at the end   What
a sucker   Looks disgusting and to tell the truth it never
          works   Don't even know what you're supposed to do
with that prick   I suppose you squeeze it between your teeth
like a toothpick   It's not very exciting and in fact I can prove
it   it never fits   Unless   I tried   Too big
                          You postpone
                          You squeeze it   Unless it's to rub your
gums if you have weak gums   That's possible   But they charge
      extra for it   Those bastards   Anything
                                Anything to get your money
      The tricks the motherfuckers will invent to get you
Makes sense to postpone   You tell yourself next time
                              next time when I go out
to buy cigarettes I'll get a new one   It haunts you   literally
in the morning   even if there are a few good brushings left
   in your old one   It hurts after a while   But you keep
                                      forgetting
                                      postponing
                                      procrastinating
You touch them   You feel them   You handle them all over   Once I
felt one for twenty-five minutes in a drugstore without even buying
it   The guy in the drugstore was looking at me as though I was
      some kind of queer or something
You touch the bristles
        the handles
        the little hole at the end of the handle   I have touched
them all   Soft Medium Hard Stiff Curved   How the hell do
you know which one to choose   It's excruciating and you can't
                              you can't
because the damn things are locked up in plastic cases and you're
not allowed to open the cases   That's for sure   And besides
you always think it's useful at first when you pay for it but in the
end there is no hope   They are useless those crummy little plastic
cases   Especially since you can never get the damn paper that's
glued on them off   So you don't feel the brush in any case it
      would not be sanitary   All you can do is feel the plastic
cases   Feels good as a matter of fact   Nice and smooth   But
still   you can't make up your mind   Toothbrushes always seem
too expensive or else too cheap for what they are   That's a good
point: The ones at 39 look too cheap
      The ones at 89 too expensive and the ones at 59 you can't
                              trust

Also they make some with plastic bristles   Plastic my ass
Never trust plasticity
Never

Also (that's another thing to consider) the hard ones make
your gums bleed   They always say you have to brush UP
                                                           and D
and never s-id-e-w-ay-s   That in itself is a   goOd
                                                           W
Could waste two or three boxes just on that alone!   poiNt
Skip it!

It's like a game
        a game with very tricky rules   A POKER GAME   let's say
Somewhere in Las Vegas or else in Los Angeles   just to get away
        from the toothbrush.

Almost lost my pants (you say game but who knows the game may have been rigged)
Doesn't matter the money has to come from someplace Yours is gone   Finished
        It breaks off between your teeth   But you forget again
                                                What an obsession
        You remember the next morning even though it hurts   And here we go.
Finally you can't take it any more
        You rush out of the game   You take off like a rabbit   Your pants
down to buy the first one that looks decent   DR. SOANDSO But finally
you're never satisfied   Too hard
                            Too soft   Next time I'll play roulette you tell
yourself (what a mess!)   Next time I'll buy myself a medium one
you tell yourself   A game
                       A game of course in L.A.   I remember now:

                       That's what makes life bearable
                       and to think of it
                            to talk about it
                            to get if off your chest helps
                                                helps pass the time.
What an obsession!   Perhaps I should have a second one in reserve one never
                     knows once you're in that's it if I lose it I'm lost it
                     won't matter much win or lose I won't be able to repla-
                     ce it no no extras that's for sure and it can happen once
                                                                    once I
                     knew a guy who lost his toothbrush in his room No kidding!
What a story! He spent three days straight looking for it. Three days.
Imagine that. It was a yellow one. Of course he could have dropped the
whole thing and gone out to buy another one. But not him. Not that stu
bborn sonofabitch. I can't understand guys like that. He looked everyw
here: under the bed in the closets in the kitchen in the refrigerator i
n the stairs under the carpets in all his pockets. It was like a game..
. It became an obsession. I remember I came to visit him and he asked m
e to help. We looked all over: under the bed in the closets in the kit
chen in the refrigerator in the stairs under the carpets in all our pock
ets. He looked in mine and I looked in his. What a maniac. Very frien
dly. He even asked me to take off my clothes to make sure. By then I w
as becoming very suspicious. No he said it's just to make sure. Do not
trust anybody. Some guys are real fanatics when it comes to their perso
nal properties. And once you get involved with them it's damn hard to b
reak off. Once you get started with something or somebody you've got to
go on to the end. Things have to have a beginning and an end. Lucky fo
r him he finally found it. We could have gone on like that for days and
days. 365 days just looking for a lost toothbrush. All over the place.

It's easier to go out and buy yourself a new one But not him Must have been in

Los Angeles before
bility And of all
ghed like hell But
to wash it off and
guy I told him tha
l be like new No n
himself another on
in his room This t
er to find He said
r much to me but w
se That's really s
en after we talked
e poker game and a
ems to think about
toothbrush just li
e yellow one The o
As a reward He ins
th And also for ha
warmly but of cour
e first garbage ca
in he wasn't looki
t lucky for him we
uld have gone craz
wl Imagine It's in
ning after he brus
preferred a bit of

y bucks or something would have been nice for a beginning For the reward The m

oney has to come f
one possible versi
That simplifies ma
he poker game This
for the record Ass
urse this then des
er I threw the too
wntown past the ga
e the whole busine
en I stumbled into
ked me if I wanted
moment or so and t
K and before I kne
yself in some kind
a bunch of guys wh
hat could a guy do
ng a bit here Losi
proximately I must
s and some loose c
(Let's forget abou
ty bucks the freak
s much more import
happened) I shoute
around the table l
d of nuts or somet
o me YES I shouted

the poker game tha
places in the toil
that guy what a du
use it again But n
t if he uses a str
ot that guy He rus
e immediately whil
ime a red one Supp
in case you mispla
hy did he say misp
omething Finally I
for a while I told
ll that I told him
But before leaving
ke that That's gen
ne that had fallen
isted For what the
ving wasted my tim
se I didn't keep i
n I saw down the s
ng out of the wind
found his toothbru
y Happens sometime
credible Must have
hed his teeth Of c
cash instead of th

rom someplace Luck
on It happened one
tters Both the los
way it's much easi
uming this is a no
cribes how it star
thbrush away I was
rbage can Going We
ss about the noodl
this bunch of guys
to play poker with
hen said Trying to
w what was happeni
of crummy basement
o looked very susp
That's how I got i
ng a bit there But
have had close Eve
hange in front and
t the yellow tooth
guy didn't give me
ant)(tell it strai
d DOUBLE OR NOTHIN
ooked at me as tho
hing But that's wh
DOUBLE Or NOTHING

t's the only possi
et bowl Yes We lau
mb guy I told him
ot him No not that
ong detergent it'l
hed out and bought
e I waited for him
osedly red is easi
ce it Didn't matte
lace instead of lo
agreed with him Th
him I had to go Th
I had my own probl
he gave me his old
erosity for you Th
in the toilet bowl
damn thing was wor
e So I thanked him
t I threw it in th
treet making certa
ow What a waste Bu
sh otherwise he wo
s In the toilet bo
fallen in that mor
ourse I would have
e toothbrush Twent

or no luck this is
day in Los Angeles
t toothbrush and t
er to remember But
rmal kind of disco
ted Supposedly aft
walking towards do
st (This was befor
es Much before) wh
who immediately as
them I hesitated a
control my voice O
ng to me I found m
playing poker with
icious to me But w
nto the game Winni
two hours later ap
n more to 150 buck
beside me Suddenly
brush and the twen
as a reward This i
ght exactly how it
G and all the guys
ugh I was some kin
en the idea came t
not thinking about

anything just shoving all my dough Everything in the pot And hell with it all

FULL HOUSE FULL HOUSE FULL HOUSE FULL HOUSE FULL HOUSE FULL HOUSE FULL HOUSE
FULL HOUSE FULL HOUSE FULL HOUSE FULL HOUSE FULL HOUSE FULL HOUSE FULL HOUSE
FULL HOUSE FULL HOUSE FULL HOUSE FULL HOUSE FULL HOUSE FULL HOUSE FULL HOUSE

FULL HOUSE   and that bastard thought he had me with his   FULL HOUSE
FULL HOUSE   FLUSH...there was no way he could have gues   FULL HOUSE
FULL HOUSE   sed my FULL HOUSE...just a pair of ladies s   FULL HOUSE
FULL HOUSE   howing but three deuces in the hole...he co   FULL HOUSE
FULL HOUSE   uld have read me for a STRAIGHT...his was o   FULL HOUSE
FULL HOUSE   bvious...all black...some guys are real jer   FULL HOUSE
FULL HOUSE   ks...and he tried to bluff me raising twice   FULL HOUSE
FULL HOUSE   like a motherfucker...when he raised 50 buc   FULL HOUSE
FULL HOUSE   ks the second time I thought I was going to   FULL HOUSE
FULL HOUSE   shit in my pants...I must have had about 15   FULL HOUSE
FULL HOUSE   0 bucks in front of me by the time he raise   FULL HOUSE
FULL HOUSE   d the second time...but what a pot...must h   FULL HOUSE
FULL HOUSE   ave been a good 5 or 6 hundred in it...mayb   FULL HOUSE
FULL HOUSE   e more...all the other guys had stayed in t   FULL HOUSE
FULL HOUSE   o the last card but then when he showed a f   FULL HOUSE
FULL HOUSE   ourth spade on top of his other three spade   FULL HOUSE
FULL HOUSE   s and raised like he had it they all chicke   FULL HOUSE
FULL HOUSE   ned out...not me though...that little redhe   FULL HOUSE
FULL HOUSE   aded punk thought he had me with his obviou   FULL HOUSE
FULL HOUSE   s FLUSH...there was no way he could have gu   FULL HOUSE
FULL HOUSE   essed my FULL HOUSE...I had never seen that   FULL HOUSE
FULL HOUSE   guy before...nor after...nor any of the oth   FULL HOUSE
FULL HOUSE   er guys...and let me make this clear...this   FULL HOUSE
FULL HOUSE   was not the same guy as the guy with the lo   FULL HOUSE
FULL HOUSE   st toothbrush...this was later...it happene   FULL HOUSE
FULL HOUSE   d down the street...past the garbage can...   FULL HOUSE
FULL HOUSE   so I raised him another 50 bucks...he flinc   FULL HOUSE
FULL HOUSE   hed that little punk...hesitated...you coul   FULL HOUSE
FULL HOUSE   d see that...mumbled something in his teeth   FULL HOUSE
FULL HOUSE   ...a dirty word...with a little twist of th   FULL HOUSE
FULL HOUSE   e mouth...I raise you another 50 he finally   FULL HOUSE
FULL HOUSE   said just like that looking at me in the ey   FULL HOUSE
FULL HOUSE   es....what a sonofabitch OH...I was sweating   FULL HOUSE
FULL HOUSE   under the arms and in the crotch too...my j   FULL HOUSE
FULL HOUSE   ockies sticking to my balls...finally I pus   FULL HOUSE
FULL HOUSE   hed all the dough I had in front of me into   FULL HOUSE
FULL HOUSE   the pot to see his hand...cool as a rabbit.   FULL HOUSE
FULL HOUSE   ..on the surface but inside burning like he   FULL HOUSE
FULL HOUSE   ll...I was almost tempted to raise him anot   FULL HOUSE
FULL HOUSE   her 50...takes guts...the kind of guts I do   FULL HOUSE
FULL HOUSE   n't have...that did it...I don't have to gi   FULL HOUSE
FULL HOUSE   ve all the details...all the emotions and r   FULL HOUSE
FULL HOUSE   eactions...after all it's only a game...but   FULL HOUSE
FULL HOUSE   what a game...I'll use that exactly how the   FULL HOUSE
FULL HOUSE   whole thing happened approximately...but fi   FULL HOUSE
FULL HOUSE   rst he'll have to be able to take it...HE'l   FULL HOUSE
FULL HOUSE   l have to learn how to play because when he   FULL HOUSE
FULL HOUSE   first arrives in America he's so dumb he do   FULL HOUSE
FULL HOUSE   esn't even know how to play poker...eventua   FULL HOUSE
FULL HOUSE   lly I'll teach him...I'll make a gambler ou   FULL HOUSE
FULL HOUSE   t of him too...but in the beginning nothing   FULL HOUSE
FULL HOUSE   ...just as dumb as the guy with the FLUSH..   FULL HOUSE
FULL HOUSE   FULL HOUSE

FULL HOUSE FULL HOUSE FULL HOUSE FULL HOUSE FULL HOUSE FULL HOUSE FULL HOUSE
FULL HOUSE FULL HOUSE FULL HOUSE FULL HOUSE FULL HOUSE FULL HOUSE FULL HOUSE
FULL HOUSE FULL HOUSE FULL HOUSE FULL HOUSE FULL HOUSE FULL HOUSE FULL HOUSE

Nothing literally nothing what a dumb guy it's only later on that he
learns the game but that redheaded jerk he knew the game that's fo
r sure I really felt bad for him when I grabbed the big pot 5 or
6 hundred bucks so bad for that poor jerk that I told him look
here man I'll give you another chance the whole bundle on th
e line in one blow everythin D g take it or leave it that'
s generosity for you he loo O ked at me with a blank loo
k on his face and then sai U d ok and that's how it ha
ppened and of course I wo B n with a lousy pair of j
acks I believe so finall L y when I got out of the
place I must have had a E t least 12 or 13 hundr
ed bucks in my pocket   but I'll know for su
re only when I make m O y grand total at the
end then I'll know f R or sure how much I'
m supposed to have   won because the m
oney has to come f N rom someplace but
if that's not luc O k then I don't k
now what luck is T and for once yo
u might say I h H ad it assuming
even now for t I he record tha
t everytime a N guy speaks h
e tells a tr G ue story th
en this is how finally the
game ended after I turned up
my three deuces and grabbed th
e big pot it was then that I dec
ided to double up everything of co
urse I didn't say it aloud but I tho
ught of it and I can still see the poo
r guy's face when I said to him ok doubl
e or nothing his face was all green he mig
ht have pulled a knife on me or a gun or eve
n a machine gun like in the movies after all w
e were not too far from Hollywood you never know
with guys like that but he didn't move he simply m
umbled something again what a mumbler and then he to
ok a sip from his glass but funny thing though everybo
dy could see that his glass was empty yes they were serv
ing drinks in that basement either he didn't realize his g
lass was empty or else he made believe the poor sucker final
ly he got up and sort of shrugging his narrow shoulders he sai
d see you around speaking to all the other guys I suppose certai
nly not to me directly because I was not going to be around very l
ong but still he said that unbelievable the things a guy says when h
e knows he's had it and I am quoting only what he said not what prob
ably was going on in his mind his narrow little mind that little jer
k so many guys like that lousy louse losers it's like the time on th
e boat just before the boat arrived in New York there was a guy play
ing poker and losing everything he had brought with him from the old
country and still he wouldn't quit he kept playing and playing I rea
lly felt sorry for him particularly since I didn't know the game the
n it's only later on that I learned but at the time I knew nothing y
es literally nothing but I don't have to go into all the details now

I
don't
have
to
get
carried
away   But there was that tremendous poker game

that went on for three days straight (and three nights) I was really tempt

ed but I didn't want to lose my fifty bucks   Finally I walked away.

He could do the same   Have the same thing happen to his fifty bucks.

No he's too busy with Mary on the boat But sometimes it happens A guy come

s to America An immigrant He's got a few bucks to get started (a new life)

he gets caught up in a poker game or a crap game (on the boat) and by the

time he lands (in New York usually) it's all gone:

> Most of these guys have to work as dishwashers
> (or janitors) when they arrive or else it's st
> raight to the factory for them (eight hours or
> more a day) hands bleeding dreaming of the old
> country

(I knew a guy like that once)   It's always the same story.

Beginner's luck ... Bullshit!

Luck is something that goes with the weather. If it rains you're fuc

ked. That much I know. Like that time I was walking down the street

and it was raining and I was sure it was a lucky day for me just beca

use I woke up that morning feeling happy (the sun was shining when it

happened) but by the time I was walking down the street it was rainin

g like hell and I slipped on the pavement and fell and almost broke m

y leg. I didn't break it but I could have.

                    And people talk to you abo

ut LUCK!

> Talk to that guy (the little redheaded punk) about luck (yes do it)
> with his flush and I pulled a full house on him (3 kings & two tens)

He simply said SEE YOU AROUND but you could tell who he was speaking to ....
                                                              to
be honest he was looking at me straight into my eyes I didn't look back
I simply looked above his head past his red hair. I
  simply wanted to get the hell out of there.....   Q U I C K

    takes guts

to do that that fast   I played two or three more rounds   Faking it
really   Literally giving away a few bucks to get the first card and then fol
                                                                         din
             only one more hand I kept saying to   g
             myself and dammit if I didn't win a
             nother pot with only a lousy pair o
             f jacks something like 25 or 30 buc
             ks more but even that counts   :

pays for a few boxes of noodles.

             The other guys had really cooled off after the

             big hand and I felt like they admired me - who

             wouldn't - but it's not certain maybe they wer

             e just being nice to me to get their money bac

             k (tough shit!) that money BABY that's for the

             room and the noodles the coffee and the toothp

             aste and all the rest of the stuff I didn't sa

             y that (of course) I didn't even think that at

             the time I didn't think anything at the time I

             was too chicken I don't even know when or even

             how I got out of there I didn't even know in f

             act the next day I don't even know now HOW the

             whole thing started. Must have been in L. A.

It came to me only when I was on the bus. The next day. Greyhound bus. On my
way to New York. (Yesterday I arrived in New York that's how I'll start on the
boat). But then I was down to about 1200 dollars or less. It must have been w
hen I thought up the whole idea of DOUBLE OR NOTHING   ---------------------
                                                          DOUBLE OR NOTHING

That's it! I said to myself . . . But by now I must have about a thousand l
eft maybe less or a little more but just enough to where I will have to figure
out everything down to the last penny down to the last detail   and tomorrow
we start   Lucky I remembered the typewriter for a moment I thought I had l
ost the pawn ticket (I had pawned the typewriter in Las Vegas) it was in my
raincoat pocket (I had a raincoat in those days) I would really be fucked no
w without a typewriter couldn't afford to buy a new one even if I cut down on
the noodles the coffee the tomato sauce I couldn't make it those damn machines
cost a fortune even when used and with a used one you never know what will give

I don't have to go into the TYPEWRITER now   except when the screw
                                                  fell off   yes

    Must have been (conditionally) about the 127th day:

    127 boxes later a screw fell off the typewriter It
    has to be Something like that always happens to th
    ose damn machines and then you fuck around for day
    s trying to fit the little screw into the proper h
    ole Particularly when you don't have the proper to
    ol to work with at the time it happens - 127th day

WRITE IT BY HAND   (that's what the little voice of reason tells
                                                  you
                                                  in
                                                  the
                                                  back
                                                  of
                                                  your
                                                  mind)

But that's impossible
Can't even reread my own handwriting   And then after a while y
ou get cramps in your fingers and you can't go on particularly a
t the speed I plan to write the damn thing (minimum 12 pages a d
                                                             a
                                                             y
                                                              ‿

    By the 127th day when the little screw fell off, I
    must have had about 127 times 12, if you count onl
    y final pages, approximately 1524 pages IMPOSSIBLE
    nobody can work that fast even if you waste two or
    three boxes trying to screw the little screw in th
    e proper little screwing hole in the typewriter...

    No use anticipating of course Maybe the little scr
    ew won't fall off around the 127th day Maybe it'll
    happen later or even earlier One never knows But u
    ndoubtedly a little screw will fall off It always-
    -you can bet on it--happens And you screw around f
    or days trying to fix the damn thing so that the m
    achine can go on . . . . .to the END

In any case I'll describe the whole thing step by step And of course that's

without counting all the pages I'll throw away (all the garbage) The First
                                                                  Second
                                                                  Third
                                                  (and possibly) Fourth
                                                                  drafts
                                                                  ..

TOUS LES BROUILLONS AND ALL THE CORRECTIONS.

Could add up: 1 2 3 4 5 6 7 8 9 10 to infinity and eternity 12345678910.

A guy's got to think ahead. Could think of a name for him for instance. A
nice name. Got to be nice to him. Buddy Buddy for a while ME & YOU & HE.

There'll be other guys too (other characters if you wish) to think about too.

        365
        days   that's a lot of days

        Let's try something for now: JACK!
        If I had a chance to change my name
        that's what I'd choose for myself : JACK!
I love that name.   Except that in his case it should be JACQUES and not
                                       JACK!
In French it's JACQUES -- can't get around it since he comes from France --
        -- that's got to be made clear from the beginning --
        -- on the boat when Mary asks him what's his name --
        -- my real name is Jacques he says just like that --

What a liar!
I suppose I'll have him do muchthesamething I did. Travel: LOS ANGELES or
LAS VEGAS and all the other stinking places I've been too and eventually he
ends up in NEW YORK (it's quite obvious in order that we may converge or me
rge). And little by little we'll coincide. We'll overlap. HE & I.   TO
                                                                         GE
                                                                          TH
                                                                          ER
I'll even make a gambler out of him. Teach him the game. Not immediately!
He's too inexperienced in the beginning but eventually. And besides you've
got to be able to speak the language or else they take you for everything y
ou've got. Even if it's only fifty bucks. During the coffee breaks (79 ce
nts a jar -- on sale) in the factory (CHRYSLER - a damn good car) I'll have
him get involved in a few games. A few quick crap games. But he loses all
the time (at first): HURTS to lose all the time
                 HURTS like hell near the heart
                            near the guts too But he has to lear
n. Doesn't help to feel sorry for him (or for myself). It's a waste of ti
                                             me and of course a
                                             waste of money too
and when it comes to money he'll learn QUICK.

At that rate you'll never get the damn show on the road:

        416 dollars just for the room
        then the noodles on top of that (?)
Got to start all over:
        365 boxes (one pound each) at 29
        365 times 29 makes $105.85 (correct)
Could start adding up just to see where I stand: 416 plus 105.85: 416
                                                                              105.85
                                                                                   521.85

Here goes half of my earnings -- almost -- if you can call it that.

I've got to work out a system immediately to keep track and to keep above the su
rface. Best way of course is to make a list and keep adding up as you go along.
No doubt about that. With a list you never get lost even when you're lying even
when you're telling a story. True or not true. True or false. A list makes it
look credible. You have to make lists in life if you want to survive. All sort
s of lists or else how can you go on?
        or else you forget 1/2 or 2/3 or 1/5 or what you want to say and that
leaves 1/2 or 1/3 or 4/5 of what you want to say that is said. That's not tooto
o bad considering that most of what you say or want to say is crap anyway. LIES
or   LEFTOVERS

Here are examples then of possible lists
_____

EXAMPLES OF LISTS:

1. List of jobs Jacques has during his first year in America.

2. List of people he meets during that period -- (365 days) --.

3. List of girls -- girls he screws and girls he doesn't screw.

4. List of things he wants to do during that time but never does.

5. List of possible names for Jacques if I decide eventually that I don't like that name.

6. List of things (clothes - souvenirs - junk - etc.) Jacques has in his suitcase when he first arrives in America.

That's the way to go! Then you take each list and you develop - you expand:

NUMBER ONE that's no problem because you can always invent a little Yes jobs are easy to invent Travelling salesman G rocery store clerk Parking lot attendant Dishwasher Factor y worker Waiter Shoeshine boy Pimp and of course Unemploye d or partially employed depending how much money you need.

NUMBER TWO that won't make much of a list because most peo ple after they've asked you how long you've been in this c ountry and how you like it simply forget about you even if they have politely invited you for dinner or if they casua lly say in a conversation why don't you drop in sometime..

NUMBER THREE also won't make much of a list particularly t he first part unless of course you are irresistible But wh en it comes to the second part that could go on and on par ticularly if you count real and unreal girls The types you dream about or even those you follow in the streets withou t ever having the guts to speak to them The unscrewable on es The virgins The snobs The rich broads The ugly bitches.

NUMBER FOUR is the kind of list that can go on and on to i nfinity It's just a matter of time and patience The places you want to visit the money you want to save the books you want to read the movies you want to see the girls you want to marry the things you want to say or not say Etc..Etc...

NUMBER FIVE is the kind of list that depends a great great deal on the mood of the guy writing the story In this case me Here you can use real names if you wish or made up name s even if they are not believable or foreign names or else skip names altogether and simply furnish blanks perhaps...

NUMBER SIX won't make much of a list either except if to b e stuffy you decide to list everything down to the last li ttle piece of junk like an old used up bus ticket or a rub ber band or a worn out pair of socks or a postcard that so mebody sent from a sunny place or even the guy's all-torn-yellowed-andsctochedtogether-birth-certificate or else his pipe if the guy happens to be a pipe smoker at the time...

One can make all sorts of lists like that.
But most important is never to lose track.

                              For instance right now the most
important is the list of things I need in the room   once I have the room
              list of things for the year from now to the end/365 days
before switching to the TIME OF NOODLES.

                              Or else the whole system is all
screwed up.   Everything falls apart   and you have to give up.

BUT YOU CAN'T GIVE UP   Right!   then

                                                       I won't
                                                       I swear

                              Fine. But then it doesn't have
to be logical.   Doesn't even pay to work in alphabetical order
                 Would be useless   in fact
                 Just straight down the line: n t c t t o
                                                 o o o o o o
                                                 o m f o o a
                                                 d a f t t p
                                                 l t e h h
                                                 e o e p b
                                                 s s   a r
                                                 a   s u
                                                 u   t s
                                                 c   e h
                                                 e   WHAT A SET UP!

SOAP next. yes SOAP. Just like that.   A guy's got to wash
Water Gas Electricity all that included of course. For eight
bucks a week a guy would have to be crazy not to include Gas
Electricity & Water or else he would have to GIVE UP WASHING   that's for sure.

                 No problems then so far
                 No need even to save --

                 Also it'll pass the time A shower now and then when you're
                 depressed and here we go rising from the water ~~like Lazarus~~
                 fresh like a brand new baby (boy) - smelling like a flower.

SOAP!   One bar a week?   That's too much?
                                                 That's not enough?

        52 bars for the year!
                                                 That's almost right!
                                                 That's too much!

20 for the year and that's it . . . . No argument.
                              Of course one can always make mistakes.
But how can I figure out everything without goofing?   Every penny counts and
besides how the hell do I get all the stuff into the room without attracting
suspicion once I have decided what I need in the room? That's an ENORMOUS
question - a GIANT dilemma - some wise guy would say. Time is essential
of course. Even if you buy a few items at the time they'll think you're
mad. They'll think you're hoarding away like the end of the world is coming
or like you know something they don't know. Things like that happen all the
time - nowadays.

Like during the war... the occupation... and what an occupation!!! I
just can't walk into a grocery store and ask for 365 boxes... 365 bo
xes of noodles... they'll think I'm cracked... they'll look at me as
though I'm crazy... even in the supermarket you just can't walk arou
nd with a buggy full of noodles... noodle boxes... 365 of them... it
's not normal... it's irregular... they'll think you're a salesman o
r something... only thing to do is make trips... lots of trips... up
and down the stairs... UP & DOWN...

Let's say you buy 10 boxes at a t
ime... 10 boxes in one basket... that's almost human... nobody can q
uestion 10 boxes... and if someone asks you can always say you're ha
ving a party... a family dinner... 10 boxes in one basket that's a l
ittle more than 36 trips... 36 trips just for noodles!!! 36 and 1/2.
.. trips... to be exact... but of course since you can't have half t
rips... all trips are full trips... it'll have to be 37 trips... yes
... UP & DOWN the damn stairs...

Sweating like hell... arms full of b
oxes... unless you decide to buy only 8 boxes at a time... 8 boxes e
ach trip... that makes more trips... of course... 42.625 trips exact
ly... that's idiotic... 10 boxes a trip is much easier and much fast
er too... you come out with an even 1/2 trip rather than that goofed
up little .625 trip which in itself is an impossibility since you ca
n't cut boxes in half... all trips are full trips... unless of cours
e you make 35 trips with 10 boxes and the last one... the 36th... wi
th 15 boxes... then you have only 36 trips... but the best is 37 tri
ps... 36 with 10 boxes and 1 with 5 boxes... makes more sense... yes
... 37 trips:

1 2 3 4 5 6 7 8 9 10 11 12 13 14 15 16 17 18 19 20 21 22 23 24 25 26

27 28 29 30 31 32 33 34 35 36 37 T
                                  R
                                  I
                                  P
                                  S

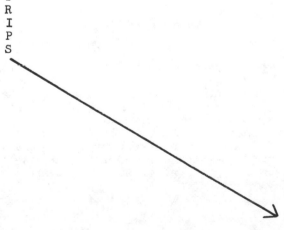

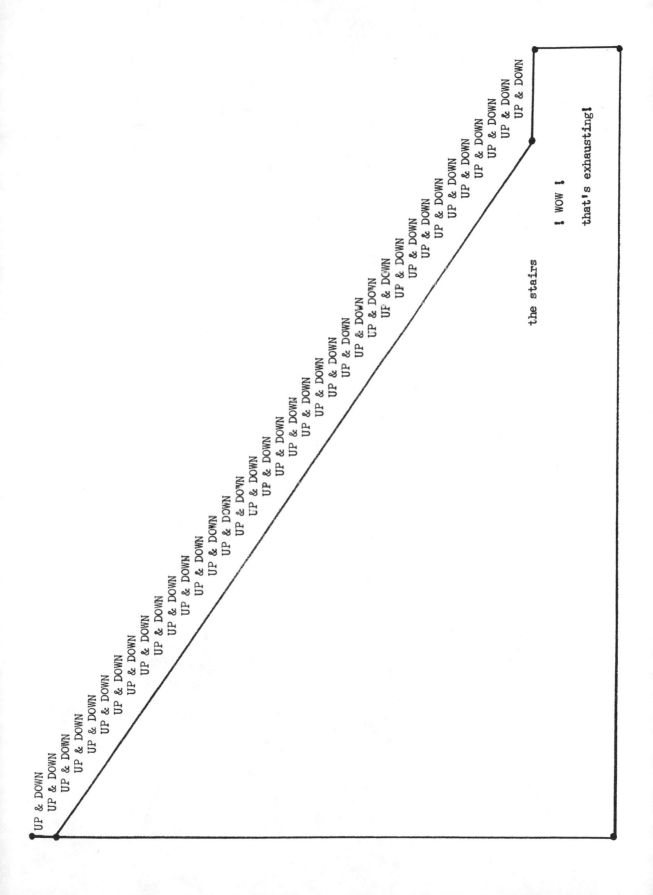

34.0

I could cut down (the UP & DOWNS) if I took 12 boxes or even 15 instead of 10
each trip   But one trip more or less   who gives a shit
                 Doesn't pay just not to go through that UP & DOWN crap again

And besides there is all the other junk too: 52 cans of tomato sauce

(10 cans a trip. That's 5 point 2 trips on top of the original 37) Of cours
                                                                             e
I'll make the point 2 a full trip with   the 5 tubes of toothpaste
                                               the 26 jars of coffee
                                               the new toothbrush
                                               the salt and the pepper

A GUY'S GOT TO BE PRACTICAL.

                          Who ever thought I would get so involved with
                          trips   UP
                          And yet   &
                          I've been around   DOWN
                          A world traveller indeed

But if there is an elevator in the place then it won't be so hard on the legs
I like the sixth floor gives you a feeling of being way up at the top or near
Even if the stairs stink like hell -- So many stairs in one's life (yes) And
                          So many closets too. . . . .!

I didn't think of that. If there is a closet in the room then I can save som
e space. Have more horses in sight. But can you trust closets? Even though
most rooms have closets. Particularly in my case (and his case too) closets
have a very special (symbolic) meaning:

          REMEMBER --------------------? "My life began in a closet
                                           Among empty skins and dusty hats
                                           While sucking pieces of stolen sugar"

                                          (PARMI LES MONSTRES, Paris, 1966-67)

SUGAR (dammit!) almost forgot! (make a note quick)   SUGAR

Nobody would believe it: "Outside the Moon tiptoed across the roof
                                         Frightened I ran down the staircase but
                                         Slipped on the twelfth step and fell..."

                                        (IBID.)

So many stairs in one's life!
And so many closets......too!

Doesn't matter. 365 boxes of noodles wouldn't fit in a closet (that's for sure)
Doesn't matter how large the closet is. I'll simply line up the walls from the
floor to the ceiling:
                          I can already see the place
                          and myself in that cubicle of boxes
                          and the horses flying on the wall paper

                          WALL TO WALL NOODLES

But I've got to be able to see my horses/   /That's essential/

Pile the boxes in the center of the room/   /What a good idea/

A square tower of noodle boxes: 12 by 12/   /That'll be great/

And walk around for exercise twice a day/   /That's essential/

Of course you'll have to climb on THE chair to take down the daily box

<pre>
                                                    ---
                                                   can't
                                                   start
                                                    at
                                                    the
                                                  BOTTOM

</pre>

or else the whole thing would come crashing down on top of mc - (bang)

I can already see myself perched on MY chair selecting the daily box :

macaronishellselbowszittispearsmanicottispaghettistwistedcurlyroundetc

readingthelabels-thecookinginstructions-theingredients-thediscourseetc

<pre>
             -would be funny as hell if one night the whole-
                                -TOWER-
             -fell on top of me buried in a pile of noodles-
</pre>

<u>HUGE HEADLINES</u>

Y O U N G   M A N   D I E S   I N   R O O M   S U F F O C A T E D

U N D E R   N O O D L E   B O X E S

M Y S T E R Y   U N S O L V E D   P O L I C E   I N V E S T I G A T E S

N O   C L U E S

Of course they'll find the manuscript (unfinished). They'll read it pe
rhaps. Judge it for sure. Edit it maybe. Publish it eventually. And
sell it probably. Criticize it certainly. Make a movie with it (quite
possibly). A lousy adaptation with a bad actor and a phony ending. Or
else they'll destroy it. Yes. Burn it publicly. Step on it publicly.

<u>HUGE HEADLINES</u>

P O S T H U M O U S   M A S T E R P I E C E   F O U N D   I N   N O O D L E S

No   those boxes are not heavy enough   you're kidding yourself   you
could work your way out   365 bars of soap would be more dangerous   but
I said 20
      20 is enough   How much for each bar? They should make little-
free booklets with all the prices for guys like us. So many prices to che
ck and no booklets.   Just that alone can discourage a guy: drive him or
you mad/nuts/crazy/ding/fou/sonné - drive him or you straight to his///your
grave/hole/box/trou - drive you or him out of your///his head/mind/tête/cul

Therefore: Got to decide -- 10 cents - 15 cents a bar -- 3 for a quarter -

                                        3 for a quarter:

(that's not unusual) that means you can either get 6 times 3 makes 18
                                        or 7 times 3 makes 21
                                either way doesn't come out even.
                                Let's go for 21 (gives you an extra bar)
3 for a quarter makes 7 quarters
21 divided by 3 and multiplied by 25 (cents) makes $1.75
                                        Add $1.75 to the previous total
and you've got a brand new total.

But where the hell is my previous total?   Definitely without a list
                                        - a list of all the lists
                                        - you're fucked up & down
                                        & sideways and all the wa
                                                                y!

Some of that crap I should be able to buy on sale (don't think of stealing at
this stage -- too early).   Next item? SHIT!   Almost forgot:
                                SHITPAPER..... of course paper for
                                                                the
crapper. Can't do without.
        Could go back to newspaper like in the olden days (he should be used
to it but not me no not me I'm spoiled by civilization and culture) but after
a while you get a sore ass from the roughness it's so rough And anyway newsp
apers cost money too and worse of all you're always tempted to read the dam
n thing to read the dates the advertisements the news the comic strips eve
n if they are outdated or all fuzzy or even if the thing is discolored No

        No newspaper. That's for sure.

        Nothing to do with the outside world --------------------- -------------
                                        ----
                                        ------everything inside------
                                        ----

Make a list QUICK
of things to do without: No papers
                           No books
                           No telephone
                           No clocks
                           No watches
                           No rubbers
                           No time
                           No social involvement
                           No human contacts
                           No deodorant
                           No cars (that's obvious)
                           No bicycles
                           No mass communication

That's a list for you and I could go on and on like that for hours.
NO NOTHING just the TIME OF NOODLES box after box down to nothing.

When there'll be no more boxes then my time will be up
                                what a set up
                                _____
                                for a   story:

NOODLES HE ROOM STUBBORN UNCLE DAVID BOAT TOOTHBRUSH

WALL PAPER SICK PEGGY TOMATO SAUCE R. F. FICTITIOUS SIXTH FLOOR TOMATO SAUCE NOODLES

COFFEE POKER PIER FRANCE TOILET PAPER CHEWING GUN I ROOM

CONCENTRATION CAMP vomit vomit HORSES CLOSET SALT BUTTER

SAXOPHONE EXTERMINATED MOTHER ERNEST DETERMINED TAURUS BRIDGE RHETORIC LOS ANGELES TOILET PAPER

STAIRS POTATOES OCEAN AMERICA TELEPHONE DISCOURSE OBSCURITIES

YOU TOOTHBRUSH SCRIBBLER UP & DOWN AFRICA TABLE PAPER PUNCTUATION SOAP....HE PLOT

$$$ POKER... BUS ??? MARY OCTOBER 1ST 8 BUCKS 365

PARANOIAC CAMP ROOM MOTHER FARM RATS DEODORANT NEWSPAPERS

VITAMINS LOULOU PLOT #4 FIRST PERSON FUCK YES NEVER CRAP

BEGINNING BOAT TOILET PAPER $105.85 shit shit LIST MILWAUKEE CRAP ALMOST I

SECOND PERSON LAMPSHADE FLYING HORSES N.Y. DOUBLE .04 TOOTHPASTE WE LIAR

JOSEPH LIES CHARACTERS 12 FATHER EGG NOODLES MR. LAWRENCE

BAGS SAOP LAS VEGAS PALUCCI TYPEWRITER GAMBLING BOX SCREW RATS

SHY 19 FRENCH/ENGLISH sperm sperm LIFE ONE YEAR CURTAINS

POSTERITY STAIRS DEATH SOUVENIRS NOODLER DETROIT NOT GLOVES NORTHERN HIGH SCHOOL THEY SEX

CHRYSLER BLOOD FOG SONOFABITCH NOTHING OR MASTURBATION SEPTEMBER 30TH RECORDINGS N O W

JAZZ THIRD PERSON 416 DOLLARS

PROTAGONIST NOODLES 365 DAYS FAMILY blood blood GERMAN PAGES TREMENDOUS WOW NO

IRRESPONSIBLE 1 2 3 365 DAYS 8 OF COURSE SLOW MOTHERFUCKER 5 6 3 CHAIR;!!?

After he lands in New York he'll have to be on his own YES uncle Arthur NO
David will be waiting for him on the pier You're sure about that NO Uncle
Sam James David Yes David is better That's what I said before A little old
man who can hardly speak English That's the irony He doesn't know that his
uncle is also a foreigner First generation YES I am the only one who knows
that uncle David is not an American and that he speaks five languages YES
but not English or at least not very well in fact very badly YES That makes
it more interesting Here we have then a guy who speaks five languages but
who can hardly speak English Five languages NO KIDDING German Russian Polish Hungarian and Yiddish that's if you count the last one as a regular
language and whose English is so lousy he can't even communicate with his
nephew when his nephew arrives in America YES That's irony for you But who
is to know that he never met his uncle before Nobody told him Nobody Talk
to me about mass communication after that A little old man who speaks five
languages but mostly Yiddish and his nephew Jacques doesn't speak a damn
word of Yiddish of course French Jews don't speak it any more A dead tongue
for them A least not the new generation
                    the left over generation
                    the reduced generation Those who didn't end up as lampshades
(I don't have to go into that but it's there in the background and will alwa
  ys be there Can't avoid it even if you want to THE CAMPS
                                                     &
                                            THE LAMPS
                                                  H
                                                  A
                                                  D
                                                  E
                                                  S   The boat is slow
ly approaching the dock. A band is playing and thousands of people maybe more
are waving their hands and handkerchiefs. It's a tremendous scene. It's diz-
zying. Noisy. Confusing. Imagine that. He's standing next to Mary on what
seems to be the upper deck in his double-breasted suit. His only suit except
for the green sweater in his suitcase. He's holding on to her hand squeezing
it tight. He can't see his uncle in the crowd. And anyway doesn't matter he
doesn't even know how he looks his uncle. Uncle David definitely. More real.

How the hell will they meet?
What will they say to each other?
Will they kiss?
Will they cry?

These are QUESTIONS that will have to be answered eventually.
Damn good QUESTIONS and there are many more to be asked soon.

The first QUESTION is simple:

Eventually Mary points to a little old man in a brown suit and an enormous
red tie with rimless glasses on his nose and no overcoat. It's summertime

therefore he didn't wear his overcoat. No hat either. THAT'S YOUR UNCLE!

she cried. I KNOW IT'S HIM! What is she? Some kind of visionary? A pro

phet or something? How did she know? Nobody knows? Instinct? Bluff? L
uck? Whatever the case she hit it right on the nose. That's for sure. I

(no I mean) Robert (?) imagined him quite different. Tall in a darkish su

it with a striped tie and perhaps an umbrella (it's cloudy that day) a big

felt hat dark blue shiny shoes. Uncle George! The things a guy invents w
hen he doesn't know. UNCLE GEORGE! Why not THEODORE? And ROBERT! What'

s going on? What a nice pair they would make together. UNCLE GEORGE with

his nephew ROBERT from France. Charming! But uncle david and jacques tha

t's not the same. Though ROBERT that's not a bad name except that after a
while everybody calls him BOB and he passes for a real American (except of

course when he opens his mouth to speak then everybody knows for sure what

he is). No good. He's got to stay a foreigner for a while or else the wh

ole story falls apart. The first year at least. Then why not something m
ore French more European more cosmopolitan. MARCEL...ANDRE...JEAN-LOUIS..

Too Catholic. EMILE? No! A bit more Jewish even though this is not -- I

insist -- a Jewish story. This whole business of names is getting on my n

erves. I'll never get him off the boat. Who says I have to give him a na
me now. Eventually yes. Particularly if in the beginning he speaks in th

e first person (or will speak). Even though it's a bit restricting. Have

him tell his own story (he's about 19 when he arrives) then he doesn't hav

e to mention his name immediately. The whole thing told from the point of
view of a 19 year old (a bit naive). Why not try it out for a while while

he's standing on the upper deck of the boat with Mary in his double-breast

ed suit holding on to her hand anxiously waiting to get off the boat to me
et uncle David on the pier and get started with his first year in America.

I was standing next to the girl from Milwaukee (Mary was her name I beli
eve). On the upper deck in my double-breasted suit. A grey suit. We met the
first day at sea on the lower deck while the band was playing. We quickly be
came good friends. It's not unusual on boats. But she refused to sleep with
me.

HE'S SO SHY HE WON'T EVEN SAY SCREW WITH ME

Not that she didn't want to. But somehow (you see) it never worked that
way. We necked quite a bit on the deck. The upper deck in my double-breasted
suit. Sort of greyish with the American tie Uncle David sent me from America
in one of the packages. And the American socks too. During the nights. It
was beautiful. Sometimes the Moon was out over the sea. And the sea so ca
lm. So...So dreamy. It was my first trip on a boat. But it was foggy in
New York when we arrived. You know the kind of fog that drips from every
thing and makes you say what a lousy weather. Scary kind of fog. The k
ind that makes you feel lonely.

WHAT A ROMANTIC

Lucky Mary was there. But it never got very far. I mean the necking on
the upper deck with the blanket. Couldn't get into her cabin because of the o
ther girl from Chicago. Fat and ugly. I slept in the big hole down below (i
n the precipice) where they shove 20 or 30 or even more guys together and it
stinks like hell. Feet and all that other smell. She must have been older
than me. Sort of blond. Cute. With funny teeth.

HIS AESTHETIC NOTIONS ARE UNDERDEVELOPED

I loved her. I can't tell if she did even though she told me she did at
that time. She was so nice to me. So understanding. So comprehensive. So c
ompassionate. We promised to write to each other regularly. And she said th
at she would try to come and see me in Detroit.

I SUPPOSE HE ALREADY KNOWS HE'S GOING TO LIVE IN DETROIT A LETTER
OR SOMETHING THE ADDRESS ON THE PACKAGES A GUY DOES NOT HAVE TO B
E A GENIUS TO PUT TWO AND TWO TOGETHER AND GUESS THAT IF THE PACK
AGES COME FROM DETROIT THEN THAT MUST BE WHERE THE GUY WHO ADDRES
SES THE PACKAGES MUST BE LIVING IN THIS CASE UNCLE DAVID OF COURSE

Milwaukee is not very far from Detroit (that's what she said) if you kno
w how to get there. Across the lakes. The Great Lakes. That's what she told
me. She even showed me on a map. I was standing behind her. Very close. I
was looking over her shoulder while she was pointing with her finger on a ma
p of America. I could feel her behind inside her blue shorts. She was wea
ring her blue shorts then and I was wearing my green sweater. What a love
ly behind.

DOESN'T EVEN HAVE THE GUTS TO SAY ASS

And funny thing is she did write to me regularly during the first six or
seven months (at least). I still have her letters.

I'LL THROW IN A FEW LETTERS SIX OR SEVEN AS SAMPLES OF WHAT SHE
WRITES HIM THAT'S GOOD FOR TWO OR THREE BOXES OF NOODLES

But she never came to see me in Detroit. That's a long story. Am I all
owed to go into that? It might take a while. But first I should describe the
encounter with my uncle. On the pier. He was wearing a brown suit and a red
tie. I had never met him before. Mary is the one who pointed him out to me
just like that. What a nice girl.

UNBELIEVABLE THE THINGS A GUY CAN INVENT

It's so easy
Easier as you go on
The first six months or so
It's the last six months that are tough
The last stretch
When you're fed up with the noodles
When you can't take it any more
When the little screw keeps falling off the typewriter
When you're down in the hole
At the bottom of the precipice crawling like a rat
In the beginning anything goes
But later on it slows down
You spend hours and hours just wasting time
With the curtains closed you won't know if it's night or day
Just keep going that's what I'll keep telling myself
With my beard down to my belly
That's another question to answer
Do I shave or do I give up shaving
And there is the problem of the toilet paper that's still unresolved
The room all set
The noodles ok
The coffee fine
The toothpaste and toothbrush all over
The tomato sauce I almost forgot once in a while for extra flavor
Then you start on the boat
Uncle David waiting on the pier
The two of them on the upper deck
He's wearing his double-breasted suit

It's easy
Easier as you go on
The first six months or so

And then of course you can jump ahead
Look into the future so to speak into the conditional rather
But nothing before New York
No past
The Statue of Liberty
Nothing before the boat
All that crap about the War the Farm the Camp the Lampshades excluded
You start just like that on the boat
First he speaks in the first person
If I don't like it I'll switch to the second person or to the third person

It's easy
Easier as you go on
The first six months or so
It's the last six months that are critical
The last stretch
When you're fed up with the noodles and the tomato sauce
When you can't take it any more and you switch to the third person

UNBELIEVABLE THE THINGS A GUY CAN INVENT

And she keeps promising that one of these days she's going to surprise him and come to see him in Detroit and this time they're going to do it together...and he believes her..anywhere (but where..? can't do it in his room--that furnished room he has with the Hungarian people...what a lousy set up!..in a park?..no not with her...has to be beautiful...the first time...in America you don't fuck just anyplace...in a hotel...a motel yes...but you need a car...and anyway he wouldn't even know how to go about getting a room...that's how dumb and inexperienced he is...later on he finds out that most of the time it's done in the back seat of cars...but that too is out of the question)...Doesn't matter because she never came to see him in Detroit.

                              -- Uncle David doesn't have a car --

I could have told him that

But he goes on and on.....

One day I got a letter from Mary. Must have been six or seven months after I was in Detroit. My English had really improved a great deal too so that I could really read her letters. I read them and reread them often.

-- Still in the first person --

It was a funny letter: Saying that she was engaged to be married and that I would understand and that everything was fine and that he was a great person the other guy an old school friend from Milwaukee who was serious.

She was a college girl from a good family (Lutheran). She must have been to be able to spend a whole summer travelling in Europe by herself. It's expensive!

To write a letter like that takes guts (at least two boxes). When I got it the letter I thought it was the end of the world. Even though we had not seen each other again since the boat. I wanted to die (tremendous!) but that's not an easy thing to do in America. After six or seven months in America things do change fast for a guy like me.

                 Dying becomes almost meaningless -- I mean you're so lonely - so cornered - so speechless - in the dark hole of your furnished room (boxes all over) and Chrysler and school in the morning if you work the afternoon shift or in the evening if it's the other way around you don't even think of dying any more -- it's hopeless - useless - yes: !
                                                            IT'S SAD

That's about it.   For now.

He can jump around like that in his story.   Feeling sorry for himself.

Since he remembers the whole thing and remembering is always a confusing process.
When you remember   you don't remember   in a straight line   never.

                Things don't have to be in C-H-R-O-N-O-L-O-G-I-C-A-L-O-R-D-E-R

                In fact   most of it is plain lies -- lies.   Bavardage.

In fact if you go on like that they'll take you for a BAVARD (you know Le Bavard)

                :   talkative
                :   loquacious
                :   garrulous
                :   discursive   GABBY

In any case I paraphrase verbatum (my translation):

                Besides the sequence of events does not matter
                and believe me if I analyze if I build hypothe
                ses if I temporize it is less by scrupules tha
                t I might let something get lost of what comes
                to my mind in bulk than to allow myself to pla
                y a little game as frivolous as it is inoffens
                ive at which I do not claim to be a master a l
                ittle game which consists primarily in holding
                your interlocutor at bay and then through sham
                resulting from a rather deplorable habit to lo
                se him with what could have been what has perh
                aps what has surely not been what would have b
                een good to have been and what would have been
                bad to have been and what has been overlooked-
                -by the overalllooker- to say and what was sai
                d which was not said and so on until finally l
                osing patience he cries out: GET TO THE POINT
                                              GET TO THE POINT

One could set up (indeed) a whole series of scenes to work with (series are always
useful just as much as lists are always useful).

                First the scene on the boat.

                QUICK make a list immediately of possible series of scenes:

1. Scene on the boat (the excitement of arriving in America. Not too much descrip-
                tion. Feelings. Lots of feelings. The people. The buildin-
                gs. The streets. The taxis. The dogs in the street. But in
                the beginning it doesn't really feel like a foreign country at
                all. America! feels like any other country at first).

2. Scene in the subway (the excitement. A bit more description. With feelings too
                and emotions. The girl. The legs. The ass. Uncle David al-
                most asleep. The people. The negroes. The suitcase. In the
                beginning it feels quite different. The subway! feels somew-
                hat like it's not the same at first).

Nothing does.   That doesn't mean much. It means that being in America
                       doesn't feel like being in a foreign country
                                 feels like being in the same place as before
                                           same as in your own
                                                      country
if you have one.

Unless of course you come from a place like Japan or India or Arabia
                       or some place like that
         then of course it feels different
               many things are different   :

First there is the language

               that's different

               Since Robert doesn't speak a word of English he does
               feel like a foreigner when he tries to speak   But
               when he does not open his mouth then he can almost
               pass for an American   (with his American tie socks
               and green sweater).

In the beginning he is not as surprised by what he sees as he had expected to be.
That's always the case.   That's a good point in fact.   Nobody is.
Things are a bit the same all over.

               The first impression is important (however)
               The first scene (the arrival of the boat in NEW YORK):

               The excitement the landing the waving the people the buildings...

               One could go on like that for hours REMEMBERING   impressions
                                                                 colors
                                                                 feelings
                                                                 sensations

               People rushing around with suitcases   shouting
                                                       pushing
                                                       shoving
                                                       crying
                                                       cheating

He knew many of them now after nine days on the boat.   It was a slow
                              boat.

Many disappeared in the crowd and he never saw them again even though many of
them said they would keep in touch - the number of people who say that to you
in your lifetime and never do (it's unbelievable). Many wrote for a while --
but eventually they stopped writing.
                         Mary wrote for a while until she wrote
that she could not write any more. She was engaged. She wrote first. That
will be better. And he answered immediately. In English. His first letter
in English. He had sent letters in English before (to his uncle) but he had
a friend who studied English write them for him. But this time he tries his
English alone. With a little dictionary. Looking up every word to be sure.
In alphabetical order.
                    Must have been about a week or ten days later.

A good ten days after they arrived in Detroit. More than that
even. A good twelve days. Sounds better. Even more than that
since he spends almost a week in New York with his uncle, sightseeing. Let's say then that by the time he got her first letter
and answers it (he answered it the same day he got it) (unless i
t was already there when they arrived in Detroit then it throws
off the whole thing but that's looking for more complication t
han necessary).

    Let's say that by the time he got her first letter he
knows quite a bit of English. Quite a few words. That's simple enough
to assume. I don't have to make a list of all the words he knows by the
time he got Mary's first letter but I could list all the things he saw in
New York. That's a nice touristic touch:

LIST OF THINGS HE SAW IN NEW YORK:

        The Empire State Building
        The Statue of Liberty
        The B. M. T.
        The Bronx
        The Museum of Modern Art
        Macy's
        Fifth Avenue
        Central Park
        Time Square
        The Jewish Daily Forward
        Rockerfeller Center

He describes all that to Mary in his first letter (five pages at least).

Even the cafeteria where Uncle David took him for his first meal in America.

    Writing (of course) is easier than speaking. At least it's not the
same. You can say anything you want. And besides you can always
find words in the dictionary.

        He has a little dictionary
        FRENCH-ENGLISH
        ENGLISH-FRENCH
        pocket size he bought it just before
        leaving knowing that it would be use
        ful in America
        In fact the first few weeks he always
        carries it in his pocket (that's cruc
        ial and logical)
        Gives him a feeling of security.

Then the first meeting with Uncle David (that's the second scene) Uncle David
was a little old man close to sixty badly shaven (you couldn't see that from
the upper deck but when he kissed him Robert felt how badly shaven he was --
it scratched) (Should I have him cry now or wait until he's alone?)

He was a nice man even though not a real uncle (he had married a cousin of his
father -- that makes him some sort of an uncle -- unless it was a step sister
or a half sister of his father) (when it comes to human relationship Robert is
very unsure of himself) but it's not a major problem though it could become a
major problem eventually. In any event I know for sure that they don't have
the same last name (the same family name).

```
DO
I
HAVE
TO
FURNISH
LAST NAMES?
all
LAST NAMES?
```

That complicates the situation.

```
Unless
        I
            use
                real
                    names!
```

Nobody goes around giving his last name
unless he's asked to when speaking   in
                                      the
                                      first
                                      person

That's another good argument in favor of the
FIRST PERSON

As for the SECOND PERSON (the noodler) it's
out of the question.

And the THIRD PERSON (the protagonist) it's
too early.

And at this point it's useless even to mention the FOURTH PERSON.

let us therefore ignore this matter at
                                      this time

I tried to see some family resemblance in the uncle's face.

I couldn't tell at first.

Then after a while I was sure there was none.

A strange sadness in his eyes behind the rimless glasses.
Resignation perhaps?   It's more suitable.   Insecurity!

And lots of silence.

He hardly speaks.

People   rushing
           pushing
           shoving   all over.

Suitcases everywhere.

The silence between them is extremely important.

I'll go into that further.

Even in the subway later on.

That's the next scene: Uncle David wanted to carry my
                                          suitcase but I didn't let him.
                                          I insisted on carrying it my
                                          self.

He doesn't have to insist with words.

He simply insists   with gestures.

I'll have to stress the silence between them (and the gestures too).

The meeting of two strangers.

Here is a man who speaks five languages and a young man who only speaks one:

FRENCH.   And since Uncle David does not speak FRENCH (he only
                           speaks RUSSIAN POLISH HUNGARIAN GERMAN YIDDISH ...)

and Robert does not speak any of the other languages it's a damn difficult situation.

They can't speak to each other.

I have to do something about ROBERT   I don't really like ROBERT

It's neither French nor American   It's both   It's nothing.   Change it:

SOLOMON! a lot of French Jews were called that but they changed their names
          during the war. I don't think there is a SOLOMON left in France today.

A guy would have to be crazy or masochistic to keep a name like that.

                              I
                            could
                            use
                            my
                            own
                            name

                            It
                            might
                            get
                                confusing
                                  though

    because
    people
    will
    start
    identifying me with him   that's
                                                       dangerous

                                                         must
                                                         avoid
                                                         that

                              A
                          Russian
                          name   ?   Originally
                                                         his
                                                       father
                                                        came
                                                        from
                                                       Russia

    but you can't go into that

    Nothing
    beyond
    the
    boat   I
                                   mean
                                      nothing
                                          in
                                         the
                                          past
                                            in
                                          fact

                                           the
                                         whole
                                         story
                                          is
                                          a
                                         break
                                     with the past

    THE WAR   THE CAMPS   THE FARM   !

THE WAR

THE CAMPS

THE TRAIN

THE FARM   Nothing of all that as though he had not even been marked
                                                    <u>Consciously</u>.

            Or at least he doesn't know it
                    -   <u>obviously</u>.

            I do of course
              <u>necessarily</u>.

            That should come in flashes.   <u>Images</u>.

            This way you have a kind of existential situation.   A
            <u>being</u>   who springs up on the boat.

            Reborn.
            Available for any eventuality.   For action
                                                      for the future.

            FREEDOM being his most essential trait.   (no)!
            FREEDOM is something else. He doesn't know what to do with
                                                                 <u>it</u>.

            Also (<u>subconsciously</u>) he wants to forget.

            Always dreaming of the future.   Lots of dreams. At night
                                              during the day
                                                      daydreaming
                                              his life away
                                              All the things he wants
                                              All the things he wants <u>to</u>
                                                                       <u>do</u>

One the boat he builds up a whole story about Uncle David. It's easy since
he doesn't know a thing about him. He tells Mary how rich his uncle is and
how generous he is. What a huge beautiful house he has. What an enormous
car he has. Two even. And then when they arrive Uncle David is waiting
at the pier with the car. They drive away. This is really the first
time he rides in the front seat of a car. He drove in trucks before
and maybe in a taxi once or twice but never in the front seat of a
car as though the car was his.

            (Sounds ridiculous to an American but it's true)

They drive to a magnificent house in the suburbs. They talk a lot. That's
another thing. Robert doesn't know a thing about houses. Only apartments.
Crummy little apartments. Or better yet. Furnished rooms. Crummy filthy
little furnished rooms.

Uncle David's wife did not come to the boat (he thinks Uncle David is married).
But he fact he has no wife (therefore no aunt for Robert).

            The things a guy thinks he knows where in fact he doesn't know.

It's so simple to invent.

But later on you're really disappointed when the things you invent

don't come true.   That's the problem with situations like these.

Inventions.   Lies.

I'll have to rewrite that part several times.
Once I find the right tone it will be easier.

But so far I have the room worked out.   The noodles.   The tomato
                                                                 sauce.

Did I finish the coffee?
The toothpaste and the toothbrush that's settled.

Anyway I am working on the toilet paper   (I didn't think of that)!

And the sugar for the coffee (no cream) and the salt for the noodles.

Or else the stuff is UNDRINKABLE UNEATABLE.

                                    A

                                    p
                                    o
                                    u
                                    n
                                    d   or two of s
                                                    a
                                                    l
                                                    t   that should do.

                                          Five pounds!

Can't take a chance.   SALT
                              SALT
                               SALT
                               SALT
                                 SALT   is cheap.   A few pinches into the boiling
                                                     water and that's it you're set

for the day. And in case in emergency you can always swipe a few salt shakers
from a restaurant: 2
                  or
                  3   Just to make sure. I'm not going to go
                                            around spending money on SALT.

Could do the same for SUGAR.   But there it's more tricky. Won't work.
I could cut down to two spoons a cup.   NO!   Always three.   Three.
It's stupid but two spoons only and I just can't drink the stuff.
It's wasted.   SALT (definitely) I'll swipe three or four shakers.
I won't even bother
        calculating SALT   But   SUGAR (definitely) that's another matter.

Can't waste too much T.......I.......M.......E on that however................

63 cents for a five pound bag   Interesting ********** 63 cents
                                                       not ********** 69 cents

Somebody goofed there it seems   I'll save somewhere else

But not on sugar that's essential   Three spoons
                                                 three times a day
                                                 four times   ?

                                                 Maybe five
                                                 Maybe more   ?

Maybe I should have a special fund   An emergency fund

One never knows   No

I agreed   No saving

If not the whole thing falls apart   You buy everything in advance

Down to the last penny Down to nothing   If you start saving
                                                 why not a savings account?

Like all the rest   And here you are back with the rest!

Counting pennies   Slaving like an asshole

BOURGEOIS   SALAUD

Just for that I'll buy ten (10) pounds of SUGAR just for the hell of it then

One never knows   Nobody knows a damn thing

If only people would talk to each other
                  write to each other
                  listen to each other   Once in a while!

But uncle David never mentioned in his letters if he was married this is why
one can assume that he's married that's why Jacques doesn't know that his wi
fe and children died (in a series of gruesome adventures) this way he can im
agine anything he wants he sees the house in his head uncle David's beautifu
l house in the suburbs the perfect house in his mind in the suburbs he has h
is own room on the second floor and of course his uncle sends him to school.

That's the one thing he wants most go to school he is about 19 when he arriv
es in America but there is a big gap in his life between the time he left sc
hool in France and the time he arrives in New York approximately five or six
years and by the time the story ends five or six years later he'll be almost
twenty-four that's logical let's say exactly five years later that's more na
tural that means that if you divide 365 by 5 you'll have to cover a year a f
ull year of his life in 73 days:

                73 days for a year   12 pages a day
                73 times 12 makes 876
                             876 pages for one year
                                       one year of his life
one year of his life in 876 pages that's a lot of pages for one year. Unless I

cut down.

I could easily tell only one year of his life The first year That means I write only 876 pages of his life This way you don't have to go so fast You can take a bit more time each day on each page until I run out of things to say obviously.

He tells Mary about his uncle Everything he has invented about him as though it were true She doesn't believe him of course but he doesn't know that And she do esn't tell him that she doesn't believe him She simply makes believe she does.

That's the trick It comes out through the dialogue between them Very subtly at first But eventually it's so obvious that he's inventing much of what he's tell ing her that she's almost tempted to tell him stop dreaming or you'll get hurt.

But he goes on telling her You should read the letters my uncle wrote me during the past year while I was waiting for my visa I'll show them to you someday Not now because they are at the bottom of my suitcase I always keep all my letters.

You see He goes on There is a quota for French people to come to America And in my case I had to wait a long time More than a year I was lucky because you just can't come like that to America Somebody rich has to bring you Your rich uncle.

He can't stop that sonofabitch Also you have to be in good health They give you a medical examination but there was nothing wrong with me The doctor told me So my uncle wrote saying that everything would be wonderful I'll have a nice life.

I'll go to school I'll learn English The things a guy can invent out of despair In America it's easy That's why I decided to come to America instead of going t o Africa with my aunt in Dakar I would have worked in her hotel It's hot there.

"You know some people have a job during the day and go
to school at night -- (THAT BITCH) -- it's not unusual."

"I know a lot of kids that do that work their way through
college taking courses at night -- (THAT STUPID MARY SHE
REALLY WANTS TO RUIN EVERYTHING FOR HIM IN ADVANCE). Yes
takes a while longer to finish but it's the same in the
end."

He doesn't agree with that.

First you learn English he tells her.

First you learn the language and then you get a job.

I don't really know what I want to do but first I go to school.

                                        WHAT A JOKE!

Not bad for a beginning.   Full of illusions
                                 Full of shit   that ppoorr guy.

        in
     the beginning   D
                      O

                      N
                      O
                      T

                      F
                      O
                      R
                      G
                      E
                      T   T H E   T
                                 O   I
                                  L
                               E   T

                                   P
                               P   A
                               E
                               R

a   h   i
 l   i   l
  l   s   lusions s$_{ha}^{tte}_{red}$ to pieces   piece by piece
                                                              by piece

                         It's hard to be young.

<u>From</u> <u>the</u> <u>moment</u> <u>he</u> <u>walks</u> <u>off</u> <u>the</u> <u>boat</u> <u>there</u> <u>goes</u> <u>his</u> <u>illusions</u>

      Uncle David is a short wrinkled old man who wears a wrinkled brown suit

with a huge red and blue tie (you couldn't see the blue in the tie from

the upper deck only the red) and who doesn't even own a car They walk n

ext to each other without talking In fact they hardly talk to each othe

r after they kissed on both cheeks on the pier Once in a while they try

to ask each other questions in English but it's useless They can't find

the words So they simply walk together in the streets in total silence

Should take him a good three or four weeks   even more   before he can
manage a complete sentence At first he jus   t says NO   or YES even i
f he doesn't understand what people are sa   ying to h   im which is m
ost of the time This way you have a fifty-   fifty cha   nce to be rig
ht when you say YES and the same number of   chances w   hen you say N
O but with words like MAYBE or PERHAPS it'   s differe   nt You're nev
er sure to be fifty-fifty right or fifty-f   ifty wron   g These are w
ords that take a long time to master in th   e beginni   ng I mean the
exact meaning of words like MAYBE or PERHA   PS and th   at's only two

In any event

This starts his mute period   in America

Crucial these first few months   weeks   days

They walk together   They walk toward the subway s
                                          ide by side (they didn't even
take a cab Imagine That on his first day in America)
                                          There is a fever in the air Y
ou always get that feeling when you arrive in New York Every time For Solomo
n all this is new (Not For Me).

    I felt it again this time when the Greyhound bus pulled in.

    I'll have to describe that feeling: The noise
                                                  The smell
                                                  The mixture of excite
                                                              ment
                                                          of relaxa
                                                              tion

    I mean people rushing in all directions and others just standing around
as though waiting for something to happen   That's NEW YORK waiting for
the end on the one hand rushing for the end on the other hand   That's

                                          modern man for you Up
                                                    &
                                                   Down
                                                    &
                                                   Away

Lots of cabs too.

Lots of yellow and green cabs.

                                        The noise.

                                        Gives you a dizzying feeling
                                        the first day (in New York)

Never fails

        You always need to take an ASPIRIN

Never fails

And the suitcase is getting heavy Uncle David doesn't walk very fast but still
the suitcase is getting heavier and heavier Uncle David is a slow walker still
he has to stop often to change hand Solomon's suitcase is all black but still
he has to stop often to change hand it's black with a brown leather strap yes
a brown leather strap around it that's typical all foreigners have straps yes
around their suitcases it's like they didn't trust suitcases and if they don't
have straps they use rope never fails very often they use rope instead of straps
                                                                   _____

        (They'll call him SAUL for sure with a name like that

                                        that's no good)

                                Maybe it should be a rope around it?

                                No   That's too obvious!

                                You don't want to push things too   F A R
                                                                    AAAAA
                                                                    R A F

The suitcase is very important (must avoid clichés)   In fact

    suitcases are as important   as rooms in this story

                                                       Almost symbolic Almost

        LIFE BY SUITCASE   Almost what I mean Yes

But this time in his case the black suitcase with the brown strap around it
represents something more than just a suitcase   Everything he owns is
    in it   the black suitcase   Everything
                                                      (I'll make a list)

And it's getting heavier and heavier as they walk toward the subway (THEY DIDN'T
EVEN TAKE A CAB) ---------------------(that's the next scene)
                                        the subway --------------
They are on their way to the BRONX to visit one of UNCLE DAVID'S cousins
                                Unless it's just a friend
                                                friend (s) from EUROPE.

Solomon doesn't know that of course.

He doesn't know anything   Neither do I   Doesn't
                                                                  matter
                                                                        I
                                                                  can
                                                                  always
                                                                  invent
                                                                        a
                                                                  relationship

They are going to the BRONX because the man they are going to visit knew

his father (Solomon's) many years ago Before the War in Europe That much

is under
    stood
          t
           h
            e
             s   f
              u   d   o   turning
               b   n   p
                w   i   o
                 a   k   i
                  y is a   n
                                                      t

                      because of the masses of people
                      there
                      it's like P
                                  L
                                  U
                                  N
                                  G
                                   I
                                   N
                                   G   into the BELLY of * * * * * * *
                                                        A M E R I C A
                                                        * * * * * * *

Mostly black.

Of course Solomon doesn't know that they are going to the BRONX.

He has no idea where the BRONX is or what the BRONX is.

His uncle didn't say that they were going to the BRONX.

He simply mumbled something in English (or was it in YIDDISH?) like BRAWNX.

Could have been "WE ARE GOING TO THE BRONX".   Doesn't make much difference
                                                    He didn't understand anyway.

His uncle said they were going someplace.   That much was under
                                                                      stood
                                                    but where That much
                                                    was mis-under-stood
So they are just going someplace and it happens that they are going to the BRONX.
You have to. You just can't stand there on the pier once you arrive in AMERICA.
THINGS HAVE TO MOVE SOMEWHERE - - - - - - - - - - - - - YOU'VE GOT TO GO SOMEPLACE

That's true of everything
             everything   that goes UP must come DOWN
             everything

                             up
.... you double UP .. up
                             up
and for a moment it seems ..... all lost

....

It's a game of course
that's what you keep telling yourself....... BULLSHIT!

It's more than that...... it's quite serious......yes!

IT'S ALL LOST because you are convinced while it lasts
.... while the <u>dice</u> are rolling that you have
             LOST

1 to 11   1................1
                .
               . .
              . . .
            . . . .
          . . . . .
      . . . . . .   CRAP.   But then it passes again

                                 3 passes in the row
                                 pass   pass   pass

                                 4
                                 passpasspasspass 5

                                 WHERE AM I ?

                                 That's what you say to you...SELF!

NEW YORK
DETROIT
LAS VEGAS
LOS ANGELES

The new phase: that's what you call it. When I arrived in Vegas must
have been three in the morning. The guy who gave me a
ride from Bakersfield (or was it San Bernadino?) said
GOOD LUCK man
                I had slept a little in the car while he
was driving 90 miles an hour   at least   through
the desert.   WHAT a ride!

GOD BE WITH YOU he even added!   What he really really
meant I'll never know. You meet so many guys like tha
t who tell you something but you never really know wha
t they really mean or if they really mean it -- yes --

the world is full of two-bit-philosophers!

I had about twenty bucks on me...my suitcase...a black one...no I didn't have the black one any more...I had a brown one...doesn't matter...a suitcase is a suitcase...I'll go over that again...the strap too...also the typewriter...it was always with me from the day I bought it...used...not new...new they're ex pensive...that's for sure...could afford a new one only if you save....and in my case it never works...unless you have a savings account...or something...a savings device...but then you're stuck...penny after penny dollar after dolla r to the point of hiding the little book so well that you don't even remember where you've put it...not me...no savings...suitcases...rooms...typewriters.. that's for me...the rest they can shove it...all the way...

SUITCASES   ROOMS   TYPEWRITERS

that sums up a life

Doesn't mean (though) that you do much with them (evidently)...

       ...I was carrying the suitcase in one hand and the typewriter in the other...doesn't matter much if it was the left hand or if i t was the right hand...I kept changing hands...it was cold...cold like hell.. yes in spite of what people think it does get cold like hell in Vegas....only one table going at the FLAMINGO...

    ...mirrors on the ceiling | comme dans un bordel |

    didn't like that too much
it was not the right atmosphere...moved on to the DESERT INN...much better... first played a buck on the pass line...not getting anywhere...left the suitca se and the typewriter in the lobby behind a chair...a big chair...and I kept. ..so to speak...shooting my one buck a throw until the dice came to me...what a crowd for a week-day...five bucks this time...don't be chicken...blew on th e dice...

ELEVEEEN

    two-times (twice)
    in the row....... couldn't believe it...was pissed-off hadn't put a do llar on ELEVEN...pays 15 to 1...then three passes after that...the 9...(came) ...the 5...(came)...the 6...(came too)...then looking for the 10...

    ...the hard way
one buck...played it this time...pays 8 to 1...

    HARD WAY TEN

IT CAME...couldn't believe it...

    DOUBLE OR NOTHING...don't be chicken....kept saying to myself...double up.....triple up......all the way...have another ci garette...have another drink...on the house...20 bucks on the line...BIG 8..
    BIG 6...
for the boys...thank you SIR...SIR my ass...ELEVEN...........TWELVE....shit! 20 bucks...
    ...anything goes...who is to say that I am bluffing...inventing... who can prove it...nobody...
    ...nobody... it's my game...it's my hand...it's my dough.....
    it's my noodles too...it's my story...NO...it's his story....
    HIS only HIS.

-- When I walked out of there the place was full of people must have been about 5 --
-- I had myself about 150 bucks Ham and Eggs in the coffee shop Delicious dead tired --
-- And then checked behind the chair Dead beat Must have fallen asleep in the lobby --
-- My suitcase and typewriter squeezed between my legs the money in my back pocket --
-- Sitting on it to make sure Can't take chances My feet hurting like hell 150 bucks --
-- A cry in my head A crummy taste in my mouth All the free cigarettes and free drinks --

-- You've got to take advantage of all that free stuff especially when you're hot --

        I don't have to go into a long description of the whole
        night - at least not now unless I decide to use it all.

-- Next day After I woke up Put the original 20 bucks and an extra 10 inside my shoe --
-- Inside my sock first and then inside my shoe Got to be careful in places like these --
-- And I'll be damned if the first roll didn't bounce into a SEVEN just like that --
-- I had ten bucks on the line LET IT RIDE - LET IT RIDE kept saying to myself inside --
-- Chicken Left only the 20 bucks on the line Threw five move on CRAP/ELEVEN Safety --
-- Eleven ELEVEN the guy shouted as though he was happy for me but I knew better --

-- There was a mob now around the table and some guy kept calling to me ROLL BABY ROLL --

-- Must have been drunk that bastard Didn't bother me This time 25 bucks on the line --
-- And five again on CRAP/ELEVEN -- SNAKE-EYES I knew it (I knew it for sure this time --
-- Could have told him That Bastard did it to me with his BABY but crap pays anyway --
-- Seven to one CRAP then I started working for my money You bet your ass All over --

        I don't have to describe each throw in detail but just
        the general mood the approximate feeling of the game.

-- The suitcase and the typewriter were back behind the same big chair in the lobby --

Looking for the NINE   it came

Looking for the FIVE   that came too

Looking for the FOUR   came easy (3-1)

I threw a few chips ($5) on the big SIX (6) and the big EIGHT (8)

Then looking for the FIVE <u>again</u>   Unbelievable:

> I kept shooting with my left hand only my left hand for
> luck you might say just because I started with the left
> hand.
>
> I shoved another pile of chips (green and some yellow)
> in my pocket (25 dollar chips and some five dollars in
> my pocket) my left pocket (pants pocket) must have bee
> n close to 200 bucks.
>
> This time I was going all the way a big pile on the line
> green and yellow chips I didn't even count I just push t
> he stuff on the line didn't even make neat little piles.
> Just pushed it but the guy made neat little piles for me
> to make sure.
>
> I wish I could have sat down my feet were killing me and
> too many cigarettes. My throat was sore. I grabbed ano
> ther one another free cigarette and bang BANG eleven ELE
> VEN the guy shouted as though he was happy for me.
>
> Rake it in BABY (where is the guy?) ELEVEN and another big
> pile in my pocket (my coat pocket this time) and I still h
> ad plenty in front of me.
>
> Couldn't go on like that forever that's for sure DOUBLE OR
> NOTHING go ahead DOUBLE OR NOTHING the little voice in the
> back of my head kept saying to me or somewhere around ther
> e (I mean the back of my head).
>
> I didn't have the guts I left only 10 bucks on the line and
> MOTHERFUCKING STUPID ASS it passed (&) it passed (7) and it
> repassed (7) let it ride let it ride it's a good sign go on
> double up double it up DOUBLE OR NOTHING.
>
> I said it aloud while shoving everything I had in front of
> me on the line (except for the green and yellow chips that
> I had sneaked in my pocket) except for one green one on th
> e SEVEN always cover the seven MAN.
>
> I blew on the dice and rolled still throwing with my left
> hand SEVEN IT IS!
>
> The mob around the table was jumping up & down UP & DOWN &
> sideways too and screaming and puffing and feeling good fo
> r me and encouraging me to go on. There must have been at
> least hundred or hundred-fifty of them standing around the
> table supporting me and quite a few good looking girls but
> I was too busy to notice the girls I just raked in the $$$

ROLL BABY ROLL (here comes that bastard again – sideways) That's it!   I KNEW IT.

I KNEW IT

It's like the story of Palucci and his Gang

you know   Palucci
             Sticky
             Zutalors
             Mirabelle
             Elephant
             Bug

What a story:

It all started in my head the day the Six of them
decided to steal the Eifel Tower to sell it to the
Turks. Then with the money they went down to Monte
Carlo to break the bank playing roulette.
                        The Six of
them surrounded the table and before you knew it they
each had 20,000 a piece (francs of course)
        20,000 times 6 that's a lot of dough (even if
it's only francs).
                But they lost it all the next day or
a few days later in Las Vegas playing the slot machines.
That's the way it goes.
                I knew them well I mean the whole
Gang even if it sounds unbelievable. 20,000 apiece. And
they blew it.
                It's quite normal in that kind of a story.

But what a coincidence (talk to me about coincidence):

Just as I woke up in the lobby in my big chair my suitcase
and my typewriter squeezed between my legs sitting on the
money in my back pocket a guy came over to me -- quite a f
riendly guy -- and what a coincidence it was none other t
han Palucci himself.
                He started talking to me. Told me
all about his new life. No more gambling he said. He'
s finished with that. He's in politics now. Explaine
d to me that the way to save America was for him & hi
s Gang to take over the government. It's as simple
as that he said to me. I didn't argue with him. I
was too tired and my feet were killing me. Bad.

That's quite a streak you had yesterday he said to me.   I
saw him coming. Either he wanted to borrow money (for his
campaign) or else he was sincere. I didn't really answer.
I smiled. YES. I did mumble a little something like NOT
BAD but I could have made more if I had gone all the way..
.. I mean DOUBLE OR NOTHING .. towards the end. Oh well I
said that's the way the cooky crumbles. He laughed at me.
That's exactly what he said to me whatever that means.
                                                And
then he disappeared. It was like a dream. A bad dream.
                                                Could
have been a dream
        I dream all the time in situations like these. I
wonder where the rest of the gang was?
STICKY/ZUTALORS/MIRABELLE/ELEPHANT/BUG   ?

I didn't have time to think about them and anyway it doesn't fit into the story
it merely confuses matter because it was impossible for him to tell me what he
told me when I woke up in my chair in the lobby of the Desert Inn with the suitcase and the typewriter squeezed between my legs it was impossible because I had
not had my streak yet I mean the big streak except for that lucky 150 bucks you
remember in my back pocket the night before before the ham and eggs in the coffee
shop so the whole story is a joke Palucci is a liar that's for sure or else he
does not exist that kind of coincidence never happens even if you're lucky like
hell you just can't mix reality and fantasy like that just for fun you just can't
it doesn't work or else the whole system is all screwed up all fucked up etc.....

    I KNEW IT
    I knew it the moment that guy came back with his ROLLBABYROLL
                                 rollmyassbaby.

I left only about ten or twenty bucks on the line and started throwing silver

dollars all over the table: on the seven
                                  on the crap-eleven
                                  on the no-pass-line

what's a few bucks!   even if you're contradicting yourself.

And I threw the dice.............FOUR
                          FOUR IS THE NUMBER   (that's what the guy said)

                          Everybody could see that.

I looked for it (the four) three or four times.   Got a few $'s back
                                          Lost a few too....

But I knew I had shot my load. BANG!   SEVEN!   (the guy shouted like he was
                                                  happy)

I could have told him I could have told it to all the guys around the table

There comes a time when you know you've got it when you can't push your   L
                                                          U
                                                          C
                                                          K
                                                          .

That's when a guy with some sense gives up the whole thing and quits and walks
away and certainly I deserve a medal for that: I WALKED AWAY FROM THE TABLE
                                                       WITHOUT EVEN LOOKING BACK
                                                       WITHOUT EVEN LEAVING A TIP
                                                       FOR THE GUY WHO SHOUTED ALL
                                                       MY GOOD NUMBERS AND THE BAD
                                                       ONES TOO   TOO BAD

I had left my suitcase and the typewriter hidden behind that big chair
(the same one mentioned before).

I asked if they had a room.

I was dead.

The guy behind the desk was friendly even though I hadn't shaved in three days.

The guy behind the desk said it would be $18.00 for a single.

    18 bucks for a room! WOW! What a story I could write in a room like that.
                    Imagine!
    18 bucks though (you couldn't do it on noodles -- that's for sure).
                    Impossible!
    18 times 52 that's 936
              936 bucks just for a room alone   WOW!

I started walking out of the place when I felt the wight of the chips in my
pockets Silver dollars ($1) Green chips ($25) Yellow chips ($5) in my pants
pockets and also in my coat pocket (the sport coat) I was loaded like a mu-
le In fact it was so heavy I couldn't walk straight I was staggering all o-
ver the place I must have looked funny from the back like a guy who is bow-
legged or better yet like a guy who's got the shits (merde que je me suis.)

I found a little corner in the lobby all by myself and started counting my chips.

1200 * * * * x * * * * * * * * * * PLUS.

Close to 1250 - - - - - - - - - - - - as a matter of fact.

To be exact I had exactly 1248 bucks - and that's without counting the 30 bucks
                            in my shoe (remember the 30 dollars sta-
                            shed away in my sock first and then ins-
                            ide my shoe) -

My eyes were burning My throat was like an open sore My legs were swollen and my
ass was sore too I hadn't taken a crap in three days and I had such a filthy tas
te in my mouth I felt like throwing up all over the place and on top of that (be
lieve it or not) I had a blister in the palm of my left hand and lucky for me at
that point (damn lucky) as I was digging in my left pants pocket I discovered (I
should have guessed) a little hole at the bottom of that pocket Had I gone on pl
aying and shoving green chips and some yellow ones too in that same pocket the l
ittle hole would have become a big hole for sure that's inevitable and the whole
damn pile of chips would have fallen out for sure and I might not even have noti
ced it and some bum standing around might have stood right next to me picking up
my chips from the floor as they dribbled out of the hole in my pocket and imagin
e what would have happened after a while if I had been so-involved-so-engrossed-
in-the-game to pay attention to the guy picking up my dough from the floor or ev
en worse what would have happened if I had noticed the guy eventually and I woul
d have been too chicken to say to him That's my money man you're picking up from
the floor and he had been a bastard and given me an argument and suddenly the wh
ole pocket cracked and all the green and yellow chips had fallen out on the grou
nd and then all the other guys around the crap table had rushed like scavengers-
motherfuckers to pick up my chips and I helpless like an ass just because my fee
t were killing me shouting like mad you bastards that's my dough you're all pick
ing up there and then all of them laughing at me shouting back you're a liar you
're a thief you're an imbecile you're a lousy gambler you're a nothing punk jerk

. . . . you're a . . . .

Lucky I stopped when I stopped.

Lucky I stopped on time . . . .

I almost cried I
                                              a
                                              l
                                              m
                                              o
                                              s
                                              t did . . . .

I walked O V E R to the cashier's window ------------------

$$$$$$$$$$$$$$$$$$$$$$$
$$$$$$$$$$$$$$$$$$$$$$$
$$$$$$$$$$$$$$$$$$$$$$$
$$$$$$$$$$$$$$$$$$$$$$$
$$$$$$$$$$$$$$$$$$$$$$$
$$$$$$$$$$$$$$$$$$$$$$$
$$$$$$$$$$$$$$$$$$$$$$$
$$$$$$$$$$$$$$$$$$$$$$$
$$$$$$$$$$$$$$$$$$$$$$$
$$$$$$$$$$$$$$$$$$$$$$$

CASHIER

The

B

I

G

<u>C O P</u>   next to the window smiled at me

I didn't say a word

Couldn't believe it

Do you want it in 100 dollar bills - or smaller?

YES   ---   NO!

Give it to me in   10 dollar bills -   All tens │I almost said in one dollar
                                                  │bills but the guy behind th
                                                  │e glasspane would have thou
                                                  │ght I was crazy or deranged│

          10 dollar bills make a nice little bundle   --   anyway you
                                                                 look
                                                                   at
                                                                   it

I took my bundle (all tens) and walked all the way downtown (Fremont Avenue)
carrying my suitcase in one hand and the typewriter in the other - switching
hands from time to time because of the weight (the suitcase being heavier th
an the typewriter) it was a little OLIVETTI portable which I had bought used
the day I started thinking about the noodles (or was it before?) - I found a
room for six bucks in a crummy hotel next to the bus depot I was exhausted I
pushed the bed against the door just in case put the money inside a sock and
shoved the sock inside my jockeys right against my dick this way it was safe
because nobody would think of looking for the money there unless the guys is
a queer or a fanatic

          In five minutes I was asleep   1
                                           2
                                           3
                                           4
                                           5   WHAT A DREAM   :

iwasswimminginbeangreenwaterahugeoceanandthewaveshadnumbersonthemfromonetotwelve
imaginethatbignumbersinblackanditwastryingtodrownmeandiwastryingtoswimasfastasic
ouldatthesametimegrabbingasmanyofthenumbersaspossiblehandsfullofthembutifeltmyse
lfsinkingasigrabbedthewavesandwhenmyhandswerefullofgreennumbersididntknowwhattod
owiththemicouldntputtheminmypocketsbecauseiwasswimmingnakeddammitthatsnottrueiwa
sswimmingwithmyclothesonthatswhyitwassodifficulttostayontopofthewateronthesurfac
ebutitdoesntmatteritsonlyadreamikeptsayingtomyselfandanythingcanhappeninadreame
venifitsabaddreamorelseiaminventingthewholethingandafterwardsyoumakebelievethati
twasadreamwheninfactthatsortofthinghappensallthetimeaccordingtofreudandcompanyor

              in fact I slept like an angel   nowater
                                               nobeans
                                               nowaves
                                               nonumbers either
              justanenormoushardon rubbing against my moneysock
              inside my underwears   (coming out of it)
That's better   - - - -   better than P O K E R !

YEAH

Sounds better more credible more logical than the poker game in L.A.

Craps is more human and since the money must come from someplace (one or the
                                                                    other)

Why not craps instead of poker?

        But now I have two possibilities for the money   CRAPS   or   POKER
                                                          ****
                    and other possibilities might still come up

        Important though is to remember to shove the bed against the door.

        Important also is to remember that the whole idea of the room and
        the noodles and all the rest came to me just as I woke up after I
        had the dream about the money-water and the huge hard-on rubbing
        against my money-sock in my jockeys (that's a very good touch).

Later I'll get the rest   More details   when he arrives in

Las Vegas   Eventually everybody gets to

Las Vegas   It won't be the same for him
            .
            .
            .
            .
        . you're getting everything confused .
                                             .
                                             .
                                             .
                                    . his story and my story. . . . .

        it's not the same. . . . . and entirely different moods
                                He's so shy it won't work. . . . .

IN THE SUBWAY

It all started there

He had never seen so many black people (all that in the first person) in his life.

He was thinking to himself (the things one thinks about in one's lifetime).

        Did I forget anything?

        About the landing
        Uncle David
        Mary   (she disappeared in the crowd eventually)

        Everything happened so fast he couldn't even say goodby to her
        . . . . at least not the way he would have liked to. . . . .

All that will have to be rewritten several times (it's obvious) but once you find
the right tone it's in the bag it'll go easy particularly once you have everything
ready   in the bag   in the room   in your head .

```
SO FAR      (let us recapitulate):              The room
                                                The noodles
                                                The toothpaste
                                                The toothbrush

                                                Did I finish the coffee?
                                                Can't remember
                                                CAN'T REMEMBER EVERYTHING

(that's the problem):                           The toilet paper

                                                I didn't think of that

DEFINITELY without a list
it won't work  DEFINITELY                       And the salt
                                                   the sugar
                                                And the coffee
                                                   the sugar for the coffee
                                                Or else the stuff is
                                                            uneatable
                                                            undrinkable
------------                                     ------------
```

I'll get ten pounds for 52 weeks. That's a pound for 5 weeks point 2. You get

that stuff in 5 pound bags. So you get three five pound bags and it's in the b

ag. No. That's only 15 pounds. I mean that's 15 pounds only. Too much.   It

doesn't work. Though 15 pounds is better than 10. 3 five pound bags at 63 cen

ts a bag that's $1.89 exactly. No savings. Unless you keep a special fund for

emergency. For movies for instance. Movies are important. When you can't tak

e it any more you'll sneak out and go to a movie. Even in the middle of the ni

ght. Idiot. Nobody will see me. And who cares. I'll rush down to 42nd Stree

t. They play all night. Maybe two. Or three movies in one night. But that's

cheating. Let's try without movies. Unless by the 237th day I can't stand the

damn seclusion any more. Then I'll decide. In the middle of the night. But t

hat does present a problem about the emergency fund. Of course if I don't have

an emergency fund I won't be tempted. If I don't have an emergency fund I'll d

o without. That's obvious. That's more than logical. Indeed it's selfevident

```
------------                                     ------------
```

Can one TAKE it though?   365 days (without movies) that's a long TIME!

It's WORSE than without ~~~~~~~ SCREWING~~~~~~ And the toilet paper?

Never thought it would get so difficult
                            so complex   OK.....   THE LIST:

1. NOODLES .... (365 one pound boxes)

2. ROOM .... (8 bucks a week - 52 weeks)

3. COFFEE .... (one jar for two weeks)

4. TOOTHPASTE .... (80 squeezes in a tube)

5. TOOTHBRUSH .... (one new one at 59 cents)

6. SALT .... (no problem - free)

7. SUGAR .... (3 five pound bags)

8. SOAP .... (20 bars - no deodorant)

9. TOILET PAPER .... (definitely - a must)

Tremendous!   It's easier than I thought as long as I keep going like that.

How much do I need (toilet paper)? Newspaper would be too tempting
                                    (like movies).

Nothing to distract you. Complete concentration. I begin to understand what
they mean by CONCENTRATION (concentration camps).

Some guy came up with the idea of L'AGE CONCENTRATIONNAIRE. A French guy of

course. (Doesn't work in English) (there are so many things that don't work
in English).

Indeed!   Can't translate everything he says verbatum.
               Therefore I'll paraphrase as best I can.

Indeed!   But don't lose track. Stay with it. No digressions.
               The main points as much as possible.

TOILET PAPER: Two craps a day?
               Normally one in the morning. Usually quite regular (I
               understand now what they mean by regularities) about that.
               When it comes to regularity I'm quite a regular guy though
               one never knows under the conditions in which I will be
               working, the conditions to which I will be subjected in
               my room. Perhaps I should keep track. Have a chart or
               a daily record. For the future. For posterity. Or for
               sociologists. It is indeed an unusual situation in which I
               shall find myself.

                                                            A
                                                   SHIT-CHART

               Normally they tell you on the wrapper how many sheets in a
               roll:
                                   500?
                                   1000?

                                        double-ply (of course).

Always standard size (they haven't yet invented the KING size in toilet paper)

(though they do have colors - patterns and even perfumed)

2 rolls for 27 cents (usually)

(also no FAMILY size in shit-paper that would be too much)

(they might someday You never know with those bastards)

(imagine a whole family working on a family size roll).

What's certain you always use more than one sheet at a time

Six or seven

Even more

And each crap requires several handsfull (handfulls?)

Also you use the stuff to blow your nose

Also you use the stuff to wipe the mirror after a shower

Also you use the stuff to clean your glasses (if you wear glasses)

(it's a waste).

I could measure   (how many wipes in a roll?)

I can see myself already trying out how many wipes in a roll

One could get a sore ASS from something like that (definitely).

Also you have to allow for constipation

(not in my case HEADACHES once in a while).

In the end though I guess shits and constipation balance out

(definitely I should have a little supply of aspirin)

What a difference it might have made for ROBINSON CRUSOE if he had had some

(a minor point of course but not to be neglected).

(Make a note.   ASPIRIN.   Two boxes)

(no suppositories though) (that's a great word)

(it supposes that you might or might not be able)

(disgusting little bullets up your ASS. I've never tried
(but I can imagine a guy shoving those little things UP)

Let's keep it clean   (orderly)

How many times can you wipe your ASS with a roll of toilet paper?

Who ever thought that a guy might get hang up on a question like that?

They say 500 sheets (but who ever really checked to make sure)   ?
You always grab a handfull

HAND   IN   HAND

They stood on the upper deck (it's too simple) (and besides I don't like
the name Marry - with one r or with two rr - it's too nothing. Got to be something more catchy. More like her. More American. Typically. Could it be
Peggy? That's a good one. He had never heard a name like that before.   How
do you spell it? He asked. P E double G Y. That's easy to remember)   With
PEGGY. A little blond well stacked. With clear blue eyes. And a nice round
ass. They met at the beginning of the trip. The first day as the boat (S.S.
Marine Jumper) left Le Havre. She was standing on the upper deck next to him
her hair in the wind. Something like that.

"Lovely, isn't it?"   A   HANDFULL

He didn't understand what she meant at first.

"Oh! You don't speak English?"

He understood that. Peggy moved a bit closer to him. And there he goes
feeling like crying suddenly as I watched (switching to the first person) the
coast of France recede with the horizon (he wouldn't say recede. He would no
t even think of the word. In fact in French he would think something like :
je me sentais triste en regardant la côte se barrer avec l'horizon. J'avais
presque envie de chialer. Et c'est alors que la gonzesse, une petite blonde
du tonnerre avec des yeux bleus et une poitrine formidable, est venue près de
moi et a commencé à baratiner en anglais. J'ai rien pigé à ce qu'elle disait
mais elle était gentille comme tout et moi alors j'ai plus eu envie de me sen
tir triste et de chialer pendant que je regardais la côte de France disparaît
re à l'horizon.) Disappear. Fade away (that's about it). Somebody was next
to me. Somebody had spoken to him. After all these were important years yes
very important years he was leaving behind THE TRAIN THE CAMP THE FARM we are
not going to discuss. Yes nothing of the past. A clear break. Symbolically
that is. As soon as the coast disappears he turns away from it toward the wa
ter THE OCEAN. Toward AMERICA.

"Vous êtes français?" Lovely the way she said that. "Moi je suis améri
caine." And she goes on and on with lovely little grammatical errors. Takes
guts to speak like that. "Voulez-vous marcher devant le bateau pour voir cet
immense océan mieux?" (Shows you). It really made him feel warm inside that
someone like that next to him would talk to him. Did she sense something? Y
PAS A DIRE she was really cute. You never know with girls from Milwaukee. Y
PAS A DIRE they are surprising. Loneliness? Sadness? The feeling of breaki
ng away from something important or at least from something which you just ca
nnot forget? It's possible. I'll never know. Nor will Solomon ever know si
nce he never asked her.

"Vous allez en Amérique?" What a question. Where else could he be goin
g on a boat like that?

                         She's got to become more important. Even if I have to
                         invent a little. She reappears towards the end of the
                         story. It's easy to start a story but to end it that'
                         s another matter. Of course I won't have to face that
                         problem until about the 300th day or let's say 300-350
days from tomorrow because tomorrow we begin - OCTOBER 1st - and that's it !

```
          be prepared though
     make a list of possible endings

                   W
                   I
                   T
                   H
                 PEGGY
```

(a death here and there is more dramatic)

after he gets her letter telling him about the guy she knew in college   HE
                                                                       wants
                                                                          to
                                                                         DIE

              that's one possibility
                another possibility   HE
                                                          commits
                                                          SUICIDE

other possibilities:

He decides to give up everything and go back to France -

Tries to find another girl -

Drops out of life -

Writes a tremendous letter of protest but never sends it -

Flies to Milwaukee to kill her (that's a good one) -

She flies in (in Detroit) to explain to him that everything will be fine -:

                                        -- Don't give up --
                                        -- Don't do it ----
                                        -- Don't go away --
                                        -- Stick it out ---
                                        -- Have hope -------

He spends the night walking the streets of Detroit and in the morning
                         (that's if he's still in Detroit at that time)
he's reconciled with himself and goes home to cry a good cry and get it out
of his system -

It's winter (snow all over) and he catches pneumonia and dies a quick death
two weeks later -

She completely ignores his letters and eventually he forgets about her (except once in a while) -

He decides to lock himself in his room (with the Hungarian people) to write
the story of his life (he gives up after a week or two) -

He quits his job -

Goes west (probably to Las Vegas) - But she follows him after her divorce-
-with three children-- (five years later) - they lose all their money -

```
                be prepared though
              anything can happen here

                        W
                        I
                        T
                        H

                      PEGGY
                        &
                   toiletpaper

        (a false move here and there and you're dead)
```

You could A L S O combine endings:

```
She flies in to see him
            to explain
            to justify  herself and they decide to kill themselves
                                                        together
```

But the sexual act being an ironic substitute for suicide therefore
having managed to convince his girl friend -- PEGGY -- that she has
to commit the act of felo-de-se with him Together they proceed to a
deserted spot at the top of a mountain He carries with him a bottle
of poison a revolver and a rope But in spite of the implied seriou-
sness of the situation the whole affair quickly turns badly and becomes a grotesque comedy For when they reach the chosen place PEGGY
who has removed her skirt in order to (how shall I say?) storm that
summit with more ease seduces him and he -- the protagonist! -- can
no longer carry out what he had planned so carefully So together --
it's obvious -- they find justification for their failure in a passionate act of sexual indulgence -- LOVE & DEATH being the same thing in the end That is if (of course) you decide to use this particular type of ending for this particular type of story in which LO-
VE & DEATH are combined at the end into a more effective tragicomic
                                                                  e
                                                                  n
                                                                  d
BUT finally there is no point in it: i
                                                                  n
                                                                  g
He simply flies to Milwaukee to kill her but instead she
convinces him to calm down She drops the other guy - the
one she knew in college 0 - and together they try to mak
e it work eventhough it is a senseless hopeless situatio
n
But she is such a fine girl he does not have the courage
to kill her and eventually they both drift apart which -
I could have told them that - is not unusual in situations such as these whereas the whole affair starts on the
wrong foot -- indeed I could have told them that immedia
tely even before they started messing around on the upper deck that unless he screws her it cannot possibly wor
k out for them - and it would have been so easy for them
All they had to do was ask the girl from Chicago to take
a walk on the upper deck and the whole affair would have
been quite different right from the start and officially
the letters would have been more meaningful and I person
ally would not have the problem of trying to combine end i n g s !
```
```

She was indeed a fine girl. The type he had never met before. And beautiful
besides. That's one of the reasons (among many) he got so involved with her.
And of course it helps a great deal that she speaks French, this way they can
ask each other all sorts of questions about each other, about their respecti-
ve countries, about their past, and their potential future, and what they are
thinking and feeling, and what they plan to do even if they never quite do it
: THERE ARE ALL SORTS OF POSSIBILITIES :

She was walking next to him on the upper deck the wind blowing in

her hair her hair flying loosely in the wind (his hair is all mes

sed up but he doesn't care) asking each other all sorts of questi

ons: "YOUR FIRST TRIP TO AMERICA?"   That's a good one as if a

guy like him was in the habit of going to America regularly - and

when it comes to regularities ask Solomon - he's the most regular

the most typical type of guy -

BUT   Was he the kind of guy who travels to America every summer? What

does she take him for?   A businessman?

Must be a rich broad to think like that. That's one thing about

him. He never gives up. Always hoping he will stumble on a nice

rich girl (a bit older than he) and marry her
                                         marry her immediately
(for her money and for love too of course -- LOVE & MONEY
                         a good substitute for LOVE & DEATH   )

There is indeed a touch of gigolo in him (I didn't notice that at

first but now it's quite evident) and a very pronounced CASTRATION
COMPLEX.

BUT   not the tough type at all - on the contrary: shy
                                                         not bad looking
                                                         dark hair
                                                         strong nose
                                                         bright dark eyes
                                                         straight white teeth
                                                         height: 5'10"
                                                         weight: 156 lbs.
                                                         strong nails
                                                         long fingers
                                                         size 40
                                                         shoe 10 1/2
                                                         socks 9 1/2
                                                         arms 33"
                                                         neck 15 1/4
                                                         a little scar on left knee
                                                         heavy beard
                                                         waist 32
THAT DOES IT!   20/20 vision

It's so easy once you get going:

> Everything which -- up to this point -- was
> protecting and inspiring the storyteller on
> the threshold of his tale -- the destiny of
> rationality and of teleology, the long con-
> tinuous process of thought beyond time, the
> awakening and the progress of consciousness
> and its perpetual recapturing of itself, the
> unfinished movement yet uninterrupted of to
> -talization, the return to an origin always
> open, and finally the historico-transcenden
> -tal thematic -- all this might disappear r
> evealing for analysis a blank indifferent s
> pace without any interiority nor any promis
> e whatsoever and this is only the beginning

Of course one can avoid such pitfalls but still it will be necessary to go into
more physical details later on. Give clear and precise descriptions of his phy
sical appearance before getting into his psychological make-up.   Indeed define
each trait of his character quite clearly and specifically without exaggeration

That's the only way to give a truly-credible-human personality to that type of
character. FOR INSTANCE:
        emphasize his shyness (that's part of his charm you might say)
     .... his strong nose (call it that instead of long nose)
     .... his bright eyes (which really means deep brown eyes)
     .... his dark hair (combed straight back without a part)
     .... his straight teeth (very white -- he uses Colgate--)
     .... his height (5'10" -- Frenchmen are usually not as tall as
                          Americans -- Could be only 5'8" --)
     .... his 156 pounds (that's important too because he's somewhat
                         undernourished when he arrives in America)

and of course one can go much further in dealing with all the other aspects of his
physical appearance...   ...   .

     As for his attraction to older women (that's crucial):

     They like him
     They always feel like mothering him (good point) (In fact
     this could become a major theme and a major problem too i
     n this story: THE MOTHER COMPLEX -- the search for a lost m
                                  o
                                  t
                                  h
                                  e
         THE FATHER COMPLEX   r
                    t
                    o
                    o......... After all he's an orphan
                              Doesn't like to talk ab-
                              out it but you can avoid
                              it even if you want to.)

But here we border more on his psychological make-up rather than on his physical!

I remember (he said to me once) my first few months it was always embarrassing
to talk about it...I used to blush like a kid everytime they asked me about my
parents (I record exactly what he told me)...when they asked is your family in
France (?)...I never knew what to answer...even years later...no (and after mu
ch hesitation)...they were deported...you know during the war...by the Germans
...both of them..your father and mother (?)...yes...(it's really embarrassing)
sometimes...I would also mention my two sisters (2)...they too were deported I
would say...exterminated...but that sounded like I was exaggerating like I was
making it all up...to get more sympathy...so most of the time I left out my tw
o sisters...didn't even mention them (that's quite a statement)...because...it
means nothing to them...one person more or one person less (that's exactly how
he said it)...doesn't matter...if you insist too much they start suffering for
you (good observation)...and you feel even more embarrassed...even more lonely

indeed: THE NUMBER OF PEOPLE WHO SUFFER FOR YOU IN YOUR LIFETIME !

& also: THE NUMBER OF PEOPLE WHO DON'T GIVE A DAMN ABOUT YOU TOO !

                           Like that family in the Bronx where Uncle David is taking
                           Solomon after the boat. That's where they are going with
                           the subway. Tremendous scene. It comes right after that
(The Subway Scene)   subway scene. Easier than I thought. Once you have ever
                           ything in the room it's a matter of patience and labor so
                           tomorrow morning. October 1st. Noodles all over. And I
                           count a few horses on the wall just to get a feeling of t
                           he place. The table by the window. And here we go. But
(Double or Nothing)   of course that doesn't solve the problem of the toilet pa
                           per. And also the money. People will want to know where
                           it comes from:
                                     POKER OR CRAPS?

Doesn't have to be EITHER one though EITHER one works   unless
                                                              unless I decide

to borrow the money/it's all the same/ but borrowing means you've got to give
                                                              unless
it back   unless you take
                                                                   fof
                                                                   off
                                                                   ffo
Have you ever considered the possibility of borrowing the money? Just enough
for the room the noodles and all the rest (365 days). Which means you've got
to have an exact figure (down to the last penny).   Of course it doesn't work
unless you borrow with the intention of never returning the money. Whoever l
oans it to you doesn't have to know what you plan to do with it. Good twist!
It means getting out of the country for good and never returning. You would
have to get out permanently. Assuming then that this is how you get the mone
y it kills the poker game if it is the poker game and the crap game if it was
the crap game. It's a difficult question to resolve particularly if you deci
de to have him do the same eventually. But assuming I borrow the money. And
I don't mean borrowing from a private party. That's out of the question. No
body would trust me. I mean borrowing from one of those loan places. Even I
would not trust myself with borrowed money. Nobody in his right mind would w
ant to invest in a deal like this one. Even your best friend if you have a b
est friend would be suspicious would think you're crazy would tell you to giv
e up or go to hell. This is why it's essential to find one of those loan pla
ces that loans you money without any securities credentials (or collaterals).

All right then.

Lucky there are such places.   Businesses that love to loan money to guys
like you.   Takes a long time to find out about these places when you
are new in America.   Sometimes more than five years. And of course
you need some sort of security. Credentials.   Collaterals.   But that's
easy to invent.
                Solomon doesn't know about all that   in the beginning.
Takes a good five years even more before you learn all the ropes. Neither
did I   in the beginning.   That's why the first five years are so
tough.   For him.
           For me.   For anybody in our situation.
But borrowing is not a bad idea.   But you have to have an exact figure.
You just can't walk in and say I want to borrow some money.   They'll ask
HOW MUCH?   If you don't know they immediately get suspicious and
look at you de travers.
You've got to know down to the last penny.
You've got to justify the amount. Can't say approximately one hundred, or
hundred and fifty bucks for noodles (that's just a figure as an example at
this point). Or simply 1200 dollars.   No.   You have to be more spe
cific than that.   They may even ask you for a breakdown.   Just to bug
you.
You just can't say one hundred (or one hundred and fifty) bucks or so (for
noodles).
NOODLES -!- the guy would say ARE YOU SOME KIND OF NUT or else
                              ARE YOU ON SOME KIND OF SPECIAL DIET?
You've got to invent something more credible more reliable. Even potatoes
would not work.   And then when you get the guy convinced but you start
mentioning the toilet paper for sure the guy will throw you out of his pla
ce.
                That damn toilet paper keeps recurring.   Can't get it out
                of my system. Can't get it straight either.

A roll a week give or take a bigger wipe here and there ---------- 52
rolls then.

You can't take a chance and run out.   That would really be a hell
of a note.
                                     That would certainly force a
guy out of the room.   No shit about   that!

If one runs out of toothpaste one can do without. Sugar also even if
the coffee tastes like piss. Noodles that you can always stretch out
a bit even though it's at the core of the whole system. Essential in
fact. That's survival. BUT TOILET PAPER? Dammit! How essential is
it?   One will never know.   Unless
                           Unless one goes through the whole bus
iness of finding out.   Counting the number of wipes in one roll :

Let's see what it says :

```
WHITE CLOUD          Improved!
                       Now more softly absorbent!
Kind to skin
            Because it's so comfortably soft.
No other tissue like it!  So gentle and kind..
          ..and delightfully scented too........
Absorbs faster......and still so soft.........
EACH ROLL 500 TWO-PLY TISSUES SIZE 41/2 X 41/2
```

Beats newspaper!
But what a discourse!

5 2

```
            R
      S   O
   L      L
   L      L
      O   S
      R
```

't
can   take
you   a
        chance
            &
              run
               o u t

TWO ROLLS A WEEK
                    then   1 0 4

for safety's s a k e

that's really living like a
                          k
                           i
                            n
                             g

an ORGY of toiletpaper

                    that stuff takes a lot of room
                         (though)

should have planned everything
                          s
                          o
                          o
                          n
                          e
                          r   three days in
                    advance

                    doesn't matter
                    if I don't start tomorrow

                    I'll   start the day after
                                    tomorrow
who says I have to start   tomorrow

                    O C T O B E R   F I R S T ?

I can always write OCTOBER 1st on the first page....Nobody will know the
                                              difference

That's a good date.   October 1st
                                                         ==========

Beginning of the month.

Beginning of a new season.

Beginning of the school year (for most kids).

September is always wasted   (for most kids).

In fact for ME summer vacation always ends - - - -   October 1st
                                                       ==========

                 BUT I'VE GOT TO STICK IT OUT

                 EACH DAY   day after day

each day of postponement means more money spent more time wasted
waiting for the starting day for the beginning for the launching
for the arrival
for the arrival of the BOAT   It means having less of ever
                                                           y thing

                                     and I have already eaten up a good
                                     CHUNK of the original lump of good
                                     DOUGH

2
  r
    o
     l
      l
       s   a week (then)   52 X 2 (that's easy) 104 rolls

                                    2 rolls for 27 cents - usually!
                                    (they always come two by two -)

                                    means you divide 104 by 2 and you're back
where you started (that's easy)
                                    52
                                    52 times 27 makes 14.04

        HERE WE GO AGAIN WITH THAT LITTLE   .04

Can't get rid of it and it's purely accidental I can assure you nothing calculated in that .04 There are numbers like that that keep popping up and one really
never knows if it's chance luck the stars god heaven fate destiny or coincidence
OR SIMPLY A JOKE
with me it seems to be .04 but with other guys it's number 3 or number 5 or even
better yet number 7 and of course you have guys who believe in number 13 some of
them believe 13 is good luck and others bad luck and others as soon as they come
across number 13 they immediately chicken out and then of course there are those
who when they see number 3 immediately think of the Trinity and if they see rats
or black cats then they really get scared
                         But for me 04 means nothing but coincidence
OR SIMPLY A JOKE

For me .04 simply means .04   Nothing symbolic about this number
                                               unless of course I symbolize it :

I can have the 0 stand for   nothing - DEATH
   and have the 4 stand for something - LIFE   then I have: 0 is DEATH
                                                                    4 is   LIFE

But that's like looking for NOON at TWO O'CLOCK (or approximately).

If one runs out one can always swipe a few pieces (handsfull) from public
places.
In case of emergency.
Even though that may mean getting out of the room all-of-a-sudden.
And I shouldn't (by all means):

                         AVOID ABSOLUTELY GETTING OUT OF THE ROOM

                         if not it doesn't count.

One
could
of
course
make
a
secret
exit
or
two
now
and
then   une sortie the French would say (sounds better in French)
                  U   N   E   S   O   R   T   I   E

It's like when guys are being besieged -- assieged (what the fuck you call it)
                                          -- ?
they sneak out during the night to get more provisions more ammunitions more :
HELP HELP HELP HELP HELP HELP HELP HELP HELP HELP HELP HELP HELP HELP HELP ! !

                         but there is always a T
                                                U
                                                N
                                                N
                                                E
                                                L

          OOOOOOOOOOOOOOOOOOOOOOOOOOOOOOOOOOOOOOOOOOOOOOOOOOOOOOOOOOOOOOOOOOOOOO
          OOOOOOOOOOOOOOOOOOOOOOOOOOOOOOOOOOOOOOOOOOOOOOOOOOOOOOOOOOOOOOOOOOOOOO

                         for that
                         or else they dig one

              VVVVVVVVVVVVVVVVVVVVVVVVVVVVVVVVVVVVVVVVVVVVVVVVVVVVVVVVVVVVVVVVV
              VVVVVVVVVVVVVVVVVVVVVVVVVVVVVVVVVVVVVVVVVVVVVVVVVVVVVVVVVVVVVVV

the guy who volunteers puts on some kind of crap on his face unless he is dark
naturally dark   ::::::::::::::::::::::::::::: then they tell him what to do
                   HE'S GOT TO MAKE IT
                   HE'S GOT TO MAKE IT   O-U-T & B-A-C-K

```
. . . . . . . . . . . . . . . . . . . . .
.                                       .
.         .05 would be much simpler     .
.         .05 comes out even when you add .
.                                       .
.                                       .
. . . . . . . . . . . . . . . . . . . . .
```

                              He's taking with him the lives
                                              the survival
                              of everybody in the place men
                                                      women
                                              and children

He knows that   (WHAT A RESPONSABILITY!)

Now he is out
                          u   t
He's crawling in the dark   q   e   y   What a chance to take (alone!)
                          i   l
Of course
I won't have that kind of responsability.

If I don't want to go back that's my business   (n'est-ce pas?)

But it will take strength
it will take will power to make that kind of a SORTIE or avoid making
                          that kind of a SORTIE

                              (n'est-ce pas?)

And most important never get tempted by   a cup of coffee
                                               a piece of ass
                                               a hot dog
                                               a movie

YES!

NO definitely no exit.   AVOID GETTING OUT OF THE ROOM FOR 365 DAYS

Is it possible
    plausible   ?

That's the chance one takes   Of course one can always use one's
                                   finger
                                   Dip it in water and wash one's hand
                                   afterwards

This brings up another problem:

        How long can I hang on for one stretch? Two months? Three months?
        I mean without going outside without even opening the window in or-
        der to look outside down at the street up at the sky. Even that in
        a way should not be permitted unless it is approved as an exception
        once every 37th box a quick look out of the window. But will it be
        during the day or during the night? Impossible to decide now, par-
        ticularly if I work with the curtains closed. I might be asleep du
        ring the day and again it might be the reverse I might be asleep du
        ring the night. Wait & see. And if you can't see anything then it
        will be better to forget about the whole thing. The visual is imp-
        ortant but should not take preference over other crucial problems.

<u>Movies</u>   that's another matter

Movies   are important for inspiration
                 for relaxation

You go straight to them and come right back and no stopping anywhere
                                  no speaking to anyone
                                  no looking at windowshops.

Could be done if you're strict enough with yourself but it's a matter of self-control it will take a great deal of will power a great deal of concentration.

<u>indeed</u>

Tricky to know exactly how much to save for movies in case I do decide to save for movies....

Perhaps if I start the list now it might help:

ROOM 416.00

NOODLES 105.85

COFFEE 20.04

SALT 0.00

SUGAR 1.89

TOOTHBRUSH .... .59

TOILET PAPER 14.04

Son-of-a-bitch!   I'll never get ready.   That funny little 04 is like an o-b-s-e-s-s-i-o-n-!

The time one wastes getting ready putting things away calculating procrastinating it's unbelievable it's truly discouraging it's all these point 85 point 89 not to mention that point 04 that goof you up never comes out even and even if it did so what?
I should have thought of all that before in fact I should have the first sentence all ready in my head mayben even the first paragraph on a piece of paper so that I don't forget it the opening sentence is always a real problem a guy can-easily-get-stuck with a first sentence and spend a whole year (365 days) just working on it and not getting anywhere the opening sentence or for that matter the whole opening page is crucial if not it's all dead (a dud).
Some guys read the first page and they immediately give up they don't even try to go on you've got to hit them hard with the first sentence the first paragraph the first page particularly then they don't give up they go on to the end of the page page after page turning the pages with trembling fingers expecting the worse held in suspense and BANG you hit them on the head.
What does it is the right tone the right rhythm everything has to be there in the beginning in essence and in substance.
The essential difference here whatever that means is not the material as such nor the manner in which you present it nor the message nor the language itself but to do it.
What counts is to do it.   COMPACT and CLEAR or better yet SIMPLE and DIRECT.

Take for instance this kind of opening paragraph:

> Mr. H✳✳✳✳✳✳ turned the corner and saw, in the failing light,
> at some little distance, his seat. It seemed to be occupied.
> This seat, the property very likely of the municipality, or
> of the public, was of course not his, but he thought of it as
> his. This was Mr. H✳✳✳✳✳✳'s attitude towards things that ple-
> ased him. He knew they were not his, but he thought of them
> as his. He knew were not his, because they pleased him. . . .

SUPERB!

> The character. The setting. The tone. The mood.

(Really make you feel like you want to go on)

Or take this second example:

> Yesterday my wife left me. She took her toothbrush and left
> without a word. Just like that. True, we rarely talked to
> each other, but still, on such a occasion, she could have
> said something, anything: SEE YOU AROUND, SO LONG, GOODBY!
> Hell, at least leave a note. It hurts just to think of it.
> What am I, a stranger?

FABULOUS!

> What a **beginning!** Suspense. Pathos. What language too: quick
>   precise
>   succinct

(Really makes you feel like you want to go on and on)

INDEED.

                                   You've got to stay away from the typical

        "La marquise est sortie à cinq heures."

Could start with   CALL ME SOLOMON !

in the first person   but SOLOMON ?

                        CALL ME ISHMAEL !   that's a name. Biblical (Solomon too).

but ...   .   CALL ME SOLOMON !   it's too funny.
                                              They'll call him SAUL for short
                                                                    for sure.

Though for this kind of a discourse anything would do:

                        Call me Stanley!
                        Call me Charlie!
                        Call me William!
                        Call me Richard!
                        Call me Raymond!

                        Call me   Dick!

That's what they start calling you after a while in America. They always do.

They always do it to you.

    Always cut it short.   Like they were ashamed or something

    Always do it: William --------------- Bill
                          Richard --------------- Dick
                          Raymond --------------- Ray
                          Robert   --------------- Bob

(What a friendly world) !

    BUT   Stanley --------------- Stan

    No.   That's too crappy.   Honest.

Call me more names: Call me Marcel - Call me Jules - Call me Louis - Call me Jim.

Could make a whole list and let whoever wants to decide decide which name he likes best - or better yet let him chose a name at random from the given list of names --- given anywhere and anytime at the pleasure of whoever is furnishing the list -- thus allowing whoever decides he wants a name for the person whose story is curren tly being told and he is currently in the process of reading -- assuming of course that he has the courage and the patience to go on to the end or at least far enoug h into the story to need to choose A NAME ....

                                  Why not   BORIS
                                            ?
                                            ?
                                  BORIS
                                            !
                                          !

That's a good name. Doesn't have to be Russian (even though originally his father came from Russia). Lots of guys are called Boris and they do not come from anywhe re in particular. They like the name Boris (or rather their parents did) and they call themselves (their parents rather call them) Boris and everybody wonders where the guys with names like Boris come from originally. I knew a guy who was in fact called Boris once and I liked him very much. But I never wondered where he came o r where he went. That's none of my business. In fact with a name like Boris Solo mon could have a much stronger personality. And besides there's no way you can cu t Boris that I know. No possibility of nicknaming him. You just can't say to any one whose name is BORIS: HI BO! Sounds ridiculous - HI BO!

        BORIS that's it for now. No last name though. Particularly sin ce he might speak all the time in the first person. Then he doesn't have to menti on his last name (his family name). People speaking in the first person usually d on't. That's one problem less. Unless of course they introduce themselves formal ly to somebody else or else somebody else introduces them formally to somebody els e. Then evidently you can't avoid last names. But even then you can always furni sh a false last name. Happens all the time. In hotels when you want to sneak out without paying. To the police when you're arrested. And so on. However it doesn 't pay because eventually they find out your real name and either you have to give your real name or pay the bill or else they stick you in jail. Immediately. That sort of things happens all the time.

        But still THE NUMBER OF FALSE LAST NAMES IN THE WORLD!

It's unbelievable.

One could possibly furnish a list of possible

LAST NAMES: TICKLEBROWN
                               ABRAMOWITZ
                                   MARANT
                                    PUTAS
                              SALOPINASSE
                                  BARRETT
                               MAGARSHACK
                         HOMBREDELAPLUMA
                                    MUREZ
                                 HUBSCHER

A dozen or so (real and false names)

Long ones and short ones

But that can take you a long way

Could put the list at the end

or in footnotes

It's been done before

Never works of course

It seems modern enough

but finally it's gimmicky

Particularly in footnotes

At the end would be better

It may even work

As long as you don't exaggerate

A dozen names at the most

Don't even have to spell them out
....
....
....
....
....
....
....
....
....
....
....
..

Long ones and short ones

That makes a decent list

```
Let whoever wants to choose
a name at random a long one
                  a short one
                  a medium one
or even a veryveryshort one
like PUCE
or even shorter
like POU             choose
a name at random
```
                                        In other words what you need
                                        is a list of possible names:

FIRST & LAST

        and then select or rather let whoever wants to select select
the name he or she (that's always possible) prefers anytime anywhere
to suit the purpose of his or her perusing through the discourse now
in progress

        But better yet
        leaving out all names: FIRST & LAST

                                        in order that he or she may
be able   may
have the complete freedom of choosing willingly or randomly a name (or several
names depending of course on the situation and the number of people involved
in the situation) for the person whose adventures are currently being told and
fabricated and presented and related for the pleasure or rather for the infor-
mation of the person MALE or FEMALE who is presently or potentially reading or
going to read the discourse

                        However
                        the guy (whomever he might be) who is
composing or rather fabricating the discourse could (may very well) help by
simply giving (for instance) the first letter of each name: FIRST & LAST -
with blanks for the rest of the name and let the peruser (MALE or FEMALE)
fill in the blanks with whatever letters he chooses in whatever order he
chooses in whatever language he chooses (or she) -- just like that:

```
                        A-------------------.
                        B-------------------.
                        C-------------------.
                        D-------------------.
                        E-------------------.
                        F-------------------.
                        G-------------------.
                        H-------------------.
                        I-------------------.
                        J-------------------.
                        K-------------------.
                        L-------------------.
                        M-------------------.
                        N-------------------.
                        O-------------------.
                        P-------------------.
                        Q-------------------.
                        R-------------------.
                        S-------------------.
                        T-------------------.
                        U-------------------.
                        V-------------------.
                        W-------------------.
                        X-------------------.
                        Y-------------------.
                        Z-------------------.
```

Exactly this way (like the above ↑) in alphabetical order. All names
with the same number of blanks (16) and with a period (.) at the end:

One letter (the first)
16 blanks (————————————————) evenly spaced
One period (.) at the end of each name

                              But of course indicating (preferably
in a footnote) that whoever wants to may add or subtract any number of blanks
to make longer or shorter names according to his (or her) heart's desire.

                              This may undoubtedly be of some help
to some people and may seem very confusing to other people but you cannot -
that's obvious - please everybody.

                              One could of course go further and
furnish the first letter and the last letter of each name and make things
easier for some people and more complex for others.

                              Or one could even go much further and
furnish not only the first and last letter of each name but throw in one more
letter somewhere in the middle and let the people who have the courage
the determination the patience and the imagination fill in the rest of
the blanks.

                              There are all sorts of such possibi-
lities here but evidently the best and the simplest way would be to give all
the names (FIRST & LAST) right away. Write them in in straight PROSE
from <u>left to right</u>

                without any breaks ... ...
                without any   UP
                                      &
                                DOWN
                without any breathing ooooooooo pauses   and especially
                without any ————————— in the middle .

                              Then you have what can be called:

a very simple style
a very direct form of narration without any distractions
                           without any obstructions just plain
                                         normal
                                       regular
                                       readable
                                       realistic
                                       leftoright
                                       unequivocal
                                       conventional
                                       unimaginative
                                       wellpunctuated
                                       understandable
                                       uninteresting
                                       safetodigest
                                       paragraphed
                                       compulsive
                                       anecdotal
                                       salutory
                                       textual
                                       boring
      PROSE   prose   prose   plain
PROSE   PROSE   prose   PROSE   plain   PROSE

FOR INSTANCE:

We got off the subway at 185th Street (just like that). I remember that quite clearly (in the first person). Quite vividly (with a lot of adverbs). It was a very warm, humid, and sticky day (and lots of adjectives and commas). Or was it 210th Street (and a great deal of confusion and indecision)? By then the suitcase was getting quite heavy (and lots of realism too). Particularly as we (myself: BORIS, and my uncle: DAVID) went up the stairs into the streets.

(Paragraphs too). We had hardly spoken to each other (lots of silence between them shown with white spaces or blank spaces or better yet with two or three blank pages in the middle of the scene to indicate the silences) since the moment we kissed each other on the pier. Uncle David was walking very slowly his back slightly hunched. It struck me how everything about him was brownish (that's the kind of remark one can interpret two ways or even three). His shoes, his socks, his suit. His tie too (interesting point: from the upper deck it looked red, but at close range it was really brown, or at least more brownish than red -- the tie). The suit was baggy. The shoes worn out and badly polished (that's another good point to remember, how badly his shoes were polished). His skin also was somewhat brownish but not because he was suntanned, far from that. It must have been its natural coloring. (Lots of descriptions takes more room).

It felt like I was walking with a stranger. I didn't ask myself what the Hell am I doing here (but he could have easily). And yet I wanted to be close to him. I wanted to touch his arm. I wanted to tell him everything that had happened to me: my whole life (up to here), my past, and of course my hopes for the future: school, girls, possibly a wife, kids eventually, money (of course), etc. (That's the way to go, but no sentimentality. No crap).

(New paragraph). (It's clear now that Boris is talking in the first person in a very conventional manner). Then up the stairs to the people's apartment in the Bronx. (No need to describe the place. It was the usual type of place). It was a nice apartment. Shiny clean furniture. You could tell the wife was a good housekeeper (unless she had a maid?) The man was about Uncle David's age. Maybe a bit younger. Better dressed though. He had no suit coat on but still you could tell. A white shirt with a blue striped tie. I forget the color of the stripes. The woman was fat, round, with very curly hair (that should do). Not bad looking for a woman of her age. (Should have a name for them. A lot depends on whether or not they are related to Uncle David. If they are related they may have the same name though that's not necessarily so. If they are not related then it doesn't make any difference. They might be distant relatives and not have the same last name. I really do not know. But one thing is sure they are not related to Solomon. That I can assure you. I mean Boris. That's for sure. Boris doesn't know that. I do of course. Or at least I will when the time comes. But I don't have to tell him everything. Cousins! Distant cousins of Uncle David. Makes it more authentic. In America everybody is a distant cousin of somebody else).

Jacobson I think their name was. Also there was another woman there when we arrived (a neighbor or something). She had come because she was curious to see me (she knew they were coming). She was also a fat woman but much younger than the other one (I don't have to talk about her but it is interesting to know that she was present. As he explained to me she came to see the new arrival from Europe. A French Jew, that's unusual. Normally French Jews do not immigrate. They don't even admit that they are Jewish. How can you be French and Jewish at the same time? It's not rational. And the French are extremely rational. They have been like that since the 17th Century at least. Good observation. At least that's what they claim, even though they won't admit for quite a while now that they are tragically unprepared for the 20th Century.)

Boris is a special case   you might say
                one case in a thousand   that's what he should explain to them
but then he would have to tell   them
                              the whole story about the French
                                                  the Jews
                                                  the War
                                                  the Occupation
                                                  the Deportation
                                                  the Concentration
                                                  the Liberation
                                                  the Elimination
thewarthejewsthefrenchtheliberationtheconcentrationthedeportationtheelimination

I suppose they expected him to go into all that (in details) or else why should
that woman be there?

Certainly   she must have had a reason for coming -- that WOMAN!

                That's the first real thought in Boris' mind since he arrived in

                America . . . When you first arrive in America usually your mind

                is quite blank at first . . . Takes a while before you can begin

                to think straight in the beginning . . . It's a matter of speech

How can you explain?   The German   Jews
                                            The Polish   Jews
                                            The French   Jews

                                            WHAT   A   RACE

How can you explain?
the
difference
to   them   ?

        The man. Mr. Jacobson (that's a good false name for this kind of a story)

        and his wife a fat woman with a flowery dress. It's August. Must be. Or

        maybe early September. Summer anyway. Hot like hell. And the other lady

        standing there. Mrs. Somethingorother (Madame Machinchouette). Very Hot.

        Sticky. Important. Particularly since Boris is still wearing his very he

        avy suit. Double-breasted (that's the style in France). His only suit of

        course (except for the green sweater in his suitcase). But it's not as wa

        rm in the Jacobson's apartment as it was in the subway. That's for sure..

                        THE SUBWAY SCENE!

                          what a SCENE!

                          comes before the Jacobsons ------------- obviously.

THE SUBWAY SCENE

The one thing that real
has in the subways full
f this was the right pl
take WHERE AM I he said
feeling with their brig
thout stockings and eno
fore the Jacobsons righ
s ass was small relativ
in the subway ridiculou
rder in all that) There
th a beautiful face She
with a curious smile (a
aying it) on her lips T
mmediately Boris gets a
de his body He feels it
not to show it so he ke
eways at the girl He is
igner (it's obvious) in
vid is asleep next to h
it Her legs are slightl
p of her stockings (she
wearing stockings) blac
d view from where Boris
in his seat and gets an
f her secret triangle o
f she'd noticed what he
going to cross her legs
em sideways in a differ

ly strikes Boris is
of black people For
ace AMERICA or AFRI
to himself The girl
ht clinging nylon d
rmous round firm as
t after the boat sc
ely small comparing
sly small (There ha
was one girl in par
was staring at a sp
delicious smile wou
hick lips Very dark
n enormous reaction
all the way down in
eps his hands on hi
so shy and of cours
the midst of all th
im in his seat Howe
y spread apart so t
was an exception in
k on black nice smo
is sitting But to i
even better deeper l
f flesh Just then s
was doing (his litt
DAMMIT but no inste
ent position giving

the exotic feeling one
a moment he wondered i
CA There must be a mis
s especially gave that
resses Most of them wi
ses (all that comes be
ene with PEGGY) Peggy'
it to the asses he saw
s to be some kind of o
ticular A tall girl wi
ot just above his head
ld be another way of s
black like coal skin I
A rigid sensation insi
his pants but he tries
s lap and he looks sid
e he looks like a fore
ese Americans Uncle Da
ver he could be faking
hat you can see the to
the sense that she was
oth shining skin A goo
mprove it he slouches
ook into the opening o
he moves slightly as i
le game) as if she was
ad she simply moves th
Boris a much better vi

iew a bit more open now
and now you can see all
gle A triangle of veget
is but in fact Boris ca
k shiny skin just above
control Almost explodes
ace She is definitely s
t so it seems to him AH
in his seat next to him
ened on his lap and the
d the lights keep flick
nk or do What a triangl
merica What can he do a

So it seems to Boris
the way up her black
ation A triangular j
nnot see beyond that
the left stocking to
in his pants Quickly
miling at him No que
what can he do Uncle
but still holding on
subway is speeding n
ering and poor Boris
e What darkness What
bout it WHAT A WAY T

(one never really knows)
forest Black African jun
ungle So it seems to Bor
little rectangle of blac
be exact He almost loses
he looks at the girl's f
stion about that at leas
David still seems asleep
to his newspaper wide op
ow through the tunnel an
doesn't know what to thi
a way to begin life in A
O START LIFE IN AMERICA!

                                                    by
                                                       P
He's all excited   L
inside his pants   U
                                       N   N
        - par ti cu lar ly -   NOW   G
                                   NOWON   I
                                   WON   N
                                   N   G
                                                          i
                                                          n
                                                          t
I'll have to work on that   It's a damn good way to bring out   o
                                 H I S   C H A R A C T E R   out

After all he is only 19   About 19   He did have a few pieces   a
before but never spent a whole night with a woman a whole nig   b
ht just screwing   He's really inexperienced when you think o   l
f it but that does not prevent him from dreaming all the time   a
about it   In fact that's one of those things he dreams about   c
all the time even while they are sitting in the Jacobsons' li   k
ving room he thinks about it (The other woman is still there)

Must have been a good two hours (now) since they arrived ther   a   n
e maybe more (eventually the Jacobsons ask them to stay for d   A
inner and what a coincidence   F
                      WHAT DID THE JACOBSONS SERVE FOR   R
                      DINNER?   YES   I
                                N O O D L E S   C
                                                                     A
But before that (before they ask them to stay for dinner)   N   J
              (must have been a good   two hours later)   U
                                                                             N
Boris finally asked where the BATHROOM was.   NO!   G
                                                                             L
                                                                             E

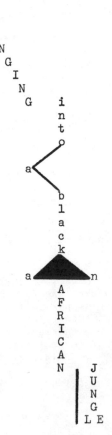

90

NO!

That's not it.

They asked him if he needed to GO (just like that).   Not immediately
                                                          But eventually

First they gave him a glass of MILK (hates milk) and then they asked him
                                                          eventually if he
needed to GO   and then
                                                          immediately showed
him the door down the hall on the l
                                   e
                                   f
                                   t (of course it could have been different)

          For as a great EGOcentric once said:

                         NEVER BELIEVE ANYTHING A WRITER
                         TELLS YOU ABOUT HIMSELF
                                          A MAN or
                         for that matter a woman COMES TO
                         BELIEVE IN THE END THE LIES HE or
                         she TELLS HIMSELF ABOUT HIMSELF or
                         she tells herself about herself

so
 •   •   •   •
HE   •
 • l   •
 • o   •   •   •   •
 • c   •   • I •
 • k   • • • • N •
 • s   himself • • and jerks off a good one.   He really needed it.
 •   •   •   •   •   •   •   •
                                                    What a day!

                                                    First day in America.

                    He does it in front of the mirror above the sink in
                    the bathroom with the girl's legs and stockings and
                    the little brown triangle in front of his eyes   the
                    whole thing like a colored picture (the images some
                    guys have in their heads in situations like these!)

But that's no reason.   It's just because.   One never knows why.   Damn right.

(FIRST DAY IN AMERICA)

Seems like just any other day at first except for the tall buildings/ the noise/
the cabs/ yellow and green/ the people/ black and white/ the subway/ and of cou
rse the strange language/ first you think it's going to be the same/ you think/
or rather you assume/ the people are the same/ except when they speak/ English/
but in fact it's quite different/ the whole world/ his whole world/ seems to be
f
 a
  l l i n g   a .. p .. a .. r .. t   /Always happens/

For him it's even more important: not only a new place
                                       a new   life
                                       a new country but also PEGGY
                                                  uncle DAVID
                            the subway ride the silence the suitcase
                            the girl with the legs spread apart and all
                            the people mostly black and the people in the
                            Bronx and that other woman (that bitch) who
                            came to see just because she was curious all
                            that down the hall first door on the left HE
locks himself in and feels like   RUNNING AWAY
                            like   CRYING ALSO

                         There is a little mirror above the sink in the
bathroom. There is always a little mirror above the sink (even in my room). Helps.
He stretches up on his toes to see himself better. His mouth slightly twisted into
a grin or a grimace (same thing). And then comes the huge feeling of guilt. Always
happens afterwards. That goes back to your childhood to your mother and all that
crap. People usually call it guilt but it could be called something less dramatic.
Guilt or no Guilt it's necessary   particularly in his case.

First day in America.

And What a Day!

First day in the room I suppose I'll feel the same way after all the excitement
of getting things ready: NOODLES
                            COFFEE
                            SUGAR
                            TOOTHPASTE
                            TOOTHBRUSH
                            TOILETPAPER and all the rest that I have not yet
discussed but will have to discuss eventually and of course the horses on the wall
counting them up & down & sideways (OCTOBER 1st) and the table by the window with
the typewriter on it and everything ready for the first sentence in my head all set
to go and the curtains closed and all the decisions made whether or not I work at
night or during the day and BORIS
                            JACQUES
                            SOLOMON or perhaps even MARCEL
                                          ROBERT
                                          JIM all ready to go with
his story: THE BOAT
               THE PIER
               THE SUBWAY RIDE
               THE PEOPLE IN THE BRONX all excited about it impatient hardly able to
wait to tell us the whole story: THE WAR
                                      THE FARM
                                      THE CAMP and I in the midst of all that stuff
real and unreal ready to go 12 pages a day one box a day of that enriched noodle
stuff 365 days to go down the white precipice and the little screw ready to fall
off on the 127th day or something like that and all the other things that will
eventually happen or not happen in the room when alone in the darkness of the mind
one awaits the flashes of light that come with imagination and a knock on the door
any door can disrupt the whole system then you wonder why such a day is important
                                              why a guy needs to jerk off
                                              why the mirror above the sink
                                                      is important
and so the first day it'll be inevitable down the corridor first door on the left
                      I TOO WILL LOCK MYSELF   me and myself
                                    me you I he all of us together. ALONE.

```
                    I
                M       M
              U           U
            S               S
          T                   T
        W                       W
      O                           O
      R                           R
      K                           K
      O                           O
      U                           U
      T         ASYSTEM           T
                   A
                PATTERN
```

A GOOD ONE HERE AND THERE NOW AND THEN
when I can't take it any more in front
of the mirror above the sink or when I
take a shower or in front of the paper
basket or better yet in front of the
typewriter just for kicks when things
go wrong or in my sleep when I'm dream
ing even if I sleep during the day but
no guilt certainly no guilt certainly
A GOOD ONE NOW AND THEN HERE AND THERE

no guilt no sticky feeling deep inside
even though that's exactly how he must
feel when he comes out of the bathroom
down the hall his legs and crotch very
much clammy sticky his eyes bloodshot


```
* * * * * * * * * * * * * * * * * * **
              ** * * **
                ***
                 *
```

That other woman is still there   when he comes out of the bathroom

```
                    BBB
                    III
                    TTT
                    CCC
                    HHH
```


They ask him some questions Questions about the War the Jews how it was during the

the War how he managed to escape In English in Yiddish Doesn't matter Uncle David

answers all the questions for him Almost as though he was the only one responsible

He should be proud and responsible because he is the one who brought him over here.

    Later on
    when Boris
    tells the story
    he changes things a bit:

I didn't say much :::: during the whole time we were sitting in the living room :::: of the Jacobsons :::: We must have been there a good three hours :::: :::: I needed to go to the bathroom but I was afraid to ask :::: :::: I didn't even know how to ask in English :::: I showed them with my hand : ::: But they were ignoring me completely :::: They kept speaking to each : ::: other :::: Uncle David the Jacobsons and also another woman :::: ::::I think she was a neighbor who came to see what was going on :::: Just curio us I suppose :::: They kept talking to each other but I could understand : ::: almost :::: everything they were saying (surprising) :::: I was really surprised :::: They kept saying how much they had suffered :::: During the war :::: I mean the Jews :::: over there :::: how much they had suffered : ::: but that included them too :::: :::: Jews like to suffer well for most Jews even though they were in America the whole time :::: during the war : ::: I wanted to point this out to them while they were drinking tea :::: : ::: from tall glasses with pieces of lemon floating on the surface of :::: the tea :::: and sucking pieces of sugar (not stolen) :::: and eating :::: cookies and remembering all the Jewish people they knew or the people :::: other people knew :::: who had been deported :::: (and exterminated) ::::: during the war while they were in America :::: suffering for them :::: Ex- cept Uncle David :::: I mean suffering the suffering that they thought all these other people who had been deported had suffered over there and grab- bing another cookie and pouring a bit more tea into the tall glasses ::::: but no more lemon :::: using the same old piece :::: all brownish now :::: floating in the tea :::: Eventually somebody :::: (the other woman) :::: I think :::: asked Uncle David if I needed to go to the bathroom :::: and he said YES :::: I THINK HE SHOULD NEED BY NOW TO GO TO THE BATHROOM ::::: It was down the hall :::: First door on the left :::: :::: When I came out of the bathroom (I stayed in there a long time :::: just to be alone ::::)::: : they hardly noticed me :::: I had a strange feeling :::: I didn't expect my first day in America to be like that :::: I expected it to be better ::

:::
There was a little mirror in the bathroom above the sink. I remember that.
I looked at my face for a long time. My eyes were all bloodshot (that's the
word they use in English). I suppose because I hadn't slept well the night
before. With Peggy. On the boat. On the upper deck. Together all night.
:::

They were still drinking their tea with cookies and sugar and lemon   WHEN
                                                                        I
                                                                     CAME
                                                                      OUT

ME!   they gave me a glass of milk
      a tall glass of thick   milk   I hate that stuff I hate it
      I had never never drunk milk   like that before
      I still remember the taste it had   a sour taste (very bad)
      I took little sips just to be polite but I couldn't finish it

DRINK your MILK!   It's good for you
EAT YOUR NOODLES - - - - - EAT YOUR BREAD - - - - - EAT YOUR POTATOES!

The number of guys who hear that sort of stuff in their lifetime!

        They were eating cookies and pound cake too and they kept shoving
        the stuff at me   It's good for you they said.

I wanted to get (the hell) out of there Walk the streets Alone To get lost in
the big city Uncle David told them we were going to spend a few days in the b
ig city (New York) He wanted to show me around We were staying with his cousi
ns in Rockaway Beach (Rockaway Beach?) Yes They have a very nice little house
(a cottage) Sounded good to me even though I couldn't understand what they we
re talking about (the things a guy thinks he understands when in fact he does
not really understand a damn thing)

                            That's when they asked them to stay -- for
dinner: "Nothing much," she said (Mrs. Jacobson), "in fact we're just having
        noodles for dinner."

                   (IMAGINE!) It must have been past six o'clock (what a day!)
But they really insisted about their staying for dinner even though they were only
serving noodles (and tomato sauce, she added).

(You've got to stretch that scene a bit this way as they go on talking he locks
  himself in more and more This must be the crucial point The starting point o
  f the silent period For three weeks A month Two perhaps He doesn't speak a
  t all A sick feeling inside A hole Like he wants to throw up all the time)

The Jacobsons are getting on my nerves. Imagine what a guy feels like when he f
irst arrives in America and he has to spend the whole afternoon of his first day
with people like the Jacobsons.   And then Detroit (that comes next).

Imagine a guy. An immigrant. A Frenchman. And a Jew on top of that. Imagine.
Walking along the streets of Detroit. Imagine the first two or three weeks. In
Detroit. Imagine what's going on in his mind. And you have a typical situation
for a good story. Imagine how he feels. Imagine how closed in he feels. Closed
up. Inside. It takes years. Five. Maybe ten. To get used to that kind of exi
stence. And sometimes a guy never gets used to it. And eventually he kills him
self or if he doesn't have the courage to kill himself he asks somebody to do it
for him.   WHAT A STINKING STORY!

Depends of course on a guy's mentality

Not all foreigners are alike

Some get rich fast

But then there are idiots all over the world

Doesn't matter how tall they are

What color their hair what color their skin

Neither Boris or I are very particular

Neither nor

And what do you do then

You save a 1000 bucks

Sometimes more sometimes less even 10000 bucks

Doesn't matter when or where or how you got it

Then what do you do

You get a room and noodles

DOUBLE OR NOTHING

And here you are back in the noodles

For a foreigner it suddenly feels like you belong

Of course sometimes it never happens

Takes a good five years sometimes ten to get used to A M E
                                                          r i
                                                        c * a

During all that time Boris felt like he wants to
                                               run
                                               die
                                               drown
                                               escape
(THE NEED TO ESCAPE -- extremely important --)   yes

He doesn't know where or how or when to go

Dreams about AFRICA (triangular African jungl
                                        jungle
                                        jungl
Dreams about the OCEAN   )
There is something about the OCEAN that seduces him
                                               seduces you

He feels it even more when he is or you are away
                                               from it
THE OCEAN   and   THE COAST
The nearness of the OCEAN becomes an obsession with him inner desire

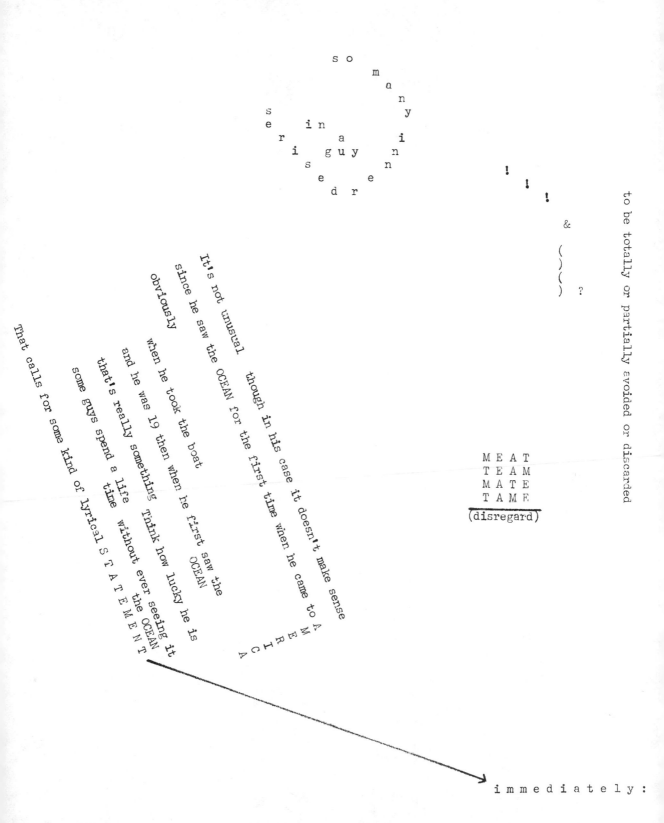

```
                    s o
                      m
                      a
                      n
                      y
        s e      i n
      r      i      a      i
      i    g u y         n
        s e              e
        d r
```

so many in a guy series in red

to be totally or partially avoided or discarded

!
  !
    !
      &
        ( )( )
              ?

It's not unusual   though in his case it doesn't make sense
since he saw the OCEAN for the first time when he came to A M E R I C A
obviously
    when he took the boat
    and he was 19 then when he first saw the OCEAN
    that's really something   Think how lucky he is
    some guys spend a life without ever seeing it
                              the OCEAN
    That calls for some kind of lyrical S T A T E M E N T

M E A T
T E A M
M A T E
T A M E
(disregard)

i m m e d i a t e l y :

```
          THE  CALL  OF
          ─────────────────
          THE  OCEAN
          ─────────────────
          ****************
SSSSSSSSSSSSSSSSSSSSSSSSSSSSSSS          SSSSSSSSSSSSSSSSSSSSSSSSSSSSSSSSSSS
       SSSSSSSSSSSSSSSSSSSSSSSSSSSSSSSSSSSSSSSSSSS
          SSSSSSSSSSSSSSSSSSSSSSSSSSSSSSSSSSSS
             SSSSSSSSSSSSSSSSSSSSSSSSSSS
                SSSSSSSSSSSSSS
                   SSS
                    S
                   ***
                    *
                    *
                    *
                    *
                    *
                    *
                    *
                    *
                    *
                    *
                   ***
                    O
                   OOO
                  )( )(
                    U
                   OOO
                    O
                    *
                    *
                    *
                    *
                    *
                   ***
------------------------------------------------------------------------
ATLANTICPACIFICINDIANARTICANTARTICOCEANOCEAATLANTICPACIFICINDIANARTICANTARTIC
------------------------------------------------------------------------
```

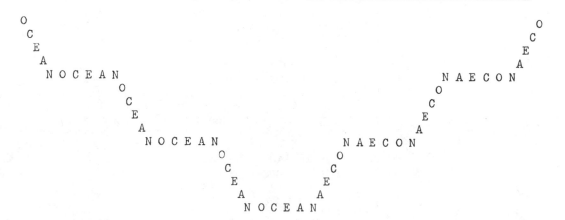

There must be a limit
                        beyond which   there is a CHANCE

That's closer to what
                    he feels at   the beginning
                                                    during the first

five years
            though it usually takes ten
                                            to get rid of that feeling

Even later on when he is in the ARMY (I suppose I'll have to send him to the army--
                    eventually--and then describe that period--it
                    will be one of the middle chapters--200 boxes
                    later--but it depends if he gets drafted orif
                    he volunteers--two years in the army is a lot
                    when you consider the shit they throw at you)

He can't get rid of that crummy feeling (they'll call him FRENCHY for sure).

THINGS ARE SHAPING UP: I have the scene on the boat
                            the first meeting with Uncle David on the pier
                            the subway ride
                            the girl with the legs
                            the afternoon with the Jacobsons
                            the masturbation in the bathroom

THINGS ARE SHAPING UP: From there I'll take them to Rockaway Beach
                            I'll call them Rabinowicz
                                    Rabinowicz that's a good name
                            (or something like that) Uncle David's Cousins
                            Polish Jews who came to America before the war
                            (or about that time)

                                                        (s)
THINGS ARE SHAPING UP: It's not too difficult to get thing going   As you
        ↑   go along people keep popping out   I now have:
        r
        e   PEGGY on the boat
        a   UNCLE DAVID on the pier
        l   THE GIRL (anonymous) with the legs in the subway
        l   THE JACOBSONS (and the other woman too) in the Bronx
        y   THE RABINOWICZ (cousins) in Rockaway Beach

                            The girl in the subway of course is a secondary charac-
                            ter unless I decide to make her a primary character and
                            have Boris screw her eventually of course it won't be e
                            asy to arrange his first day in America and Uncle David
                            sitting next to him in the subway (he looks asleep but
                            it's not certain he could be faking it) and more import
                            ant there is the language problem for Boris who doesn't
                            speak a damn word of English how the hell do you commun
                            icate your feelings By gestures
                                                By signs
                                                By symbols
                                                By silences
                                                By simulation
                            these are questions one must consider eventually as the
                            characters keep popping out all over the place suddenly

(suddenly) I'll have too many CHARACTERS!

Many of them won't last of course: they'll drop out
                                        they'll fade away
                                        they'll disappear
                                        they'll die maybe

Still that doesn't solve the problem of the person -- of the point of view:

                                  FIRST PERSON
                                     or   ?
                                  THIRD PERSON

    <u>FIRST</u> <u>PERSON</u> is more restrictive   more subjective   more personal   harder

    <u>THIRD</u> <u>PERSON</u> is more objective   more impersonal   more encompassing   easier

I could try both ways:

    I was standing on the upper deck next to a girl called Mary... No Peggy.
    He was standing on the upper deck next to a girl called Mary.. No Peggy.

    (comes out the same). Might be better therefore to start with a little

    description: THE SEA∼∼∼∼∼∼∼∼
                       THE SKYLINE OF NEW YORK ^ ^ ^ ^ ^ ^ ^ ^

It was almost night ...

(that's something else) Maybe the whole story should take place at night

only night SCENES would give it an eerie feeling (" # $ % ' & * ? ? / ")

(wouldn't work).

You could alternate: one night scene
                         then
               one   day scene

               day when he is with people (the subway ride
                                 the landing on the pier
                              the Jacobsons the bathroom)

               night when he is alone   (loneliness and dreams
                                   the room and the factory
                                   the camp the train the farm)

               DAY for the outer world
               NIGHT for the innerself

Perhaps you should have the day scenes first and the night scenes last

    (it's more logical).

    Maybe I should write the day-scenes during the day
                   and the night-scenes during the night
                                    (it would be more
                                         dramatic)

PERSONALLY   I don't give a damn if it's more dramatic - I think I
should simply write the damn thing straight and not -
definitely - not mess around with night-scenes during
the night and day-scenes during the day - doesn't make sense particularly if I decide to work with the cu
rtains closed then there won't be any nights any days
just electric time on top of the noodle time 365 days
one after another until I can't stand the damn lights
and the damn noodles any more - page after page - sen
tence after sentence - paragraph after paragraph - if
paragraphs there are - chapters after chapters - if c
hapters there are - and plot on top of plot - I didn'
t think of that - though - plot --------------------

PERSONALLY   I don't give a damn about plots as long as the storie
s move along who needs plots - plots or no plots it's
for suckers - doesn't make any difference - it's like
the nights and the days I won't be able to notice the
difference and nobody else will either - plots are in
fact useless even if plotful stories are more logical
- but that does not mean that I will skip the plot in
toto - I may have to consider the possibility of a mi
nimal plot - even if it's useless and illogical - wit
hout a plot stories read like pieces of diary and are
not always credible - nobody believes what is being s
aid - some guys in fact insist on a plot or else give
up before starting - but ----------------------------

PERSONALLY   I can do without and will answer those who insist on
a plot - whomever they are - I don't have to be speci
fic - by saying that they are a bunch of pricks - for
what I really need now is not a plot but to get going
to get my ass going - to write - write the damn thing
and then shut up though in fact I should shut up imme
diately and write the thing without babbling all over
the place or else the whole story is wasted - anyways
you want to look at it up and down or sideways - reg-
ardless of the situation in which you have cornered y
ourself in order to get the damn thing started irreg-
ardless if you ever finish it - but -----------------

PERSONALLY   I don't give a shit if I never write the damn thing -
let somebody else do it as long as I have the room to
sleep in and the noodles to survive I can always lock
myself in and make believe that I am doing it whereas
in fact I am not doing a damn thing in the room excep
t eating - day after day - my noodles - crapping - my
noodles - day after day - taking showers - usingup my
toiletpaper - wasting the time of noodles and the ele
ctric time too - making believe that in the room alon
e all by myself for 365 fucking days I am composing -
inventing - writing - the greatest plotless masterpie
ce of all time -------------------------------------

anyway you want it
anyway you see it
anyway you look at it   H O R I Z O N T A L L Y
anyway you take it
anyway you hear it

                                                    or--------

```
--------→       V               S Q U A R E L Y              SSSQQQUUUAAARRRREEELLLYYY
                E               Q           L                Q                       L
                R               U           E                U                       E
                T               A           R                A                       R
                I    or-------- R           A    or--------not R                     A
                C               E           U                E                       U
                A               L           Q                L                       Q
                L               Y L E R A U Q S              YYYLLLEEERRRAAAUUUQQQSSS
                L
                Y
```

for finally:

It all boils down to the ROOM
                    the ROOM is at the core of the whole thing
            without the ROOM nothing can be done
                    the ROOM is crucial
                    the ROOM is the starting point
            and the ROOM is also the finishing point
whatever the cost of the ROOM nothing can be done
            without the ROOM   so
                                                                              here
                                                                                we
                                                                                go

416 dollars just for the ROOM (imagine that) that's a lot of dough
And besides

how the hell do I get all the stuff into the ROOM without attracting
                                                    attention (?)

Unless I work all night (tonight!) 37 trips (UP & DOWN) for the noodles
                                                                    alone

and more trips yet for the coffee sugar toothpaste salt toilet paper (52 rolls)

and all the other crap (?) I need to survive on the edge of the precipice feet
                                                                            first

Let's say approximately 10 or 15 trips (UP & DOWN) more should do it

They'll think I'm crazy nuts mad irrational lunatic irresponsible cracked dumb

        For indeed beyond the ROOM (one should say before) there are all kinds
        of problems: for instance: the toilet paper -- two rolls for 27 cents--
        Of course you get better quality for 29 cents And even better for 32 cents
        But you can't go overboard particularly for stuff like that since it gets
        flushed away anyway.
                            You could of course do it the easy way
                                            or the hard way

        the easy way is half of 52 or 26 (comes out even)
        the hard way is half of 27 or 13.5 (comes out uneven)

        either way comes out the same: 52 times 13.5
                                            or   makes $7.02
                                        26 times 27

$7.02
___

I'll have to make sure about that -- just in case I made a mistake:

                                        But in fact:

        It doesn't matter
        in this case here
        since you decided
        on
            2 rolls a week: It simply means that I double UP:

                        Double 7.02
                            7.02 times 2 that's 14 bucks .04:

                    EXACTLY WHAT I SAID (ORIGINALLY) EXACTLY

ORIGINALLY -- when Boris first arrived in America -- he never thought he would
get so involved with such matters -- and it's not the end it's only the beginning -- take cigarettes for instance -- originally Boris -- or for that matter
even Me -- didn't smoke either before or after he arrived in America -- Never:

                                    But now I do -- he does too --
                                            I do

                            CIGARETTES!   Almost forgot:

        How can you survive
        How can you exist
        How can you work   (without)   CIGARETTES?

Right now about a pack a day (give and take an extra smoke here and there)
But under pressure could be more -- a pack and a half -- can't tell now --
two maybe -- you could cut down of course -- d
                                              r
                                               o
                                                p   the whole thing --
        Nobody's forcing you

        Nobody's pushing you - d
                            - o
                            - w
                            - n   the white p-r-e-c-i-p-i-c-e.....
                                                            .....
                                                            .....
                                                            .....
                            THAT'S FOR SURE.....

Get a job -- work during the day -- write during the night -- write the damn thing
at night -- in the evening after work -- with the money you now have you could cer
tainly live it   -- UP
            up   & DOWN -- start a savings account:
                                        BANK   TRUST   COMPANY
                                                OF
                                                AMERICA

IT NEVER WORKS!

you start writing at night and then soon you fall asleep:

ZoZoZoZoZoZoZoZoZoZoZoZoZoZoZoZoZoZoZoZoZoZoZoZoZoZoZoZoZoZoZoZoZoZoZoZoZoZ

you start going out every night looking for pieces of ass:

(o) (o) (o) (o) (o) (o) (o) (o) (o) (o) (o) (o) (o) (o) (o) (o) (o) (o)

I assure you
IT NEVER WORKS!

and soon it's all shot to hell.

Either way doesn't stop you from SMOKING (that's for sure)

a pack a day/ maybe more/ you tried before/ in Detroit/ yes/
when I had the time/ but didn't know how to say it then/ no/
in Los Angeles/ when I didn't have the time/ 20 pages/ yes/
here and there at the most/ each time/ and it's never/ no/
finished/ it never gets anywhere/ a guy needs a year/ yes/
365 days at least/ a whole year to himself just for that/
then maybe you can do it/ maybe/ maybe you can finish it/
something serious/ something profound/ something good/ yes/

it may sound ridiculous/ to most people/ and it's a heckuva
thing/ indeed/ to suggest/ and I agree with them/ who wants
to lock himself up in a room for a year and waste out one's
life on paper/ you've got to be nuts/ nobody cares after al
l/ it's my life/ one year of it blown to hell/ what a joke/
but it's my decision/ my responsibility/ my life/ my bread/
my guts/ my room/ my noodles/ my time/ my money/ my coffee/

if you give up now you'll never forgive yourself/ a pack a
day/ just another jerk working his ass off and that's all/
takes guts/ of course/ a whole year locked-up cooked-up in
a room with noodles/ what a joke/ without cigarettes it wo
uld be unbearable/ no doubt about that/ it's quite obvious

nobody/ of course/ forces you to do it/ to be a scribbler/
Boris either/ nobody/ he could as well be a painter/ a sal
esman/ a social worker/ a soda jerk/ a plumber/ a cook/ or
even better a professor/ a singer/ if he had a voice/ a pi
mp/ eventually/ a musician/ a jazz musician/ that's not as
idiotic as it sounds/ if you consider the facts/ he starts
playing when he goes to high school/ NORTHERN HIGH/ that's
in Detroit/

COURSES IN: American History (from the beginning to the present)
             Government (the Senate the Congress & the President)
             English for Foreign Students (twice a week or more)
             Physical Education (Golf Tennis & Swimming especially)
             Music (marching Band & Orchestra - First Saxophonist)

YES he plays the saxophone (TENOR SAX). He didn't know a damn thing
about music at first but one day he was walking in the streets   of
Detroit (he walks in the streets a great deal in the beginning) And
there was that school: N O R T H E R N H I G H S C H O O L   He
                                                              goes in

```
HE————————————————————————————WALKS
                              RIGHT◄————————IN
```

Full of Negroes: 〰〰〰〰〰〰〰〰
                  •••••••••••••••
                  ‖ ‖‖‖‖‖‖‖‖‖‖‖‖‖‖‖

On the EAST SIDE

Talks to the Principal ✕✕✕✕✕✕✕✕✕✕ Talks to him about courses for foreign students
       the Principal ✕✕✕✕✕✕✕✕✕✕ Talks to him about courses in   English
                                                                        History
                                                                        Government

He doesn't really know what he wants.

All he knows is that once he got started he definitely wants to play something

                              trumpet
                              clarinet
                                saxophone   (but not the piano - too tough)

          It was ERNEST who got him started (what a guy!)

          Tremendous person for a negro (his best friend)

          Can't remember how they met

          Must have been in the auditorium when he heard the music

          All the kids blowing their horns:

                              trumpets
                              clarinets
                                trombones
                                 saxophones

                                             (Tremendous scene!)

What a picture!

That's it I'll make him a SAX player for a while doesn't matter if it's not
auto=biographical one can always invent a little it's normal it's just a ma
tter of not getting confused with what's real and what's not real what he r
eally did and what he really did not do what he wants and what he doesn't w
ant.

                                             (Tremendous place!)

NORTHERN HIGH SCHOOL.......... Can't remember a single face in the place
                              Can't remember how he got into the place
                              Can't remember how he even managed to speak

He was just walking down the street one day in Detroit about two or three w
eeks later and then he saw this big building it was a school anybody in his
right mind would have guessed that just from the look of it he walked right
in just like that and told the principal that he wanted to learn English mu
st have been two or three weeks after he arrived in Detroit from New York a
fter having spent a week or so in New York with uncle David sightseeing all
the big buildings the Statue of Liberty Fifth Avenue Macy's Rockaway Beach.

Can't remember a single face   EXCEPT ERNEST's!

and some of the other guys who played with him later on on weekends at the

BLUE BIRD but this was a good two years later -- I'm not even sure I'll be
                                                able to get that far with
                                                story might run out of BO
                                                XES before that NOODLE --

What a group!

                    TONY ON PIANO
                    RED ON GUITAR
                    KENNY ON BASS
                    BILLY ON DRUM
                    ERNIE ON ALTO

                    (who the hell was on trumpet?)

                    BORIS (eventually) on TENOR

                    DAVIS! Davis or something on TRUMPET

                    That makes a septet (sextet without Boris)

                T H E   R A Z Z B E R R Y   C O M B O

Took him a good two years before he could play with them regular   but they
liked him right from the start   and also there was that other kid   once
in a while (makes it an octet with him) on trombone   with a funny Armenian
name or something Tachoukian Kachouian real funny Toungaian Dammit   had a
tremendous sound for a white guy   Boris of course is white too but he
learned quickly   it was Mr. Lawrence who got him started   After   they
left the Principal's office Boris heard the music as they were walking down
the corridor past the auditorium   what a noise   they were on their
way to Mrs. Something's office for the English course   After he left   her
office (she was a very nice person   told him he could start right in) he
went back to the auditorium to listen to the sound   he just walked into
the big room   guys all over the place in every corner blowing
their brains out and Mr. Lawrence on the stage   what a nice man   he was
sitting at the piano   he was white with fat cheeks and a very red nose an
enormous voice   but what a man what a swell guy for a music teacher

-- What can you play?
-- Nothing.
-- That's not much ... Ever studied music before?
-- (Boris lied a little) ... Yes ... in France before I came to this country.
-- You're from France? ... (What a question).
-- (Boris had to tell the truth) ... Yes.
-- Where did you pick up your English?
-- (Here and there Boris should have said) ... Euhh...
-- It's not bad ... Except for the accent (he must have been lying a bit too.

Boris blushed. What a guy wouldn't do to pass for a real American. What a
                                                                Scene!
-- What do you want to play?
-- Euhh ... Anything ... I would prefer the trumpet.
-- Don't have any.

IF they DON'T have ANY trumpets LEFT hell with it THEN.

   -- Look in that room over there ... I think there's a clarinet left.

   -- (Clarinet! ... Why not!)

YES. -- There was a clarinet left in that room over there and that's how
Boris got started on the clarinet before he switched to the saxO
phone (tenor)...same fingering as the alto (sax) explained Mr...
Lawrence...I'm not going to argue with a music teacher particula
rly a nice teacher like Mr. Lawrence...and anyway Boris was much
too happy to say anything...he took his clarinet and started....
squeaking on it....but in half an hour or so Mr. Lawrence taught
him the fingering and the basic
SCALE -
            DO
            RE
            MI
            FA
            SOL
            LA
            TI
            DO
         - he had written on a piece of paper...it was hard at
first for Boris to get the first straight sound out of that tube
but eventually he got it...must have been Ernest who showed Bori
s how to squeeze his lips tight...bite the mouthpiece MAN until
your lips...your mouth...hurt -
                           DO
                            dododo
                           DODOOO
                        MI
                            mimimi
                            miMImi
                        SOL
                            solsol
                        SOOOOL
                - Boris would have pref
erred a trumpet or a saxophone (tenor or alto it didn't matter a
bit at that time since he didn't even know the difference)....he
felt stupid with his clarinet...Ernest was blowing the alto saxo
phone...what a sound he had on his horn...like Charlie Parker...
that's what or whom he said he was trying to blow like...as..for
Boris (later on) (much later) (two or three months) (he did pick
it up rather quickly) (must have had natural talent) he played a
bit more like Dexter Gordon (particularly when he switched to th
e tenor sax)...at least that's what he said to me...the things a
guy imagines about himself when he doesn't know any better...but
he was serious about it...I can hear him telling me the whole st
ory (26 or 27 boxes later -- if we ever get that far):

"You know I really wanted to blow like Dexter Gordon. Ernest sounded more like
Bird on his alto until he too switched to the tenor (that's right -- I almost f
orgot -- Ernest also switched from the alto to the tenor about the same time Bo
ris bought himself his first tenor saxophone with the money he saved working in
the evening in a grocery store) then he started sounding more like Lester Young
Indeed Lester puts more heart into it than Dexter but Dexter's style is more mo
dern than Lester's particularly the way he holds his horn when he blows like so
me enormous phallic symbol all twisted in front of him golden and superb and.."

He goes on and on like that telling me how he was blowing his saxophone
                                    how he was holding it (for a while
at least because eventually he went back   to holding it on the side)
in front of him like Dexter
          because it's more modern
                        telling me how he's always imitating great solos
                            and how in two or three months he was
really good
          good enough in fact to play with Ernest's group THE RAZZBERRY COMBO -
"not every night at the BLUE BIRD but once in a while" a little solo here &
there   telling me how hard he worked at it 12 or 15 hours
a day (no kidding) in fact telling me how in fact that's all he did most of the
time   that's all he care about most
of the time in the beginning in Detroit (that stinking fucking place)
                        telling me how something had to crack to give up in
                              that stinking fucking place
                        telling me how sometimes he would simply play scales
and chords up and down - UP & DOWN - for hours
                        and hours:

```
DO              DO              DO              DO      DO
RE                                                      RE
MI       MI     MI      MI      MI      MI              MI
FA                                                      FA
SOL             SOL             SOL             SOL     SOL
LA                                                      LA
TI                                                      TI
DO              DO      DO      DO      DO              DO
```

12 or 15 hours a day (it's hard to believe) but this was before he started working full time in the factory at CHRYSLER because at first he only worked partime
in a grocery store   in fact at first he doesn't have   to
have a job   right away when he arrives in Detroit (that stinking fucking place
where his uncle took him) because Uncle David helps him out the first few weeks-
two or three- with a few dollars a week for the room and the food he needs to su
rvive   but eventually he gets a partime job and later on a fulltime job -
at CHRYSLER - and besides he has 50 dollars with him when he arrives in America-
imagine that-   50 dollars to arrive with in America that's qui
te a lot of money for a foreigner - that's why he can do what he does in the beg
inning:

```
        DO
      RE
    MI
      FA
        SOL
          LA
            TI
              DO
```

                        Got
                    to use that (a damn good touch) this way

                        I can also bring in the whole negro problem
That's the only way to learn how to become a real
                        true AMERICAN
In fact this whole business with his negro friends in Detroit is extremely im-
portant -- particularly his friend ERNEST...as we shall see a little further on.

DETROIT
ERNEST

ERNEST'S MOTHER these are important facts. And indeed his first piece of ass

(o) in America was a shade as ERNEST explained to him they were call

ed. A cute little brownish girl with an exotic name: DAISY or some

name like that. (NO) it was more Spanishy than that: CARMEN. I ca

n always invent something. In fact I'll change all the names eventu

ally. Has to be. Even the name of the school even the name of the

music teacher: Mr. LAWRENCE. And Mrs. SOMETHING the English teache

r. I'll change all the names. You just can't go around using real

names in something like that or else you're in serious trouble.   Ex

cept ERNEST (what a great guy!) ERNIE they called him (what a fabul

ous guy!) And very conscious of his race. Must be involved in the

movement now. ERNIE was a smart guy. BORIS and HE were real good f

riends. His only friend you might say in the beginning until BORIS

met JOSEPH. But that comes in much later (if ever) around the end.

JOSEPH
DETROIT

JOSEPH'S UNCLE these are also important facts. I almost forgot about JOSEPH.

That's another guy who'll have to come into the picture. And what a

picture! JOSEPH. I'll make a whole list of all the guys who eventu

ally have to come into the picture this way I can have a nice cross

section of America. UP & DOWN & SIDEWAYS. Then what I can do event

ually is make pictures (HUGE PICTURES) with all sorts of people and

all sorts of places. I'll make a picture on the floor of the room w

ith my noodle boxes. Pictures of places and of things too. Like an

enormous MAP of AMERICA with my noodles. Boxes all over the floor o

f my room. And then I'll walk on it. On the map. I'll plunge   in

it. Swim in it. Drown in it. State by State. Box by Box. It

will be tremendous. And after a while I'll be able to eat the MAP.

FABULOUS!   AMAZING!

Who ever thought of that?

-A NOODLE MAP OF AMERICA-
*
*
*

This whole story is getting
more and more
SYMBOLIC

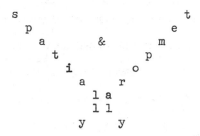

```
          s                              t
      p                              e
      a              &            m
      t                        p
        i                  o
          a          r
            l  a
            l  l
              y      y
```

PRODIDIOUS!   STUPENDOUS!

-A NOODLE MAP OF AMERICA-

with all the states in noodle
*
*
*
*

-alabamaalaskaarizonaarkansascaliforniacolorad
oconnecticutdelawarefloridageorgiahawaiiidahoi
llinoisindianaiowakansaskentuckylouisianamaine
marylandmassachusettsmichiganminnesotamississi
ppimissourimontananebraskanevadanewhampshirene
wjerseynewmexiconewyorknorthcarolinanorthdakot
aohiooklahomaoregonpennsylvaniarhodeislandsout
hcarolinasouthdakotatennesseetexasutahvermontv
irginiawashingtonwestvirginiawisconsinwyoming-
*
*
*
*

50 of them that's almost a coincidence if one were to cut down let's say to
50 rolls one would have one roll of toilet paper for each state of the U.S.
50 rolls would be plenty but that is an entirely different problem because
50 rolls of toilet paper can't possibly make a noodle map of america unless
50 rolls of toilet paper are substituted to make a toilet paper map instead
50 boxes of noodle are of course more logical even though it does not cover
52 weeks the time of noodles for indeed it would be madness to try living on
50 boxes of noodle even if the boxes are giant size with enough for one week
50 boxes would still leave me short by two weeks which may prove essential!

NOODLE MAP/NOODLE MAP/NOODLE MAP/NOODLE MAP/NOODLE MAP/NOODLE MAP/NOODLE MAP/
NOODLE MAP/NOODLE MAP/NOODLE MAP/NOODLE MAP/NOODLE MAP/NOODLE MAP/NOODLE/

therefore insert here a map of america with all the states in noodle boxes
with names of states in noodle names fifty of them or perhaps skipping o
ne or two states such as alaska and hawaii thus staying within the con
tinental boxes and having only forty-eight states to cope with which
in itself is more practical within the context of this discourse a
nd easier to handle too even though it will not be easy to map o
ut the whole thing with square or rectangular boxes since this
is strictly symbolic or better yet merely allegorical a stat
e for a box a box for a state independently of the shape a
nd a noodle for a person independently of the person's c
haracter and mentality on the fictitious level then yo
u will have eventually a perfect or almost perfect c
ross section of america and moreover with such a m
ap inserted in the discussion you also have at y
our disposal a point of reference or several p
oints of references for all the places and p
eople mentioned in the course of the narra
tion and at the same time the possibilit
y of keeping track instantly of all th
e activities the people will be doin
g and the places they will go to a
ssuming they do things and go pl
aces and so on and furthermore
have the advantage of a syst
em which permits you to re
arrange at will and at r
andom that which seems
not to fit into your
noodle map of amer
ica symbolized b
eautifully by th
e noodle boxes spr
ead on the floor sid
e by side of your room
and into which you can p
lunge swim and even get lo
st without any effort and co
nsequently your taks will be g
reatly simplified will become mu
ch more plausible and much more lo
gical considering that with such a m
ap everything will fall in place autom
atically and therefore allow me much mor
e freedom to deal with other matters which
are more important than such trivial matters
as keeping track of all the activities all the
people and all the places mentioned in this disc
ourse in progress unless of course I decide sudden
ly to skip the whole thing drop the whole idea and r
eplace the noodle map of america by a toilet paper map
as suggested above but this would not necessarily resolv
e the problem for indeed a toilet paper map is not much be
tter than a noodle map not much of a substitution thereof so
that an entirely different idea a totally new concept might be
needed to unable us to work out the details of the problem of ke
eping track of all the people places and activities mentioned in t
his discourse even though such a concept or idea requires a great de
al of imagination and patience both of which are at this time rather l
imited but eventually one can always invent something to pass the noodle
time away even if it is not something as complex as a symbolic noodle crap

NOODLE MAP/NOODLE MAP/NOODLE MAP/NOODLE MAP/NOODLE MAP/NOODLE MAP/NOODLE MAP/

a noodle a noo
in other words
if not a noodl
e map of ameri
ca then a subs
titute of some
sort something
perhaps less o
bvious less co
mplicated more
human somethin
g to keep trac
k to measure a
ll the activit
ies people and
places or simp
ly to record m
y own activit
ies in the roo
m such as taki
ng craps showe
rs and leaks a
s well as thos
e places where
I will not und
er any circums
tances be allo
wed to go to s
uch as restaur
ants movies wh
orehouses sinc
e I will not b
e permitted to
leave the room
at least physi
cally for it i
s indeed alway
s possible for
one to get out
of a room ment
ally if not ph
ysically symbo
lically if not
in reality sim
ply by inventi
ng first a pla
ce to go to an
d second by fi
guring a meth
od to get to t
hat place in q
uestion in spi
te of the fact
that one is de
liberately loc
ked in the roo
m for the purp
ose of putting
together all t
he pieces of a
life piece aft
er piece forev
er and ever ho
wever futile i
t might become
toward the end
the a noodle a

NOW THEM

This does not solve the problem of ERNEST. Last anybody heard from him
he had gone into the Air Force. Eventually BORIS finds one of ERNEST's
letters somewhere which confirms what has happened to him. And that in
fact solves the problem. But at this stage BORIS starts an argument wi
th me because he does not like what I am doing to ERNEST. But since I
have a great advantage over BORIS as his progenitor. Since I literally
control his existence. If for some reason he argues with me and I find
I do not like what he says to me I destroy him. One Two Three. I tear
him up and throw him away. I wipe him out. I erase him and all the re
st with him. There is no point in going on with a story that doesn't s
atisfy both the creator and the created the teller and the told the pro
ducer and the product. That's quite obvious. And in a way it's an easy
way out. I throw the whole thing out of the window. Noodle tomato sau
ce coffee typewriter toiletpaper toothpaste toothbrush BORIS sugar etc.

NOW THEN

Let us continue peacefully. I'll describe the whole scene in the audit
orium when BORIS walks in. First he looks around. Listens to the musi
c. Stands in one corner of the big auditorium feeling somewhat embarra
ssed. Somewhat like a stranger. Then he takes his courage in his hand
and walks up to Mr. Lawrence. Then after that he meets some of the kid
s. ERNEST is one of them. ERNEST is immediately very friendly. BORIS
doesn't like the clarinet in the beginning. But nobody else is blowing
clarinet. That gives him a chance to play in the orchestra. He has in
fact the whole part to himself. Three or four weeks later when he mana
ges to read music he is given a spot in the orchestra. Must have had s
ome natural talent. Must be in the family. Hereditary. Though neithe
r his father nor his mother played music. That's rather curious indeed.

NOW THEN

since we are dealing with personal matters let's make this clear right now:

      his father was a painter
      his mother nothing
      just a mother
      and his sisters
      do we mention the sisters or do we skip the sisters
      if we mention what happened to them then immediately
                 people start feeling sorry for us
      it always happens when you say your sisters died
      the oldest one was quite a good musician
      played the piano
      six years of lessons
      it's a lie of course
      everybody lies a little
      the youngest one nothing
      except for a few ballet lessons

that should do for the personal matters but it's a good place to bring it in

particularly since after a while Boris invents real well all sorts of things

about his father
    his mother
    his sister (s)   also
about his friend (s)   ERNEST
                      JOSEPH

for instance: the first time he gets a chance to blow a saxophone
               it's Ernest who lets him use his
               the first time he gets a chance to drive a car
               it's Joseph who lets him use his

          he uses Ernest's mouthpiece too just wipes it a bit on his sleeves
          because it was all wet
          HEY MAN DIG THAT CRAZY FRENCHMAN
          that's what Ernest says to him when he blows the sax for the first
          time

          NOT BAD NOT BAD FOR THE FIRST TIME
          that's what Joseph says to him after his first driving lesson

          Eventually Ernest and Joseph will meet when Boris introduces
          them to each other but that's much later somewhere around the 276th
          box

          but soon after Boris and Ernest meet in the auditorium Ernest takes
          Boris to his house to meet his mother and his father and his sister

ERNEST'S MOTHER: she was tremendous
                                   BIG & FAT
                                   but sexy as hell
                                   one night they danced together
                                   the night she had the birthday
                                   party   Boris's birthday
                                   party   his first birthday
                                   party   his first birthday in America.

If he is 19 when he arrives
he must be 20
for his first birthday in America
            that makes sense
If he arrives let's say in August or thereabout and he is 19
then his first birthday in America should be the following year
                            that makes sense
depending of course on his birthdate
let's assume he was born in Taurus on May 15
then the night he danced with Ernest's mother at the birthday party
must be the 15th of May the year after he arrived in America
                       that makes sense
                       It's rather amazing
        in America   that his first birthday party
        in America should have been arranged by the parents
        of his best friend
          his best negro friend rather than by his uncle
          or friends of his uncle
it shows to what extent people are thoughtful and how anything can happen
in America the same way anything can happen in a fictitious discourse
                         But still
              this business of giving exact dates
                    and real names
              might become very tricky in the end
           it might indeed be better and safer not to mention
          any of this because I have a feeling that if I go
      on giving specific details like these eventually
they'll think I am talking about myself all the time
whereas
in fact
this is not so   I insist on this point
               I am inventing most of this
therefore
who cares what they think Boris is Boris at least until
             I decide I don't like the name Boris any more
But in any event   Boris is not to be confused
                       with a real person
                       dead or alive
and above all not to be confused or identified with
                  me he is strictly fictitious

As for myself
A pure invention
THE NOODLE MAN if you wish
THE TELLER
THE SCRIBBLER   thus whether you say "They danced together"
                  or "We danced together"
           doesn't make a bit of difference

it's all a matter of point of view
        a matter of how you look at
                  it
                sideways   straight
                detravers   obliquely
              upsidedown pardessous
            parderrière alltogether
          horizontally particularly
         verticalement toutdetravers
                    it
                at how you look of matter a

IN FRENCH OR IN ENGLISH

doesn't matter
~~~~~~~~~~~~~~~~

```
            L
      E           E
   C                 T
  N                   T
  A                   H
   D                 E
            M
```

That's good enough
it was almost two o'clock in the morning when they started dancing
and that's about when Boris began to realize that she wanted him
that he wanted her that perhaps she wouldn't mind getting screwed by him
he could feel her big thighs against his legs through the thin material
of her dress she must have been completely naked under the thin summer dress
with flowers all over it was summer no it was spring since he was born in May
May 15 to be exact nice month Taurus good sign has to be spring then it must be
a spring dress she's wearing unless she wears summer dresses in spring
because she cannot afford spring dresses in spring that's possible
but it's an entirely different matter which should not enter into play at this time
but whatever the case it was a very thin dress and I am sure she could feel him too
rigid and clumsy ready to explode at any moment right through the thin dress
That's good enough

About a dozen people were present at the party: Ernest
                                                 Boris (of course)
                                                 Ernest's mother
                                                 Ernest's father (nice guy)
                                                 Ernest's sister (14 years old)

                                                 that makes five what you could
call the family   then there was:

                                                 Two buddies of Ernest with their
                                                 girl friends and two other buddies
                                                 without their girl friends

                                                 that makes six more what you could
call the close friends of the family

                                                 And then there was the Armenian
                                                 kid who plays trombone

                                                 that makes with Boris two white
guys and ten colored all together exactly a dozen.

Earlier in the evening some other people had dropped in for the cake with the twenty candles but left immediately after the cake thus you might say that by the time they started dancing only the family and the close friends of the family were left everybody was in a good mood except for one person Ernest's father who had fallen asleep on the livingroom couch but that does not mean that he was in a crummy mood on the contrary it simply indicates that he was loaded which is not unusual at birthday parties and this way things are much simpler for everybody and particularly for Boris even though nothing really happened that night except that they danced until about four in the morning and by then Boris was certain that she wanted him like mad even though she had not said so explicitly but kept rubbing her big thighs against his clumsy rigidity right through the thin material of her dress Boris was ready to explode instantly in his shorts like a motherfucker but finally nothing happened that can be interpreted in a bad way no nothing except that when Boris finally got home he couldn't stand it any more and masturbated a good one in front of the mirror hanging above the sink in his bathroom on his toes with the picture of Ernest's mother's enormous ass in front of his eyes but it was only an illusion the reall ass was asleep next to Ernest's father drunk like hell in their double bed in Ernest's apartment while Ernest was screwing gently the girl friend of one of his friends who came to the party on the back seat of his father's 1948 Buick basically then this is how the birthday party ended

But the real thing between Boris and Ernest's mother happened some four or six weeks later 12 or 15 boxes later sometime in June when Boris and Ernest had reached that stage in their friendship when they told each other everything for instance Ernest told Boris that he had screwed his friend's girl friend on the back seat of his father's car however Boris didn't have the courage to tell his friend that he had made it with his mother and it's understandable even though friends are persons you can abuse persons who supposedly forgive whatever you do that is immoral such as screwing mothers and scr ewing Ernest's mother was indeed a difficult action

most the end of June but he'd been busy
l means have done so before this was al
had given him of course he should by al
ther for the lovely birthday party they
p by Ernest's pad and thank Ernest's mo
his mind he had made up his mind to sto
but not for home because in the back of
est and they shook hands and Boris left
ht to dig some sound crazy man said Ern
man maybe we'll go to the Bluebird tonig
s home I suppose but I'll see you later
ust noplace in particular answered Bori
n Ernest asked where you going man oh j
Finally then when Boris left the statio

ng the laundry always does on Saturdays
e blushing cleaning up the house or doi
ose answered Ernest without noticing th
r mother where is she she's home I supp
d blushing a little as he asked and you
the laundry but to make sure Boris aske
ng up the house or something like doing
nest's mother must be home alone cleani
aving gone to the baseball game when Er
not lying about his father and sister h
orking in the gas station and Ernest is
ut a step to deduce that if Ernest is w
cause Ernest told him so and there is b
a baseball game with Ernest's sister be
w also that Ernest's father had gone to
w Ernest was working and in fact he kne
decided to screw Ernest's mother he kne
bullshit with Ernest so that the day he
at he would stop by the gas station and
he too worked on Saturday but before th
d got the job in the grocery store then
tion that is before he quit Chrysler an
t work he visited Ernest in his gas sta
gas station sometimes when Boris did no
rk at Chrysler but Ernest worked in the
a Saturday on Saturday Boris did not wo
was not working that day must have been
worked all day in the gas station Boris
ver since it was summer vacation Ernest
gas station just around the corner howe
e he usually works after school a Mobil
orking that day in the gas station wher
hday party Boris knew that Ernest was w
ne about two three weeks after the birt
basically this is how it happened in Ju
en if it had to be with Ernest's mother
eeded sex more regularly than before ev
had entered his manhood and therefore n
ing passed his 20th birthday he felt he
neliness and of guilt a period when hav
of a period of deep introspection of lo
to admit it was for Boris the beginning

BETTER LATE THAN NEVER that's what he told himself
I'll tell her I've been busy like hell and that he
really hadn't had the time to stop by to thank her
for the lovely party she had given him for his bir
thday and what a delicious cake she had made for h
im and how appreciative he was of the whole evenin   soft
g and particularly how he enjoyed the way they dan
ced together he'll throw that in just to see if sh
e reacts and then he'll play it by ear and see wha
t happens next and he began to get all excited whi
le walking towards Ernest's pad feeling himself al
ready rigid and clumsy inside his pants as he walk
ed faster and faster around the corner towards his MOTHER ....
                              She was a bit like a MOTHER to him too after all
                              he is an orphan with a rather curious upbringing
                              but still it's not easy to fuck your best friend
                              's mother just like that might be pushing a litt
                              le maybe a sister that's almost normal but Ernes
                              t's sister is only 14 years old that's really im
          normal   moral and his father what a nice guy what a disg
                              usting mentality Boris has and particularly sinc
                              e Ernest's father was so nice to him and to Erne
                              st too sometimes he would let Ernest have the ol
                              d 1948 Buick and one day in a park Ernest told B
                              oris you want to try man he showed him what to d
                              o and for a while Boris drove the car around the
park what a sensation it was really very exciting
as he walks up the stairs he can feel it harder a
nd harder I can't go on like that I can't I can't
wandering all over the place getting all worked u
p about something which might never happen I woul
d do better getting back to my list and not waste   hard
any more time fucking around with Boris's best fr
iend's mother perhaps eventually I'll get there a
round the 256th box but until then stick with the
toiletpaper the toothbrush the coffee the soap su
gar salt tomato sauce the wall paper and the hors
es and forget about Ernest's mother it's all an i
llusion a fiction a lie the only truth now is the NOODLES ....
                              Nothing else but the NOODLES and the toilet paper
                              I did that though I really never decided how many
                              wipes in a roll one grabs a handfull three or fou
                              r sheets at a time who the hell counts who the he
                              ll would be crazy enough to measure three or four
                              fistsful for each crap sometimes more when it's s
          sticky   ticky but otherwise use your judgment still I sho
                              uld try one roll just to see or at least time one
                              shit and then decide from that not a bad idea but
                              I really don't need to go now I went this morning
                              wait until tomorrow but then it'll be too late to
                              morrow morning I begin October first and that's i
                              t quite regular about that one crap a day does it

WHERE THE HELL IS MY ROLL?

WHERE THE HELL IS MY LIST?

Don't tell me I've got to start all over D
                                             A
                                             M
                                             M
                                             I
                                             T Estimate the cost as you go along
                                                 can't
                                                 go
                                                 on forever!

First let's see how much there is altogether: must have walked out of there
                                             with at least 1200 bucks if I
                                             am correct but some of it was
                                             spent:
                                                      the room in Vegas
                                                       the food on the road
                                                       the bus fare
                                                       the magazines
                                                        the candy bars

                                                 a good fifty bucks
                                                 or maybe even more

It's hard to keep track even though I must have counted that money at least
20 times. Make a list. A pack of cigarettes here and there and each time an
other buck shot to hell. Must have spent over a hundred bucks since Los Ang   Y
eles. Where did it all go? Yes where? That's a good question at a time like   D
this. Besides the bills I still have a bit of change left. 87 cents exactly   O
counting pennies. Can one make it on that for a year? 365 days. Some people   B
manage on less. So many guys in the world who manage on less than one thous   O
and a year. It's pitiful when you think of it. But who thinks of these guys   N

Forget it. Start adding up again. Got to keep it straight. Single space
                                                       and
                                              down the line:

```
Room...........................  416
Noodles........................  105.85
Tomato Sauce...................    7.80
Coffee.........................   20.04
Toothpaste.....................    3.45
Toothbrush.....................     .59
Soap...........................    5.25
Sugar..........................    1.89
Toiletpaper....................   14.04
```

Salt is free.
So far no problems.
It's easier than I thought.

Now we go for the TOTAL the grand total up to this point.
I S E V E R Y B O D Y R E A D Y ?

(turn the page)

five and four is nine and five is fourteen and nine is
twenty-three and five is twenty-eight and nine is thir
ty-seven and four is forty-one carry over four four an
d eight is twelve and eight is twenty and four is twen
ty-four and five is twenty-nine and two makes thirty-o
ne and eight is thirty-nine carry over three three and
six is nine and five is fourteen and seven makes twent
y-one and three is twenty-four and five is twenty-nine
and one is thirty and four is thirty-four carry over t
hree three and one is four and two is six and one is s
even four and one is five for a grand total of: 574.91

```
        this way: 416
                  105.85
                    7.80
                   20.04
                    3.45
                     .59
                    5.25
                    1.89
                   14.04
        TOTAL     574.91
```

Correct.   So far then (conditionally) I have spent exactly in dollars and
cents: 574.91. Of course if you add in French it comes out the same event
ually but it's much easier particularly for a guy like Boris. It's not un
usual for a foreigner to add and calculate and do his multiplication table
s in his original language - his native tongue - even after he's been in a
country for twenty years and knows the language fluently. It's a very com
mon practice. The number of guys who still calculate in their native tong
ue in America is a real phenomenon. Unbelievable. Polish German Greek It
alian Yiddish (of course) Hungarian etc. For Boris of course it's French:

cinq et quatre neuf et cinq quatorze et neuf vingt-tro
is et cinq vingt-huit et neuf trente-sept et quatre qu
arante-et-un et je retiens quatre quatre et huit douze
et encore une fois huit vingt et quatre vingt-quatre e
t cinq vingt-neuf et deux trente-et-un et huit ça fait
trente-neuf et je retiens trois trois et six neuf plus
cinq quatorze et sept vingt-et-un et trois vingt-quatr
e et cinq vingt-neuf et un trente et quatre trente-qua
tre et je retiens trois trois et un quatre et deux six
et un sept et je ne retiens rien quatre et un cinq voi
là c'est fini et ON arrive au même grand TOTAL: 574.91

It's just a question of being careful and of not goofing in your additions
down the line and of course of keeping track of all the numbers you must c
arry over (je retiens in French) after that everything falls in place more
or less and you have a total not necessarily a grand total since we are on
ly in the middle of the discourse and there is more a great deal more to c
ome. Unbelievable in fact how much more there is to come. And that's wit
hout counting all the different drafts (tous les brouillons) and versions.

Most important then is to keep moving therefore assuming that so far I have
estimated approximately 574.91 of my expenses and assuming that I had abou
t 1100 bucks left from my 1200 when I arrived in New York give or take tw
o or three cents here and there but assuming I round it off to 1100 even
including the 87 cents in change I know I have for sure and I divide th
at 1100 by 52 then that gives me exactly to the fourth decimal 23.2692
a week It's not an even number but it's a beautiful number to live on
a week and even if I round it off to 23 point 27 that's a nice littl
e sum of money when you think of it 23 dollars and 27 cents is bett
er than nothing especially when you consider the number of guys in
the world who survive on less compared to the number of guys who l
ive on more you are indeed in better shape than most Boris for inst
ance lived on less About 20 dollars a week when he first arrived but
quite true his room was taken care of by his uncle at least for the f
irst few weeks before he got the job full time the afternoon shift fro
m four to midnight at Chrysler then he started paying for his room hims
elf but until he got his first pay check Uncle David payed for his rente
d room It was only five bucks a week in those days Five bucks including k
itchen privileges but what a stinking room in Detroit with a Hungarian fam
ily Yes it's always the room that creates the problem the damn room in my c
ase 8 bucks a week leaves me 15 bucks or so 15.2692 or 15.27 if I round it
off 8 bucks a week for a room it's really something (6 would be tremendou
s) for all the rest of the stuff and that's without counting the stuff I
might get free or even figuring in an emergency fund How the hell can a
guy survive on the edge of the precipice falling in feet first hanging
on by my fingernails horses flying all over and noodles all around no
odles for breakfast lunch and dinner all in one pot What a situation
Where the hell did it all start Must have been in Los Angeles after
the poker game or else on the bus or somewhere else Perhaps when I
was working as a dishwasher in a cafeteria and couldn't take it an
ymore Not bad that should hit them hard Dishwasher that's a good on
e for Boris It'll go into the list of jobs Boris gets All the crummy
jobs he gets during his first year in America Unbelievable the number
of crummy jobs one gets when one first arrives in America I'll have to
remember that The list of jobs Now I remember it was in New York when I
was living with Loulou and not in Los Angeles I was mistaken all this ti
me The noodle idea was conceived (originally) before Los Angeles yes in N
ew York with Loulou when he and I shared a room in the Bronx which in thos
e days cost only 6 bucks a week for two and we did our own cooking That lef
t us a little less than 10 dollars a week for food transportation and ente
rtainment I was making 15.75 a week Loulou was not working he was a paint
er It was I poor sonofabitch who did all the work and the cooking too Wh
o supported the two of us with my 15.75 a week 15.75 clear that is afte
r all the deductions Slaving like a jerk as a dishwasher but that incl
uded lunches and of course also all the food I smuggled out of the pl
ace for Loulou That lazy bum he refused to work just like that He wa
s a painter An artist and he didn't want to get his hands dirty but
he ate like a pig Eventually he and Boris became buddies but after
the end of this story Therefore Loulou doesn't really come into t
he picture But still what an appetite With less than 10 bucks a w
eek we really had to stretch Therefore noodles was the only food w
e could afford Noodles for breakfast lunch and dinner except that d
uring the week I was better off for lunch than Loulou I had all sort
s of choice in my cafeteria But on weekends noodles all day long Must
have been when the whole noodle idea was conceived From my days with L
oulou in New York living it up on noodles with less than 10 bucks a wee
k for the two of us but Loulou used to tell me not to worry that someday
we'll laugh at the whole thing and when you're famous you'll write a book
about it a big book about noodles and rooms and New York Boris and America

I really liked Loulou too bad he doesn't
come into this story because Boris meets
him much later after this story is finis
hed but what a guy Loulou I would do any
thing for him smuggle all sorts of goodi
es for him ham sandwiches he loved ham p
otato salad too and especially pies appl
e pies he had a passion for apple pies i
n my pockets the stuff dripping like hel
l inside my pants in the subway on my wa
y home to the Bronx juicy crushed apples

what a mess.............................
what a mess indeed I hope Boris does not
have to go through all that shit with Lo
ulou but even if he does it'll be a damn
good experience for him but of course it
does not have to happen in New York it c
an happen just anywhere in America you d
on't have to be specific there are cafet
erias all over doesn't even have to happ
en in Detroit after all Boris does not s
tay in Detroit his whole life eventually
he takes off and slowly works his way to

the West Coast.........................
Los Angeles and then back East to New Yo
rk where it all started a kind of circul
ar journey Journey to Chaos remember Uni
versity of California Press 1965 and fin
ally he dies that's a beautiful ending h
e dies of starvation in a crummy furnish
ed room in the Bronx a circular story fr
om beginning to end from room to room or
better yet from boat to boat boat to boa
t is better than from room to room makes

more sense.............................
and besides this way he does not die and
he goes on to the end and in between mee
ts Loulou yes and eventually he makes up
his mind to take off by boat he can't ta
ke it any more America is for the big bi
rds that's what he tells himself I'm fed
up I'm going back to France or better ye
t he decides that France is also for the
birds and he goes to Africa to live with
his aunt and work in her big hotel at le
ast this gives great unity to his life a

nd to the story........................
but of course he never leaves never find
s the kind of courage one needs to leave
and therefore he stays in America for th
e rest of his life but in between Loulou
comes into the picture and that's why it
is necessary to say a few words about Lo
ulou even if he doesn't appear at all in
this portion of the story but somebody s
omeday might want to use Loulou for anot
her story so one page only one on Loulou

LOULOU was six feet tall with
a tremendous appetite sort of
blondish an enormous hooked n
ose very white teeth a square
chin and bushy hair on his ch
est he always wore suspenders
even at night with his pyjama
s it was so funny I could not
stop giggling in our double b
ed with his ice cold feet sho
ved against my ass he was not
a bad painter an abstract pai
nter he rarely came out of th
e room during the daytime whi
le I went to work in my cafet
aria he stayed home and paint
ed the room every week the ro
om changed color one week the
place was all black the follo
wing week all pink the entire
spectrum of the rainbow in th
e course of time but best was
the week he went wild and dec
ided to do it in multicolor h
e did the ceiling bright yell
ow and each of the four walls
in a different diabolical col
or one wall was dark brown an
other purple the one with the
window he did orange and bott
le green the one with the doo
r the place looked fabulous b
ut the landlady was furious w
hen she came up that Sunday m
orning to collect the rent sh
e almost threw us out but I m
anaged to calm her down by te
lling her that it was tempora
ry another time Loulou painte
d all the furniture fire engi
ne red it was not bad in fact
quite an improvement and sinc
e he had quite a bit of paint
left over he also did the bat

```
OOOOOO      U     U    L           OOOOOO      U        U
O    O      U     U    L          O      O     U        U
O    O      U     U    L          O      O     U        U
O    O      U     U    L          O      O     U        U
O    O      U     U    L          O      O     U        U
OOOOOO       UUUUUU    LLLLLLL     OOOOOO       UUUUUU
```

hroom in red everything the sink the shitpot the pipes and even the mirror it was very
sexy but it got to a point where I would dream in technicolor and the damn paint did c
ost me a lot of money it had to come out of the money we had left after the rent was p
ayed the rent always came first then the noodles seven boxes a week 29 cents a box for
a total of two dollars and three cents the rest of the money was for transportation en
tertainment and Loulou's paint every Saturday after I came home from work we would tak
e the subway downtown to buy the paint at the same time we would catch a movie on Fort
y-second street in those days you could get in cheap 75 cents which normally would hav
e been a dollar fifty for the two of us but somehow Loulou always managed to sneak int
o the place quite a guy Loulou of course we avoided as much as possible eating out unl
ess we couldn't take it any more then we would grab a quick hot dog after the movie wh
ich we shared equally two bites a piece was all a guy could get but it was delicious w
ith a lot of mustard Loulou always took the first bite I the second he the third and I
the fourth but by the fourth bite there was very little left but I didn't mind because
I loved Loulou and I think Loulou loved me too and Boris too too bad I can not use him

Too bad! Really too bad that it is in the part of Boris's life which does
not come into this story that   Boris eventually meets
Loulou and thereafter
Loulou and   Boris travel together -
        extensively - all over the country
                circular journeys : from East to West
                                       from West to East
First they meet in   New York   everybody does
and then they move to   Detroit
and after that it's   Chicago   one always goes through
                          Chicago   on the way West to
                          Los Angeles   with a little detour by
                          San Francisco   and then Eastward again
but don't forget to stop in Las Vegas   for the crap game
and finally it all ends in New York   in a furnished room
with noodles all around and flying horses all over writing a circular story.

                  What a journey
                        journey to chaos
                   a circular journey
                        a journey to the end of the noodles
                             to the end of the story
                             a circular story
                                        a story that never
ends since he cannot find the courage to leave
                     the courage necessary to go back to France
or to go down to Africa   BUT should he have found that kind of courage
this is approximately what would have gone on in his mind in French
                                        in French because
most foreigners when faced with a serious decision think in their original
language -- in Boris's case French:

```
je m'en fous! ** j'en ai marre! ce con de pays me tape sur les nerfs...c
'est de la merde::de la pourriture (POUH!)-- j'en peux plus- je fous  le
camp. je me tire/etvoilà/je me taille!unpointcesttout! Je me BaRrE//  je
laisse tout t-o-m-b-e-r **aurevoir** TOUT LE BORDEL. -Fini-Finie l'Améri
que: L*AM*ER*IQ*UE c'est pour les cons pour les oiseaux ^^^^^ les nouill
es pour les cons-tipés øøø pour les anculés ¿¿¿ Cette salope (o) de PEGG
-Y avec toutes ses conneries son baratin: "tu verras comme c'est bien l'
Amérique ton oncle t'enverra à l'école et tu deviendras intelligent et t
utu deviendras fameux et tu seras riche (et puis quoi encore) ($$$) tout
le monde est riche dans ce fumier-de-pays et tout le monde parle anglais
(YES...OF COURSE...GOODBY) et tu te marieras et tu auras des gosses (1.2
.3.4) et une petite maison (et quoiquoi encore?)..." Viens pas nou(ille)
s raconter tes histoires/tes histoires à la con/-/j'aurais dû lui fourre
r-lui enfoncer--ma grosse bite dans le cul--cette petite conne--ça....ça
au moins....ça lui aurait fait du bien cette gonzesse de rien du tout de
mes deux)(:)( Maintenant c'est fini foutu je me tire SALUT LES COPAINS!Z
Tiens! vous me demandez ce que je ferai et ce que je ne ferai pas (*)oui
belle question (*)? ET bien MOI je (jjeejjee) vais vous le dire ce que je
feraietaussicequejeneferaipas::et bien moi JE ne servirai pas ce en quoi
je ne crois plus que ça s'appelle mon cul ma bite ou mes couilles (ma fa
mille (1) mon pays (2) ma religion (3)) tout cela je m'en fous je m'en b
alance x-x-x- AMEN et AINSI SOIT-IL! ! SaluT la ViE.  Je fonce dans le t
as::pour rencontrer::pour la millionième (100000000) fois #### la réalit
é de mes salopes d'expériences::et pour forger //// dans la dégueulasser
ie demonâme (SALAUD) de marace (SALE JUIF-abat-jour)--oui dans les nouil
les de me mon âme(rica) le fétus de ma conscience ¿ de mon A-venir^^^^^^
```

And so, having decided that Boris would spend the rest of his life in America, there was nothing else to do but go on and on to the end, especially since eventually he too would lock himself in a room with noodles to crap out his existence on paper (52 rolls); but the money had to come from somewhere, if not some poker game in Los Angeles, then some crap game in Las Vegas (can't be both) though there is still the possibility that the money was stolen -- borrowing is out of the question, takes too much involvement and all sorts of collaterals to get it -- stolen money is not a bad idea, on the way back (I don't have the time to describe the whole trip but it's implied), instead of gambling, or instead of borrowing, he knocked up (knocked down, knocked out?), shit, he hit some guy on the head in Vegas (that'll teach him a lesson), and headed for Chicago (no, New York), and when he arrived (by bus) he had about 1100 dollars left in his pocket. And so, the first thing he thinks of doing is grab a boat, and even a plane, anything, and get the hell out of this funcking country, back to France, even though this would ruin the whole set up, mess up the circular aspect of the trip, but who wants to be locked up in a crummy room for 365 days (or 52 weeks) when one can be enjoying life with 1100 bucks or so, in Paris, yes walking UP & DOWN the Champs-Elysées, the Eiffel Tower, Saint-Germain, Montparnasse, even the Riviera. With that kind of money a guy can do almost anything he wants (RIEN N'EST IMPOSSIBLE A L'HOMME), in fact a guy could easily write the whole story in French or even in two languages at the same time (simultaneously with parentheses):

> Hier Boris est arrivé à New York (Yesterday Boris arrived in New York). Il pleuvait (It was raining). Son oncle l'attendait au bateau avec une belle voiture (His uncle was waiting for him at the boat with a beautiful car). Il avait rencontré une fille bien sur le bateau (He had met a nice girl during the trip on the boat). Un fil d'Ariane (An Ariadne thread). Une fille de Milwaukee (A girl from Milwaukee). Ils se sont aimés (They loved each other). Et ils ont pleuré un petit peu quand ils se sont separes sous la pluie (And they wept a little when they said goodbye under the rain) mais elle lui a promis de lui écrire régulièrement et en anglais surtout (But she promised to write to him regularly and in English mostly) dès qu'il serait installé à Detroit (as soon as he would be settled in Detroit). C'était touchant (It was sad)

One could last a good six months like that if one were to watch out every penny carefully. Six months living it UP rather than living it IN. After all who wants to be locked UP (cooked UP) in a room with noodles for brea kfast lunch and dinner and tomatosauceonceinawhile. FOR WHAT? A guy wou ld go crazy. Six months like that is madness! Imagine what a year (12 m onths - 365 days) would be like. It would be impossible to keep it UP. A guy would die. And then they would find the manuscript (unfinished and u nimproved) in the middle of the noodles: THE DIARY OF A MADMAN (in Engli sh) - HISTOIRE D'UN FOU (in French). I can already see the guy two or th ree months later with a beard down to his waist walking around the room l ike an animal in a cage. Horses flying inside his head. Skinny like a n oodle. Dirty filthy disgusting raving. Eyes bulging out of his head. Weak sick. Banging on the walls with his fists. Vomiting his life insi de the noodle boxes. FOR WHAT? A lousy 1100 bucks approximately! Doesn 't make sense. Would be so easy for him to get a boat ticket (one way on ly) and spend six lovely months in Paris. Six months on 1100 dollars tha t gives him $183.333 a month. Let's say he blows 200 bucks for the ticke t leaves him approximately 900 perhaps a little less if he buys himself a new suitcase for the trip (suitcases are important as we shall see) still that's a lot of money. He could live quite comfortably for six months on that. Life is cheaper there. There a guy can easily get a room for thre e bucks a week (that's without a bath of course but who cares). 52 times 3 makes only 156 bucks. Lots of guys did it that way. Hemingway. The l ost generation. That doesn't mean though that the guy would be lost. On the contrary. And noodles are cheaper there too. Easily 20 cents a poun d if not less instead of 29 and that's without figuring the possibility o f a devaluation of the franc. Working conditions are better too. One co uld get a room with a view on rooftops or on the Seine with Notre-Dame in the background perhaps in the Latin Quarter and bien entendu the whole th ing would have to be written in French in a much more conventional manner

But again a guy could forget about the whole thing forget about Paris and the
Champs Elysées and Montparnasse and the Eiffel Tower and Rue Saint-Denis avec
tous ses bordels forget about writing it in French or in English and simply s
pend the money on himself buy himself a new suit and a new tie to go with the
new suit a pair of shoes or two a belt and clean underwear and socks silk and
wool socks for the winter and the hell with the story but then six months lat
er he would feel it right there in the guts when he would realize what he has
done that there is nothing to show nothing no story nothing but wasted time a
nd wasted money and deep down his well dressed soul   inside his guts where it
hurts nothing but a feeling of emptiness the hol
low of his failure and of his frustration then h
e would realize how stupid he had been how bette
r off he would have been to lock himself in the r
oom instead of squandering away his 1100 bucks o
n clothes on movies cheap novels pieces of ass o
r even eating plentifully in good restaurants th
at's what he would realize six months later if n
ot sooner but too late of course as he would con
template his existence from the hollowness of hi
s new suit ready to hang himself with his new tie
because there is no more money and no story no lo
vely story he could have written in the room if he had had the guts to lock h
imself in the room with his life and his noodles without any further discussi
on without further deliberation digression hesitation just simply saying to h
imself tomorrow we begin straight into the room and we stick with it down the
line and up and down one box a day twelve pages a day 365 days and no more fu
cking around it starts in New York on the boat with Peggy and Uncle David wai
ting on the pier it's raining always rains on days like these makes it more h
uman more real particularly when the three of them start crying like idiots o
n the pier not knowing why how beautiful yes that's the way to go all the way

A L L   T H E   W A Y   from the bottom up just the way memory functions
W A Y   T H E   A L L   from left to right first then from right to left

---

go to the bottom of the page

---

ower yes definitely the room or rooms will become symbolic after awhile
s been a dead rat in the wall for months or else it smells like caulifl
o expensive for what they are and the smell always the same like there'
the same when it comes down to describing them dirty filthy and much to
have to be plain white but basically all rooms all furnished rooms look
ss at night that's a good touch and shitty wall paper though it doesn't
h the table by the window and only one chair and bedbugs chewing your a
e country something like the place I had when I arrived in New York wit
erhaps a symbol or two for instance the room rooms all over all over th
want to reveal his inner-self then I'll have to invent something else p
irst of all because he's not that smart and secondly because he doesn't
ecially if he tells his own story he cannot afford to analyze himself f
s definitely no psychology everything on the surface very objective esp
ou get all wrapped up with all sorts of cheap psychological problems ye
t that's tricky once you have an obsession it's hard to get rid of it y
eme to give unity to his life or perhaps something like an obsession bu
thing will fall in place particularly as soon as I find some sort of th
e into the picture this way things will keep going and eventually every
y Peggy and Uncle David that's so and only later on other guys will com
ny people in the beginning in the beginning in fact there should be onl
and you'll never get him off the boat that's for sure can't have too ma
f you get involved with all these guys you'll never get the story going
ul to him but of course he never sees any of these guys again because i
Nebraska Kansas Texas lots of guys from Texas California sounds beautif
me of them give him their addresses come and see me if you ever come to
fun of him too because he's so naive everybody does in the beginning so
im what he should do in America and how he's going to love it they make
Peggy she's alright but there are other guys on the boat too who tell h
for example on the boat he meets quite a number of people besides Peggy
re else anything can happen in this type of discourse anything anywhere
e of all the people he meets there of course he could meet them somewhe
of the time or taking craps that's true but Detroit is important becaus
t waste too much time the time a guy wastes in a lifetime sleeping most
hen back to New York to finish the circular journey this way I would no
roit and have him work his way to Los Angeles that would work too and t
s scene and after that the Jacobsons in the Bronx and then you skip Det
sential the boat scene quickly then the subway scene that's a tremendou
op in Milwaukee to see Peggy but first the scenes in New York that's es
could skip Detroit and have him work his way West immediately with a st
on the pier and then after that they split up and it's Detroit though I
I can already see the whole scene the three of them weeping like idiots

---

start here and work your way up

```
---------------------------------------------------
continue at the bottom of the page
---------------------------------------------------
```

skcolc mrala fo noitseuq eht kcab sgnirb hcihw emit fo melborp eht ht
iw decaf si eroferedt dna ecnarF ot kcab og ot tekcit taob a yub ot y
rassecen egaruoc eht evael ot egaruoc eht sdnif reven eh ecnis ylralu
citrap taht retfa mih ot neppah lliw tahw esilausiv gninnigeb eht yln
o s'ti dna aciremA ni raey tsrif sih gnirud hguorht og ot sah eh tihs
eht .siroB roop revo lla gnikael sepip htiw moorhtab gniknits dloc rod
irroc esoht nwod srehto htiw erahs uoy htab etavirp a evah neve t'nod
uoy secalp tsom ni rodirroc eht nwod ti htiw kcits tihs taht lla or r
ia hserf eht skrap eht steerts eht tegrof dlrow edistuo eht tuoba teg
rof dna derit er'uoy nehw peels dna desolc sniatruc eht htiw krow uoy
ecnis rettam t'nseod yad eht gnirud ro thgin ta yrots eht etirw od ot
evah uoy tahw od ni yats dna eldoon eb ot sah ti fi neve raey elohw e
ht rof ffuts yub ni flesruoy kcol efas er'uoy nehw moor eht fo tuo em
oc ot reven si esruoc fo gniht tseb eht rewolfiluac netter emos ro ta
r daed a no pets ot gniog er'uoy nehw wonk reven uoy dna ereht ni kra
d s'ti roolf htxis eht ot thgin ta pu og uoy nehw sriats eht ni ylral
ucitrap tnemtrapa dehsinruf a ni llems eht fo rid teg reven eno tnemt
rapa yhtlif ytrid gniknits a eb dluow ti llits tub tnemtrapa eguh yre
v a deedni evah dluow eno aciremA ni raey tsrif sih gnirud detner sir
oB taht smoor eht lla rehtegot tup ot erew eno fi smoor eht htiw euni
tnoc s'tel gnieb emit eht rof tub tnemom a ni ti ot kcab emoc ll'I tn
emele doog a s'taht sey ecnatsni rof skcolc mrala tnemele dnoces a ni
gnirb dluoc I smoor eht dnoyeb meht diova t'nac uoy tub sgniht yhtlif
esoht etah I ecim tsael ta ro osla star sgub deb htiw smoor smoor kra
d smoor llams smoor gniknits erutinruf ymmurc htiw smoor doog sa tsuj
s'ti tub tnemele na tsuj s'ti emeht a ton s'ti ytinu fo tnemele na sa
yrtnuoc eht revo lla smoor fo seires a naem I aedi bad a ton s'taht l
obmys a sa moor eht em nrecnoc dluohs moor eht ni deen I sgniht eht d
na smoor eht ylno gnieb emit eht rof yrots tnereffid yleritne na s'ta
ht tub naimemrA s'eh hsiweJ ton s'eh tub ecnarF morf semoc osla ees u
oy hoesoJ aciremA ni secneirepxe rieht ssucsid meht fo owt eht nehw y
lralucitrap retcarahc gnitseretni na ekam ll'eh hpesoJ tuoba togrof t
somla I no retal hpesoJ osla dna dneirf laer a si tsenrE tsenrE rof e
sruoc fo tpecxe elpoep tsuj sdneirf ylirassecen ton ereht steem eh el
poep eht lla osla dna tiorteD ni sah eh smoor eht lla fo tsil etelpmo
c a tsil a ekam tsom ta deneppah tahw ebircsed ot evah t'nod I hguoht
neve noitautis suoiruc rehtar a rof sekam ti dna pu tes dab a ton nam
dlo eht tis ybab ot dah eh gnineve eht ni tub eerf saw moor eht esuac
eb gninnigeb eht ni mih ot lead doog a ekil demees ti nam dnilb a hti
w moor rehtona ot devom eh elpoep nairagnuH eht htiw moor eht morf se
mit lareves devom ydaerla sah eh rehtom s'tsenrE swercs eh erofeb rev
ewoh stnap sih ni no-drah suomrone na htiw deticxe lla mih tfel ew er
ehw rehtom s'tsenrE ot yaw eht no sriats eht pu siroB tegrof ton tsum
ew esuaceb rehtom s'tsenrE tsenrE hguorht dna tsenrE steem eh yllautn
eve erehw s'taht dna muirotidua eht otni sklaw eh yad taht dna loohcS
hgiH nrehtroN fo lapicnirp eht ot skaeps eh retal syad ruof dna elpoe
p nairagnuH eht htiw moor eht sdnif eh nehw s'taht dna elpoep ecin eh
t dna moor ecin eht ekil t'nseod eh esuaceb tuo sevom siroB retal sya
d eerht ro owt yletaidemmi tub ylimaf hsiweJ ecin a htiw mih rof moor
ecin a dnuof sah eh mih sllet divaD elcnU tiorteD ni evirra yeht nehW

```
---------------------------------------------------
work your way up from right to left this time
---------------------------------------------------
```

..........After all this..........here <u>WE</u> are in the middle..........

```
                              M I D D L E
                              I
                    M I D D L E
                    I         D
                    D         L
          M I D D L E         E
                    L
                    E
```

me
myself
I   After all these   contorsions
                                      contraptions
                                      circumvolutions

                          Here WE are <u>converging</u>   into
                                                                  one
                                                                  another

you
he
we   & the other too   THE SUPERINTENDANT
                                      THE OVERALL-LOOKER

one
two
three   & four   the camp
                                                                 the room
                                                                 together

and yet WE must go on for a while augmenting while converging
                                  decreasing while augmenting

as WE augment towards our end
              towards the end   at least for a while longer

and yet

so many days   left
so many boxes   left
so many pages   left
so many words   left   and so many stories   too
                                      right on   WE   go!
```
```

full speed then step by step and up and down and **sideways** too and
upside down and so on to the end now uncle david is almost comple
ted almost out of it and peggy too but the subway scene and the g
irl with the legs and the jacobsons and rockaway beach all that r
emains to be seen to be worked out down to the last detail of wha
t follows to be told analyzed scribbled and recorded and invented
and the number of boxes left also and all the necessary crap also

TOUT OEUVRE N'EXISTE COMME OEUVRE QU'A PARTIR DES ACTES CRITIQUES
QUI CHERCHENT A LA CERNER TOUT ACTE CRITIQUE APPARAIT COMME COMME
NT DIRE UN APPAUVRISSEMENT DE L'OEUVRE CAR UNE OEUVRE EXISTE POUR
AINSI DIRE QUE PAR UN EXCES DE RICHESSE QUE C'EST BEAU TOUT ÇA ET
QUE C'EST EMMERDANT SIMPLEMENT D'Y PENSER ET DE LE DIRE DE LE RED
IRE SANS SAVOIR VRAIMENT CE QUE ÇA VEUT DIRE CAR TOUT CE QUI DANS
TOUT EST DIT N'EST JAMAIS DIT PUISQU'ON PEUT LE DIRE AUTREMENT AI
NSI J'AURAI DONC DORENAVANT ET DEJA DIT TOUT CELA MAIS ÇA N'A PAS
D'IMPORTANCE PUISQU'IL FAUT EN FINIR UNE FOIS POUR TOUTE QUE CELA
SOIT VRAI OU NON REEL OU IRREEL PLAUSIBLE OU IMPOSSIBLE QUE CE SO
IT CITÉ OU INVENTÉ RACONTÉ OU DÉGUEULÉ A LA FIN C'EST DE LA MERDE

r i g h t   o n   t o   t h e   e n d

Every morning (except Sundays	ALARM CLOCKS	and sometimes Saturdays - but
	ALARM CLOCKS	
even that is not sure):	ALARM CLOCKS	One could write a whole
	ALARM CLOCKS	
book about	ALARM CLOCKS	A whole il
	ALARM CLOCKS	
lustrated book. And people	ALARM CLOCKS	waking up in the morning. R
	ALARM CLOCKS	
ed eyes and bloodshot eyes	ALARM CLOCKS	staring at the ugly faces.
	ALARM CLOCKS	
Ugly faces of	ALARM CLOCKS	all over in e
	ALARM CLOCKS	
very corner of the world.	ALARM CLOCKS	Motherfucking little thin
	ALARM CLOCKS	
gs. Even the name is disgust	ALARM CLOCKS	ing. Frightening. Help! Ah!
	ALARM CLOCKS	
Sauf qui peut! Shouting.	ALARM CLOCKS	Screeching. Squeaking or
	ALARM CLOCKS	
banging in your head. And of	ALARM CLOCKS	course ringing. Ringing like
	ALARM CLOCKS	
hell in every corner of the	ALARM CLOCKS	world. Everywhere at every
	ALARM CLOCKS	
time of the day but particula	ALARM CLOCKS	rly at five in the morning an
	ALARM CLOCKS	
d at five-thirty and at six.	ALARM CLOCKS	At seven. Lots of them at s
	ALARM CLOCKS	
even. That's when most peopl	ALARM CLOCKS	e get up to get to work at ei
	ALARM CLOCKS	
ght even if it means being la	ALARM CLOCKS	te a few minutes. Seven-thir
	ALARM CLOCKS	
ty. Eight. It goes on and	ALARM CLOCKS	on like that for a good par
	ALARM CLOCKS	
t of the morning (except for	ALARM CLOCKS	those that ring in the eveni
	ALARM CLOCKS	
ng - for those people who hav	ALARM CLOCKS	e to work the night shifts an
	ALARM CLOCKS	
d have to sleep during the	ALARM CLOCKS	day). Much less by nine o
	ALARM CLOCKS	
'clock (that's already a time	ALARM CLOCKS	for the rich guys). But from
	ALARM CLOCKS	
five to eight what a racket!	ALARM CLOCKS	The whole working class must
	ALARM CLOCKS	
get up. It starts in one	ALARM CLOCKS	place and then it doesn't
	ALARM CLOCKS	
stop for a long time.	ALARM CLOCKS	It starts in your roo
	ALARM CLOCKS	
m. Then next door. And next	ALARM CLOCKS	door. Then next door to that
	ALARM CLOCKS	
next door room. And so on.	ALARM CLOCKS	Then down the street and up
	ALARM CLOCKS	
the next building. When one	ALARM CLOCKS	shuts up another one gets go
	ALARM CLOCKS	
ing. All over the city.	ALARM CLOCKS	All over the country. A
	ALARM CLOCKS	
ll over the world as a matter	ALARM CLOCKS	of fact. And if the other pl
	ALARM CLOCKS	
anets had people on them then	ALARM CLOCKS	they would also be ringing al
	ALARM CLOCKS	
l over the universe. Drag	ALARM CLOCKS	ging poor slobs out of bed

ALARM CLOCKS telling them to get their asses out of bed. Got to get up quick

right now. ALARM CLOCKS Get up! Upppp! UUUUUUPPPPP! Work! Got to Work!

Think of all the fucki ALARM CLOCKS ringing in the world. No language barr
               n   i
It starts in one place g and it goe ALARM CLOCKS on from five to eight with e
                          s   r
out a stop. And if you think of it   ALARM CLOCKS Never.   s
                              it never stops
Because of the time element. The difference of time from ALARM CLOCKS one

place to another. The r   n of the E   Five o'clock in New   ALARM
                 o   o   A   York
                 t   i   R   CLOCKS Six
                   a t   T
somewhere else. Six in Chicago. Seven H in Salt Lake City ALARM Nine on the

west coast. Los Angeles and Frisco. And then ALARM CLOCKS Tokyo Calcutta.

Jerusalem. Athens. Rome. Paris. ALARM CLOCKS London. Oslo. And back to
                                                                     NEW
You go around the world ALARM CLOCKS like that. When it's five here   YORK!
                                                            it's six
a little f ALARM CLOCKS and seven a little f u r t h e r. A chain reaction
      u r t h e r on
ALARM CLOCKS   you might say. On and On. All around the world. In

both direct ALARM CLOCKS If you think you know what's going on you're kidding
           i
For indee o d   ALARM CLOCKS   ring around   yourself.
         n s   the world without ever stopping
all day long   ALARM CLOCKS
    day after day after day. All   the time.   Put them all
                                   ALARM CLOCKS
together then you have a tremendous racket. Frightening. If a guy could he
                                             ALARM CLOCKS   ar
around the world he would go crazy. All the same little damn ringing boxes .
                                                   ALARM
torturing you out of your sleep. In every corner of the world. With a
                                                  CLOCKS
slight time de.............lay.   When one goes o
                                      f
                                    f another starts.   It's sel
Of course. It would be interesting to know   ALARM CLOCKS   torture-f
            when they were invented.
                          ALARM CLOCKS   Who the hell invented the
Must have been an aristocrat. All kinds of guys. Some   ?m
                  ALARM CLOCKS   j m
                                        u p out of bed immed
Others   ALARM CLOCKS Others get furious.   iatel
turn on the other side and   y
ALARM CLOCKS   ignore the first ring. Fanatics. So much depends on th
                                                    at
in the mor ALARM CLOCKS   initial ring.
        ning (and in the evening too for the night shifters). The rest   of
the day can be fucked   ALARM CLOCKS
                             up because of the way your clock rings.

ALARM CLOCKS they must have invented
them at the beginning of the 19th ce
ntury with the rise of the working c
lass just another one of their trick
s ALARM CLOCKS once I bought one mus
t have been in Detroit they even mak
e travelling ALARM CLOCKS that's pus
hing a bit yes in Detroit when Boris
started working in the factory and h
e had to get up at five-thirty in th
e morning except Sundays to get to w
ork at CHRYSLER by six-thirty the mo
rning shift (what a bitch of a life)
eventually no more ALARM CLOCKS just
the TIME OF NOODLES that's good enou

gh for me I'll get rid of mine no shit about it all you have to do is forget

it somewhere dump it in a garbage can throw the damn thing out of the window

step on it like you step on a bug or a cockroach or some other little animal

and then the white juice comes out of it like sperm like used up sperm that'

s what I'll do with it that damn alarm clock I bought in Detroit or else you

can simply lock it up in your suitcase without winding it and it's dead it's

silent no I'll get rid of it throw it away it's safer I'll sell it perhaps y

ou can always get a buck or two for something like that in fact I should sel

l everything I have down to the last detail keep only the essential only the

things I need essentially in the room that too should come in at the beginni

ng make an inventory of all the things Boris has in his suitcase when he arr

ives in America the black suitcase with the strap around it a cheap one of c

ourse no rope though around it that's for bums all the stuff in French biene

ntendu I mean his shirts his underwears his socks his shoes his books also h
e has two or three it'll be interest
ing to know what he brings without g
oing into all the details what he br
ings with him to America from the ol
d country a kind of summary of his f
ormer life also what he reads at tha
t time later on things will change a
guy can't stay the same his whole li
fe that's for sure at 19 he's somebo
dy else than what he is or will be a
t 29 therefore make a list of all th
e things in his suitcase until there
is nothing left from what he origina
lly brought with him when he first a
rrived on the boat with his suitcase

Everything. Until there is nothing left except for one or two small souvenirs
he can't get rid of. It's normal. For sentimental reasons. And then ev
en these disappear eventually. Always happens. He loses them. And
by the time there is nothing left from the original things that
were in his suitcase and in his pockets when he arrives in
America then he should be at the end of his story. A
t least at the end of the first stage of the sto
ry of his life. In America. Things happen fast
in America. It completes the cycle. He is now total
ly American. From shoes and socks to haircut. Even thoug
h he still speaks with an accent. Takes years to get rid of yo
ur French accent. That's very symbolic. Suitcases too could be sym
bolic. He carries his life in his suitcase. Now it's taking shape. Roo
ms. Suitcases. Funny how things begin to happen when you start talking about
rooms. First you have to describe the furniture. The table. The chair.
By the window. But with suitcases it's even better. You can really
spend hours describing all the things a guy has in his suitcase
when he first arrives someplace. And it doesn't even have
to be in America. Everybody has a suitcase somewhere
in his room. Even imaginary rooms and imaginary
suitcases work the same way. Things always happ
en in them. Suddenly there is a mirror in the room a
nd that mirror suddenly gives an added dimension to the ro
om and of course to the whole story. Like in that other story:
AND I FOLLOWED MY SHADOW. A long time ago. The kids walks into the
room. On the farm. A dirty filthy room. He hasn't seen himself in a mi
rror for almost five years. Sounds incredible but it's true. He gets undress
ed. Naked. He stands in the middle of the room. And bang he sees himse
lf in the mirror. What a shock! A disgusting picture of himself. A
theme! And after that everything begins to fall in place soon.

After all these years. A symbol. When he sees himself in the mirror after all

these years. Five years. Can't believe it. It was like he was born

again. Reborn. First he didn't recognize himself. He had

grown much taller. Skinny as hell though. So sk

inny it was frightening. That's the cu

rious thing about this story. Even whe

n you're starving you go on growing. In spite of

the camp and the suffering. I mean when you're a kid. But

he was only twelve when they shipped him to the camp. Five years lat

er he was seventeen. Doesn't work too well but it'll do for now. In any event

it won't come into this story. But you could use the mirror. I supp

ose if you didn't keep on growing you wouldn't feel the hun

ger as much. Then you would stay a midget your w

hole life. Can a guy shrink? After fi

ve or six months of noodles I might beg

in to shrink. Fortunately I don't grow anymore t

hese days. Except of course for the beard down to my waist

and the hair down to my shoulders. Christ like almost. Naked in the

room. After a while if the heat is good I could work naked. Saves a lot on cl

othing and laundry. Naked in the middle of the room. But what about

the mirror? Must be one. All furnished rooms have mirror.

In the bathroom usually above the sink. Obviousl

y. There's always a little mirror abov

e the sink. But not necessarily in the

room proper. However if I do without clocks. Wi

thout newspapers. Radio. Telephone. And so on. Why a mi

rror? I should do without a mirror too. Definitely. If there is on

e cover it up with a blanket. Might be unbearable. Mirrors give a little dime

nsion to a room. A little depth. Three-dimensional depth. Then whe

n you have nothing else to do you look at yourself in them.

If you look at yourself in the mirror as though you were somebody else, if you
make faces at yourself in the mirror, that should occupy time for a while, and
this way, between scenes, and boxes, you can observe your own suffering, becau
se a guy always suffers in situations such as these, it's normal, particularly
Boris, that poor kid, after he jumped off the train (during the war) one night
and fell into a ditch where a farmer found him, and they put him in a room, na
ked, a nice sunny room in a farm house (I was working on the description of th
e room -- in those days I still fucked around with descriptions -- and I had a
ll the furniture almost in place, including the table by the window, nothing t
o rave about, just crummy old furniture in a farm house, but compared with wha
t Boris had in the camp it was almost paradise, and that's when the idea of pu
tting a mirror in the room came to me), and the first thing he did when he got
in the room, after he looked around, a bit scared, was to jerk off, or at leas
t he was starting to do it, holding on to it with his left hand, when he saw h
imself in the mirror, and that's when the shock came, the shock of not recogni
zing himself, after all these years, five years, because he had changed so muc
h, much taller, but skinny like hell, his stomach sticking out, his eyes bulgi
ng out, he really looked atrocious standing there in from of the mirror with h
is erected dick in his hand, and yet he suddenly (almost as in a dream) became
aware of himself, aware of being alive instead of being dead, as he saw himsel
f, or at least someone he thought was himself, in the mirror, because everyone
has an idea of himself in his mind, and even though he did not recognize himse
lf, it made him aware of himself at some different stage of his life, of being
someone else than what he was before the camp, and this awareness, this self-r
ecognition of what one is, but not necessarily of what one was, or the idea of
what one thinks one is, because everybody has an idea of oneself in one's mind
at one time or another, and I suppose Boris did too, or will have an idea of h
imself in his mind (of course I'll be the one who will create that idea of him
self in his mind, but first I'll have to create him before the idea can be the
re, or does it work the other way around, first the idea and then the man him-

self, that's a very tricky point, it's almost impossible to know, for in fact
you cannot explain that which you do not know in advance, and therefore it is
up to the guy who reads the discourse to determine that fact, but that does n
ot necessarily mean that it is a philosophical point, it can merely be a fict
itious point, because only in fiction, and not in reality, does such problems
arise, otherwise life would be unbearable, and it is already hard enough to c
ope with it), but Boris has a rather fuzzy idea of himself in his mind, and t
his is why he is so unstable, but if there is one thing about Boris that is t
ypical (or for that matter about every guy in his situation, guys who come to
America), it's his loneliness, his inclination towards loneliness, of course,
but everybody is lonely, doesn't matter where you are, never fails, people do
not admit it publicly, but in private most of them are scared shit of their l
oneliness, and what do they do, for instance, they lock themselves in a crumm
y room, for 365 days, without even considering the consequences, all alone, a
nd try to spit out their lives, or the idea of their lives, on paper, thinkin
g that this way they will exorcize their inner-self, or the equivalent of it,
but in the end it does not work, they remain the same as before, it's insane,
it's not logical, but if there is a mirror in the room, even a small mirror a
bove the sink in the bathroom, I'll keep it, just for the company, just to ha
ve somebody to look at, but I won't go out, that's for sure, out of my way to
buy one, can't afford it, I have enough trouble with all the rest of the stuf
f, the food in particular, to start bothering about a mirror, that's for sure
at this stage, and this is why the whole thing has to be planned in advance o
r else it falls apart, systematically, like the plan of an attack, exactly, b
ecause the least little error can mess up the whole set up, and if that happe
ns you're finished, dead, and everybody else with you, therefore, assuming he
is 19 when he first arrives in America then if I register him in high school,
he's already too old to be at ease with the other kids, even though in his ca
se it's only for courses in English for foreign students, government, history
and a bit of physical education, but he does feel the difference, it's normal.

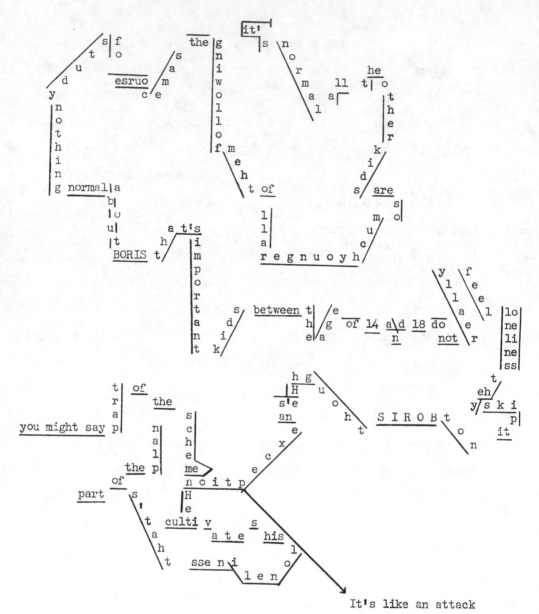

It's like an attack

The captain just got his orders   TAKE THE WHOLE COMPANY OUT he's been told

What a responsibility!   He plans (he stays up all night planning in anguish)
                                                          thinking
                                                          of all the guys
who are going to die the next day when he takes them out
                                        It's normal (he's a good captain)

It's always the same thing though some guys make it others don't and others come
back to tell the story but funny thing the captain rarely dies (it's normal) for
if he does then it's really a sad story
                        I don't have to go into all that war shit
it's just an example (an aside) -- But the mirror (that's not an aside) that's I
 -- E M I T   S I H T   T A   T N A T R O P M I│Y L E M E R T X E   T N A T R O P M

```
m b o a t s t i a a m a t s i t c l f r n f a l i a
u e n b h i h s l   i b h i n h r i u o e a t e n l
s   e o e n e w     s l   r o e n   o u t r o v i   a     l
t   v k r   a r     v       r v k   s m t n m e l       s   .
    e     y s     o       r           o e       e m l i s r s       t
                s     r                   k             y e     s h
                                                              s h
                                                              e
                                                              d
```

```
t o I h b i c m a l a I s a i a t o B h o w b i n f
h n   a e n o a   i n   u l n l h n o   a r i e n e a
e e   v e   u k s d     t   p s     l e e r s   l e     v i
s   s e n   l e   t         p o         s i       l n e l
            d             o             s           r s
                          s
                          e
```

Let me think

did I ever have a room without a mirror

No exception

It works

But it's useless   Doesn't get you anywhere

You look at yourself in the mirror and what do you see?   Yourself!

                                                    Your own disgust
                                                    ing   self!

Badly shaved in the beginning
Eyes bulging out   Skinny like hell

That's the story of life.   h l   m l   o l   L I F E
                               i i   y i   u i   in
                               s f   f   r f   general
                               e   e   e

it's u   le.   a sensible guy would give up (immediately)
     n   b   k
   bear a   unless   n
                                                                               i
Boris decides one day that he too doesn't need a room with a mirror above the s

Nothing   about that. He'll have a few ideas of his own.
      I can do

                    s ubborn like he l in fa t.
                    t   l   c

He might be shy and naive but when it comes to stubborness and determination
          shy   naive   stubborness   determination

he beats anybody.   Like the time he decided he was going to buy
                               himself a T E N O R   S A X O P H O N E

```
T
T E N O R
E                    S
N                    A X
O              S A X O P H O N E
R                    O
                     P
                     H
                     O
                     N
                     E
```

Every
penny
he
had
saved
(
foreigners
always
save
in
the
beginning
when
they
first
arrive
in
America
but
eventually
they
give
up
saving
takes
a
good
five
years
sometimes
ten
to
get
to
that
stage
)
Uncle
David
was
furious
when
he   (Uncle David) found out about the

```
                                    *
                                    *
                                    *
                        * * * * * * * * * * * *
                                    *
                                    *
                                    *

                                    *
                                  *   *
                                *       *
                              *           *
                            *               *
                            *               *
                            * * * * * * * * * *
                            * * * * * * * * * *
                            * * * * * * * * * *
                            *               *
                              *           *
                                *       *
                                  *   *
                                    *
                                    *
                                    *
                                    *
                                    *
                                  *****
                                  *****
                            ***************
                            *           *
                            *           *
                            *           *
                            ***************
```

```
                              T E N O R
                              E              S
                              N              A
                              O         S A X O P H O N E
                              R              P
                                             H
                                             O
                                             N
                                             E
```

If you ? yourself a suitcase that ? fine with people
but a tenor saxophone that ? a bit unusual particularl
y when you ? to ? money in the beginning Few people
? that They immediately ? you ? crazy or irrespons
ible Rooms and suitcases that ? fine but a tenor saxo
phone that ? too much Rooms and suitcases it ? livi
ng in one place and traveling sometimes A whole life ?
contained between rooms and suitcases The room ? you
? in one place The suitcase that you ? from one plac
e to another That ? the way to ? movement Movement
in time The time element ? important too Space and t
ime in other words Once you ? involved with a suitcas
e you ? never ? with it It ? the hardest thing to
? ? of The girl in the subway with the legs ? apart
She ? ? at his suitcase Or somewhere around there He
? the suitcase between his legs Or whatever else one ?
between one's legs His shoes No The suitcase It ? b
etter He really ? like a foreigner in his double-brea
sted suit At least in the subway scene His hair too ?
him ? like that That ? one thing about Boris he nev
er ? up ? his hair long You ? wearing but ? his h
air long ? just as good I ? ? down to his shoulder
s but down in the back of his neck almost to his shirt c
ollar More than almost ? straight back His hair yes
Dark Very dark Very thick too Slightly curly But the
suit ? what ? him ? like a foreigner and the shoes
too That ? what ? him away You ? ? him out imme
diately as a foreigner Nowadays it ? more difficult H
e ? ? a great deal From the original stuff he ? then

Uncle David was furious. Or else he was asleep. But that doesn't prevent the girl from staring at the suitcase between Boris' legs. Particularly since He's staring between _her_ legs. She was sitting her legs slightly spread apart in a rather sensual position. Just across from him. But he has to slide down in his seat a little to get a _better_ look. Uncle David's head keeps tilting side ways. You couldn't tell from where Boris is sitting if he is asleep _for sure._

_No_ better yet. He's not asleep. He's reading a newspaper. Wide open in fron t of him. _The Jewish Daily Forward_. Then a guy comes in at one of the stops. He stands _right_ in front of the girl hanging on to a porcelain loop. Boris ca n't see anything any more. Just the _top_ of the knees. But the guy moves side ways. Not consciously. Just enough to hide the girl's face _but_ not the legs. So now Boris can see _much_ better than before and she cannot see him. Perfect.

The man's belly is right in _front_ of her face. His belly or his dick dependin g how tall he is. Now he can _really_ see between her legs well. Almost all th e way _up_. At least way above where the stockings stop. This way also with th e guy in front he can really look _without_ being noticed by the girl. He sudde nly gets _all_ excited. All of America is there. Between the legs. He can fee l it in his pants but he has his hands crossed on his lap. _Nobody_ can see it.

All this time he's thinking about everything that happened to him _since_ the mo rning. The arrival of the boat. Peggy. The custom agent who asked him _numer ous_ questions. His suitcase. Uncle David. All the people on the pier. Thou sands of them. New York. The _tall_ buildings. That's a _lot_ of things to thin k about for one day. And the day is not over yet. _And_ on top of that the str ange feeling inside. All sorts of images in his mind. Mixed feelings _inside_.

And on top of that the girl's crotch in front of him. AMERICA THE CROTCH!
It's more than he can take for his first encounter with AMERICA. The great
CONFRONTATION. The enormous CUNTFRONTATION. The giant CROTCH. Why beat
around the bush. Say it straight. Loud and clear. HE HAS AN ENORMOUS --
A GIGANTIC -- A FABULOUS -- ERECTION inside his pants. That's not nice fo
r a guy who just arrived in America but it's understandable. I could list
all the reasons and mixed feelings he feels inside. People would (should)
understand:
>Anguish
>
>Fear
>
>Hesitation
>
>Loneliness
>
>Anxiety
>
>Homesickness
>
>Alienation

Shit! How do you show all that? In a sense it'
s almost impossible. How do you show all that in a sentence or two. Just
can't say it outright. You have to show it. Make people feel it. It's a
bit like being lost. No. It's like being scared. Scared like a rabbit b
eing chassed by a dog. But you don't want to show it. Nobody does. Ther
efore you make believe it's tremendous. Beautiful. A happy experience. A
dream. THE CONFRONTATION. You love it. I love it. WE LOVE AMERICA! At
least the first few days.

But it takes a good five years and even sometime
s ten to get used to it. HOW DO YOU LIKE IT HERE? The eternal question t
hey all ask. HOW LONG HAVE YOU BEEN IN THIS COUNTRY? The second question
they all ask. They must have asked those two eternal questions at least a
million times for the last century. The same two questions to all the poo
r slobs who came to America. Even twenty years later they ask the same tw
o fucking questions. DO YOU LIKE IT HERE? HOW LONG HAVE YOU BEEN IN THIS
COUNTRY? Sometimes with slight variations. Sometimes asking the second q
uestion first and the first second. They ask you as soon as they pick you

.............out....................Just a touch of an accent in your.....
English.................and............................inevitably............
....................there they go asking the eternal questions..........
.....but.....nobody ever says.......I LOVE IT HERE.......................
............................IT'S TREMENDOUS..............No!...........
..................You have to show some respect.........................
...............................some reservation.....................
..................control.........................commonsense...........
..............................Not too much enthusiasm..................
.....at first...
.......................Less stupidity................................
..................But at the same time you don't want to offend them.....
.....................................It's normal......................
.....And so....you answer the first thing that comes to your mind..........
I REALLY LIKE IT.................honest............................I DO

OH IT'S FINE. OH IT'S REALLY GOOD. OH IT'S HARD TO GET USED TO IT IN THE
BEGINNING. OH SOMETIMES YOU GET LONELY BUT EVENTUALLY THINGS WORK OUT. O
H I REALLY LIKE IT HERE BUT IT TOOK ME A WHILE TO LEARN THE LANGUAGE. OH!
That's what you say most of the time. And on top of that you always lie a
little about the number of years you've been in the country. Sounds bette
r to say OH JUST A FEW YEARS! Three or four is a good number. Because if
you say you've been in this country ten years then they don't feel sorry f
or you anymore. It's normal.

Usually in the beginning they ask the eternal questions t
o your uncle or whoever brought you to this country. Uncle David for Bori
s. Because they know you don't speak the language well. HOW DOES HE LIKE
IT HERE? HOW LONG HAS HE BEEN HERE? And the uncle answers for you. Uncl
e David answers the eternal questions for Boris in the beginning. Gives h
im a chance to feel proud for having brought his nephew to America.

Boris imagined Uncle
David quite different. Not as old first of all. Tall like his father was
or at least how tall he remembers his father was. More American too. Thi
nking is a difficult process for Boris in the beginning. Particularly sin
ce he doesn't know what to think about. Souffrir c'est penser. That's on
e of the things he thinks about. That's a good one. He had heard that so
mewhere in France before he came and he keeps throwing it in.

Once in a while you wonder w
ho is thinking. Must be Boris. As a matter of fact he only thinks in Fre
nch during the first few months. After a while he begins to think in both
languages. Simultaneously sometimes. What a confusion. Takes a long tim
e to start thinking straight in English. Particularly when you're lonely.
But you can't have him think in French all the time. Or any time he wants
to in the middle of the story. Doesn't make sense. Unless I translate fo
r him. Translate everything he says or thinks during his first year in Am
erica. TO THINK IS TO SUFFER. It's a good one even though it's backward.

SOUFFRIR C'EST PENSER
PENSER C'EST SOUFFRIR

works
e
i
t
h
e
r
way

TO THINK IS TO SUFFER
TO SUFFER IS TO THINK

He didn't invent it. He simply heard it or read it somewhere. He's full o
f crap like that. But I'll translate everything. Except once in a while a
few sentences in French here and there to make it look more realistic and a
lso more genuine. But even then you'll have to give some kind of approxima
tion for people who don't read French. Except when he uses bad obscenities

: Ah ce qu'on se fait chier ici :   : Quelle saloperie d'existence :

: Quel bordel de putain de pays :   : Les américains sont des cons :

: Ah la belle blague l'Amérique :   : Qu'ils aillent se faire voir :

Things like that you can't translate. But it's better than nothing. It's
a question of style. It's natural if you want to give the story a sense o
f reality. For instance in the subway he thinks in French. And he sees a
ll sorts of dirty images in his mind and describes them to himself in Fren
ch. And what's even worse some of these images seem to gather between the
girl's legs. Right there in the   T   spot he's staring at. That giv
es him a hard-on immediately   R   R   on the spot. That dark cor
ner where the seam of her   I   A   skirt stops his eyes. B
ut the rectangular piece   A   N   G   U   L   of flesh he can see bec
omes like a screen   on which the imag
es are reflected q   uite vividly. He
sees faces there e   ven his own face.
He sees the face o   f his mother. Al
so the face of his father. But not Uncle David's face. That would really
be indecent. It's as though he could almost touch that screen so real and
so palpable it appears. He even sees a little house there. And lots of t
rees. Lots of vegetation. But can one really remember the touch of flesh
under such conditions? I suppose. One can always invent a little. Parti
cularly if it's not possible to remember. Or else one can simply approxim
ate how it feels. For instance: Flesh is like a banana peel
                                Flesh is like a piece of white paper
                                Flesh is like a dozen eggs in a basket
                                Flesh is like a glass of wine at night
----

At that point Uncle David folds his newspaper. Dammit! Don't tell me the
subway scene is over and they are getting off already even before all thos
e images are finished. No! He settles back in his seat. And this time h
e really goes to sleep. Boris can see that from where he's sitting but he
has to look sideways. Then the subway stops. The man in front of the gir
l's face leaves. No! He simply gets a seat where somebody else just left
to get off. A fat woman. Those damn subways! They go on and on. But we
must admit that we've done some of our best thinking in subways. So let's
go on. Anyway the guy is not important. He's gone now. Gone out of scen
e. The view is clear. Boris looks at the girl. She's definitely smiling!

What a smile (real or imagined) can do for a guy but not
everybody has the courage to look people straight in the
face takes a huge effort and Boris is so shy he can only
look at the girl sideways but she looks at him square in
the face as though she understood that he was all worked
up over her little black triangle (but she does not know
that this is his first day in America eventhough she may
have a slight suspicion that he's a foreigner because of
his suit and also the way his hair is combed) and instin
ctively she moves her legs but does not cross them (as o
ne would expect) she simply moves a little on her behind
shifting her weight from one cheek to the other and as a
result the triangle disappears but now Boris sees a diff
erent figure (much more interesting) a rectangle no it's
more like a parallelogram upside down no it's worse than
that what he sees now are two shapeless flabby pieces of
flesh with a very dark line in the middle (figuratively)
it looks like some kind of furry animal and it scares th
e hell out of him however he can feel his dick throbbing
inside his pants against his left thigh (he carries left
most of the time) and that reassures him but nonetheless
he says to himself I can't go on like this and I agree w
ith him I can't go on either we must find a way out of t
his 365 days like this and we'll go crazy for sure event
hough the room idea is a good one (the suitcase that's a
nother matter it's too obvious too cheap) but in any cas
e assuming we have spent $574.91 so far (that's not coun
ting the cigarettes) then definitely it's time to get go
ing with the cigarettes or else we'll run out of time of
place money ideas patience goodwill determination breath

And now: C I G A R E T T E S

Right now about a pack a day!
A pack and a half a day or so
maybe more - nobody ever keeps track that closely - but under pressure could
be two packs - I should cut down -
seriously! With all those stories
going around about   C A N C E R -

C A N C E R of the throat
of the breast
of the chest
of the belly
of the penis   - All that jazz about guys dying around forty or
forty-two (in the prime of life) - it's a myth - a lie - a joke - of course
mere propaganda - cheap publicity!
And suppose you quit then you get fat you get nervous you get normal but you
die anyway when your time comes - cigarettes or no cigarettes - inevitably -

MORTALITY FROM CANCER OF THE STOMACH IS FIVE TIMES HIGHER IN JAPAN
THAN THE U. S. BUT AMERICAN WOMEN HAVE SEVEN TIMES AS MUCH CANCER
OF THE BREAST   AS   JAPANESE WOMEN

(as quoted from the Buffalo Evening News of all places - verbatum)

The question then can be asked WHY?
Because they are flat chested (Japanese women that is) a wise guy would SAY
ironically but without seriously considering the consequences of his words -

And yet - cancer research is discovering a growing number of these puzzles -

Describing the problems faced by the investigators one doctor para-
phrased Winston Churchill's famous phrase about the Soviet Union..:
WE ARE FINDING A WHOLE LOT OF RIDDLES WRAPPED IN MYSTERIES INSIDE OF ENIGMAS

(This is not invented but merely quoted - these are real facts - facts which
can be found in every newspaper everyday of your life - but that doesn't
prevent a guy from smoking a pack or a pack and a half of cigarettes
a day particularly when working under pressure when locked up in
a room for 365 days to spit out his life on paper as he eats
noodles everyday and counts horses on the walls all day)

Therefore let us say two packs a day under pressure it's
not too much in this case particularly if you put in 16 or 17
hours a day at the typewriter however for the time being we'll f
igure on one hand a half pack a day we'll assume everything is norma
l everything is as usual and we'll forget about the pressure then we can
agree on a pack and a half a day which means 365 packs plus half of 365 (for
the year) 365 divided by 2 makes 182 point 5 however since you cannot really
buy half a pack it'll have to be 182 even or else 183 we'll take 183 because
it gives us 20 extra cigarettes in case of emergency thus 365 plus 183 makes
548
548 packs of cigarettes for the year - that makes quite a room full - indeed
- FULL OF CIGARETTES and FULL OF SMOKE!
Now I have the noodles on one wall and now I'll have the cigarettes on anoth
er wall - of course some of the horses will have to be sacrificed - but that
negates the idea of a SQUARE TOWER OF NOODLE BOXES in the middle of the room
which was a much more sensible idea - and much more attractive - than piling
everything against the wall and thus obstructing from view the flying horses
But that's the danger of C I G A R E T T E S!

SOME REFLEXIONS ON THE NOVEL IN OUR TIME
QUELQUES REFLEXIONS SUR LE ROMAN AUJOURD'HUI

original text | **translation**

Peut-on dire qu'en dénonçant l'imposture d'un roman qui tend à totaliser l'existence et manque sa "pluridimensionnalité," l'oeuvre critique nous libère de l'illusion réaliste? Je crois plutôt qu'elle nous y enferme. Car l'objectif reste le même: il s'agit toujours d'exprimer, de traduire quelque chose qui est déjà là--même si être déjà là, dans cette nouvelle perspective, consiste paradoxalement à ne pas être là. Autrement dit, le roman, en un sens, ne peut pas échapper au réalisme. Cette hypothèque pèse sur lui depuis l'origine, depuis l'époque ou pour se justifier du soupçon de frivolité, il a dû se présenter comme un moyen de connaissance--et non pas seulement depuis le XIXe siècle. L'histoire du roman n'est-il faut l'admettre--rien d'autre que la succession de ses efforts pour "apprésenter" une réalité qui toujours se dérobe, pour substituter à des miroirs trop grossiers des miroirs plus fins, plus sélectifs. Mais, en un autre sens, le roman n'a jamais cessé de dénoncer, par sa réalité même l'illusion qui l'anime. Tous les grands romans sont des romans critiques qui sous couleur de raconter une histoire, de faire vivre des personnages, d'interpréter des situations, glissent sous nos yeux le mirage tangible d'une forme. Toute oeuvre romanesque forme bloc : on ne peut y soustraire ou y changer un mot, la prolonger ou la dévier de son cours. C'est ce qui fait d'elle un leurre. Nous croyons y trouver l'expression de notre unité, alors qu'elle n'en manifeste que le désir. Nous croyons, en nous racontant, découvrir ce quelqu'un que nous sommes déjà. Mais ce quelqu'un n'existe que dans l'oeuvre, il en est le produit et non pas la source. Et ceci parce que le propre d'un discours littéraire--c'est-à-dire d'un discours fixé une fois pour toutes--est de trouver sa référence, ses règles d'organisation en lui-même, et non pas dans l'expérience réelle ou imaginaire sur laquelle il s'appuie. A travers tous les détours qu'on voudra, le sujet qui écrit ne se saisira jamais dans le roman: il ne saisira que le roman, qui, par définition, l'exclut. . . . . .

Can it be said that by denouncing the fraudulence of a novel which tends to totalize existence and misses its pluridimentionality, the critical work frees us from the illusion of realism? I rather believe that it encloses us in it. Because the goal remains the same: it is always a question of expressing, of translating something which is already there--even if to be already there, in this new perspective, consists paradoxically in not being there. In other words, the novel, in a sense, cannot escape realism. This mortgage weighs upon it since its origin, since the period when for justifying itself of the suspicion of frivolity, it had to present itself as a means of knowledge-- and not only since the 19th century. The history of the novel is--one must admit it--nothing else but the succession of its efforts to "appresent" a reality which always evades, always substitutes for vulgar mirrors finer mirrors, more selective mirrors. But, in another sense, the novel is nothing else but a denounciation, by its very reality, of the illusion which animates it. All great novels are critical novels which, under the pretense of telling a story, of bringing characters to life, of interpreting situations, slide under our eyes the mirage of a tangible form. All fictitious work forms a block: nothing can be taken away from it nor can a single word be changed. That is what makes of the novel a lure. We think we are going to find in it the expression of our unity, whereas in fact it only manifests the desire of it. We believe, as we are relating ourself, that we are going to discover, to find, that being that we are already. But that being, that somebody, exists in the work only, it is the product of it and not the source. And this because the essence of a literary discourse--that is to say a discourse fixed once and for all--is to find its own point of reference, its own rules of organization in itself, and not in the real or imaginary experience, on which it rests. Through all the detours that one wishes, the subject who writes will never seize himself in the novel: he will only seize the novel which, by definition, excludes him. . . . .

By all means the horses should not be sacrificed/
                                      /After a few days in the room
it might be very lonely/
                    /and confusing too/
                                    /with some of the horses hidden/
                                                                /behind
the boxes and the packs/
                      /and in some places pieces of horses only showing on
the sides/
        /no/
          /definitely not/
                        /nothing against the walls/
                                              /everything in the center of
the room/
        /in the form of a large tower/
                                    /everything/
                                              /noodles/
                                                      /cigarettes/
                                                                /soap/
                                                                    /sugar/
                                                                          /etc./
                                                                              /
everything in one huge pile/
                          /and then when you are lonely you start moving things
around/
      /keeps you busy/
                    /because it's not easy to count horses on the wall paper/
sometimes you skip one or two accidentally/   /
                                        /here and there/
                                                      /and then you have to
start all over again/
                   /best thing to do is to number each horse/
                                                          /give each horse a
number/
      /starting at the top of the wall/
                                    /working across/
                                                  /and then down/
                                                                /then after a
while it becomes easier/
                      /you simply count the numbers/
                                                  /and by the time you're out
of the room/
          /you have everything in order/
                                      /something like 722 horses/
                                                                /or better yet/
976/   /
   /assuming of course you buy the cigarettes by the carton/
                                                          /that means 548 divided
by 10/
     /makes it easier/
                    /54 point 8 cartons/
                                      /or to simplify matters 55 cartons/
                                                                      /you just
can't fuck around with an extra two packs/
                                        /but I have no idea what a carton costs/
I have never bought cigarettes by the carton/   /
                                          /never/
                                                /who can afford it/
                                                                /day by day/
pack by pack/   /

DAY by DAY

PACK by PACK -- that's the story of my life -- but in the long run you do
save -- at least that's what people tell you if you buy cigarettes by the
carton -- even if they dry up after a while -- a dime here and there adds
up in the end -- but how the hell am I going to get things going -- today
-- tomorrow morning -- YESTERDAY HE ARRIVED IN NEW YORK -- that's settled
now -- but now I've got to have a plan of action -- a direction -- a plot

DAY by DAY

55 cartons of cigarettes ---   --- PACK by PACK

Right now you pay about 40 cents a pack -- 42 to be exact -- Pack by Pack
cheaper by the carton -- no doubt about that -- $3.80 a carton --plus tax
it never comes out even -- they always confuse you with pennies -- always
-- Let's say $3.86 even -- 55 times 3.86 -- takes almost a genius to work
this one out -- or at least some experience in arithmetic -- comes out to
212.30 -- just for cigarettes -- that's even more than for the noodles --

BOX by BOX

212.30 for smoke puffs ---   --- DAY by DAY

Unbelievable -- if I give up smoking I can literally double up on the noo
dles -- 105.85 times 2 makes 211.70 -- a difference of 60 cents -- really
something -- it's really something to consider -- you give up smoking and
you have a double portion of noodles each day -- except the last two days
because of the 60 cents difference -- 29 cents a box -- that's just about
two boxes short -- but can I do it -- can I give up -- is it worth it eve
n to think about it -- you get fat -- you get nervous -- you start eating
more -- you have a need for sweets -- then I could perhaps buy a stock of
candies -- candies instead of the double portion of noodles in one pot --
it's something to consider -- I quite smoking -- I could do it and manage
to have a ball -- perhaps even a little piece of meat every other day and
cookies too -- instead of candies -- so many possibilities -- canned meat
of course -- what a guy could do with an extra $212.30 -- it's incredible

Without cigarettes you'll go crazy for sure, you'll get fat, nervous, and
paranoiac. No. You've got to hang on. Cigarettes are essential, almost
as essential as noodles. Unless you give up the whole IDEA and look imme
diately for a job. And of course you stop smoking at the same time. Just
think, for a moment, what a guy could save right from the start. $212.30
for cigarettes, plus $105.85 for noodles, plus all the rest. Enough to o
pen a nice little savings account in the BANK TRUST OF AMERICA. And also
a job on top of that. Security. Normalcy. Regular meals, three times a
day, with meat twice a day. It means you have close to 1100 bucks in the
bank. Well a little less because either way I'll keep the room. A person
must have a place to sleep. A place to hang his coat and put his clothes
away and put his feet up. And who knows, even a little piece of ass occa
sionally. Then if I deduct 416 immediately, I still have enough left yes
to open my little savings account. But 8 bucks a week for a room, what a
crummy room it'll be. With a job and a little savings account and regula
r meals, I should be able to afford a 10 dollar a week room in a nice nei
ghborhood. That's only 520 bucks for the year. With a lovely view looki
ng out on the street. The 10th floor. It's higher. More freshness more
air. 520 for the room, and all the rest in the bank. And work every day
from 8 to 5 with half an hour for lunch. COCKSUCKERS! They always do it
to you. Always twisting your mind. Always tempting you with an illusion
or a dream. A savings account, and a nice room for 10 bucks a week. They
always manage to have you think the way they want you to think. How lucky
you caught yourself on time. NO - DEFINITELY - NO . I won't give up. I
refuse. Object. Protest. Revolt.   F   . I can hear their little v
                                     U
oice whispering in my ears. You   C   could do it slowly. In the
                                YOU   K   ALL
evening after work. And also on ‾‾‾‾‾‾‾‾‾‾ weekends. You could get a
job as a waiter or as a typist. You're a good typist. A taxi-cab driver
a travelling salesman. You could teach French in high school. Get a col
lege degree with a major in business administration. In mathematics. Yes
with your experience with numbers, lists, additions, substractions, lies.

Eventually Boris goes to college and gets a degree. He majors in French of course. You've got to exploit his natural talent. But this part about his college life does not come into this part of the story. It happens much later. After he comes out of the Army. Still I could start asking a few questions about Boris. A few practical questions about his life. About his past. About his present. About his future. All sorts of questions. And when you have the answers then a good part of the story falls in place and is already written. In other words questions always precede answers. And the answers become the writing itself. First you have a question and then an answer. It's part of what is called the creative process. But it could be the other way around. However that would be very unnatural. You cannot write a story by simply asking questions. Normally a story is made up of answers. Answers to questions. But of course you never write down the questions. Only the answers. Questions remain understood. Unformulated verbally or manually. In other words when you read a story what you are really reading are the answers to unformulated questions. So all that crap about fiction writing it's for the birds. Only traditional and bad fiction writers do it that way usually. The normal way. The real sensitive imaginative inventive progressive guys do it differently. Or at least they try even if they fail in the end. It's only a matter of patience and determination in any case

Yet it does not prevent some people from writing a statement such as the one that follows: "It has long been a platitude to assert that the nineteenth century was the golden age of fiction supposedly because this fiction portrayed the middle class and because its audience was chiefly recruited from that same middle class." And to go on with even worse stuff

That's the sort of thing people write about fiction. But nobody ever tries to find out the questions. The original questions unformulated on paper and yet understood in the writer's mind. The reader doesn't know that. He only sees the answers. A good reader however tries to find out or at least imagine what the original questions were. But that takes an enormous intellectual effort. And not all readers are willing or capable of such an intellectual effort. Therefore it is preferable if the writer wants to be inventive modern progressive and experimental to try a more forward method. That is to say to work backward. To give the questions as the substance of his fiction rather than give the answers. Everybody has answers but few people have real honest sensitive and coherent questions to ask. If the questions are given first on paper then the reader can formulate the answers in his mind. This does not always work of course. Because most questions cannot be answered. Then everybody is confused. I know something about that. Being guilty myself of having made such statements at one time or another. Statements which ressembled answers but which in fact were not really answers but very bad questions

For instance that kind of a statement: "Most works of fiction achieve coherence through a logical accumulation of facts about specific situations and more or less credible characters. In the process of recording or gradually revealing mental and physical experiences organized in an aesthetic or ethical form these works progress toward a definite clear goal: THE DISCOVERY OF KNOWLEDGE." More or less. Then there's little hope for

HIM ———————————————— or ———————————————— ME

There is (indeed) little hope for ME or for HIM and yet this does not prevent ME from asking HIM some questions (practical questions) about himself even though there might not be any discovery of knowledge and the answers might be totally false therefore let us start with a list of the most basic questions to which we shall give very basic answers to the best of our knowledge so as not to interfere with HIM in order that HE may remain independent and totally candid in his answers thus giving HIM a chance to shape his own destiny as much as possible even though eventually the course of his destiny might not follow its pres cribed course according to the answers HE will give to our questions:

Q. - Boris! Where were you born?

A. - Paris. France.

Q. - Date of birth?   (That's a tricky question. Invent here. Lit
                        erally. In order that the dates come out exa
                        ctly as planned.)

A. - 1928.   (Whoever reads that can calculate from that b
                        ecause if I am more specific than that then t
                        he whole story becomes dated. Whoever is rea
                        ding that can add up himself. If Boris is 19
                        when he arrives in America and he was born in
                        1928 then 1928 plus 19 that brings him to Ame
                        rica in 1947. That should work. Though it's
                        always possible to change the dates to render
                        the story more contemporary. Of course one m
                        ust be careful because of the war. The Jews.
                        The camp. The farm. Nothing too specific of
                        course. Just enough for people to feel sorry
                        for him.)

Q. - 1928? Are you sure?

A. - What do you mean am I sure? Of course I am sure. I know exact
     ly when I was born.

Q. - Ok! Let us not argue. We'll have enough problems together for
     the next 365 days (damn you!) without getting all excited about
     dates. And in any case this is not a question.

Q. - When did you come to America?

A. - After the war.

Q. - Which war?

A. - What do you mean which war?   The BIG ONE of course!

Q. - What kind of an answer is that? The BIG ONE! Either you say the
First World War or the Second World War.   But you cannot say the
Big One.   Doesn't make sense.

A. - Ok!   The Second World War.   After the Liberation.   (All that in
French of course.   The answers being translated simultaneou
sly.)

Q. - How long have you been in this country?

A. - You're kidding!   You too.   The eternal question.

Q. - Ok!   Skip that one.

Q. - How do you like it here?

A. - Unbelievable!   I refuse to answer that one too.

Q. - Ok!   I apologize... Let's try something else...   Why did you come?

A. - You see I could have gone to Africa with my aunt in Dakar who owns
a beautiful huge hotel and I would have worked with her in her big
hotel but my uncle from America wrote to me (in English) after the
war asking if I wanted to come to America and start a new life (it
was a difficult decision) but meanwhile my aunt from Africa - Aunt
Rachel - came to see me in Paris by plane and bought me a watch (a
beautiful wrist watch - in fact my first wrist watch) and she also
wanted me to come to Dakar with her and she said to me that of cou
rse the climate there is very hot but that I would get used to it.

Q. - Please! Skip the details. Be specific. And besides that doesn't
answer the basic question why did you come to America?   (you ask
a guy a very basic question and there he goes telling you
his whole life story. Helps when you're stuck. But it's
beside the point. But isn't it true of all stories? Who
knows what the right answer is. Who knows if the answers
the reader reads are really the correct answers to the qu
estions. The original unformulated questions.) (And ass
uming I make him 19 when he arrives in America and he answers 1928
to the question date of birth then the whole story is immediatemen
t dépassée et datée. Sometimes it's better not to ask questions a
t all. However if he is born the same year as I was born - 1928 -
then the story must take place in the past - unless it's a coincid
ence - in order that the two of us may not be the same person. If
however we decide to make the story more contemporary then we will
have to change his birthdate. He could be born in 1948 for instan
ce. But that means that we have to skip the War the Jews the Farm
the Camps entirely because he would not yet have been born when it
all happened. That fucks up the whole story. No it's preferable!
I mean it's better to lie a little about dates and about his past.
Or else throw the whole story into the past tense. The near past.
Or better yet into a fictitious past. But that creates another pr
oblem. The problem of time. The time element is always there yes
always there to bug you. I'll have another chance to deal with it
later I'm sure. But for the time being let us go on with a few mo
re questions just to see what happens and how we get out of them.)

Q. - Is your family still in France?

A. - No!

Q. - Where are they?

A. - Dead.

Q. - That's sad. But can you be a bit more specific?

A. - You see they were deported (my father my mother and my two sisters
but usually I don't mention my two sisters because then people thi
nk you are exaggerating) by the Germans to a concentration camp (I
think it was Auschwitz) and they never returned no doubt having be
en exterminated deliberately (X * X * X * X) we were Jewish and ev
ventually they became lampshades and this is why after the war whe
n my uncle . . . . and also my aunt from Africa (it was a difficul
t decision) because . . . .

Q. - Please! That's enough. Don't get carried away.

Q. - What did your father do?

A. - What do you mean? What did my father do?

Q. - Yes. How did he make a living?

A. - Oh! Not very well. He was an artist. A surrealist painter. Not
a bad painter. I could write a whole book about my father. But t
hat does not necessarily mean that what I would write would be abo
ut my real father. On the contrary. Everybody invents an image o
f his father. A legendary father. A mythical father image. A dr
ream father. And when it comes to my father. What a myth my fath
er!

Q. - Well said but nobody is asking you to get carried away. Be specif
ic. Just mention the essential. For instance his physical attrib
utes.

A. - Tall. Dark. Blue grey eyes. Jewish. And also quite a gambler w
hen he had nothing else to do.

Q. - Was he faithful to your mother?

A. - That I really don't know. I doubt it.

Q. - All fathers are alike. I could also write quite a story myself ab
out my father. Everybody invents a perfect image of one's father.
Nothing more deceptive more false more intriguing than your father
and I don't mean your real father. Mothers are different. Mother
s usually don't have to be reinvented because they remain real. E
ven after they are gone. With some exceptions of course. My moth
er! But who the hell cares about my mother.

Q. - What about your mother? Who was she? What did she do? How did s
he look?

A. - I prefer not to answer all these questions. I prefer to keep moth
er (my mother) the way she was. The way I remember her. With her
dark eyes full of sadness.

But finally all these questions lead nowhere (-) because in the end all you get is false answers (-) and yet could help to have a list of questions (-) very short and precise questions (-) but questions only (-) nothing more or nothing else (-) no answers (-) something like a questionary (-) or like an inquisitionary (:)

    N ame?
    A ge ?
    P lace of B irth?
    N ame of F ather and P rofession?
    N ame of M other and P rofession?
    N umber of S isters and A ge?
    N umber of B rothers if A ny?

of course it will be a bit too sketchy (-) one may have to be much more (-) specific (-) much more (-) personal (-) to get anywhere (-) definitely (--) one should cut down (-) or else give up completely (-) particularly now (-) with all those stories going around about cancer (-) some people don't take it seriously (-) but every day they come out with more reports more warning more statistics more convincing evidence (-) and another guy dies (-) mouth cancer (-) lung cancer (-) even though he has been warned (-) told & retold

```
CAUTION:  CIGARETTE SMOKING MAY
BE HAZARDOUS TO YOUR HEALTH MAY
SMOKING CIGARETTE BE    :CAUTION
```

but they insist on the MAY (-) and another guy dies anyway (-) and soon you no longer MAY (-) IT'S FRIGHTENING (!) but then if you give up (-) you must face the certainty of getting fat (-) fat like a pig (-) and nervous too (-) like a rat (-) scares the shit out of me (-) and what happens (?) you die anyway (-) it never fails (-) you die of apoplexy (-) or a heart attack (-) of anything (-) and in the end it comes out the same (-) also they claim (-) without any evidence (-) that if you stop smoking you start eating like a pig (-) twice as much as before (-) imagine (-) in my condition (-) imagine (-) in my situation (-) it would be a disaster (-) I mean once I am working in the room (-) on noodles (-) two boxes a day instead of one (-) though in the long run it would be cheaper (-) noodles are cheaper per box than packs of cigarettes (-) that's a fact (-) as we have already witnessed (-) not by much but a penny here and there could help in the end (-) unquestionably (!)

or C I G A R E T T E S

```
Q   that's the kind of corner I just got myself in because of all these  q
U                                                                          u
E   funny like hell the kind of  i m p                                     e
S                                      a                                    s
T                                       e s s  a guy can get in            t
I                                                                          i
O   unbelievable the k i n d of stupid  p r e d i c a m e n t              o
N                                                                          n
S                      idiotic  s i t u a t i o n     one                  s
                                                      can
                                                      get
                                                      in!
```

And yet the only way to get out of that c o r n
                                                e
                                                r is to ask more question
and   also make more l   s
                                                                   i s t
Therefore the list of questions previously asked about Boris is not a bad

idea at all because it gives me a beginning
                                 a starting point
                                 a way to keep going (and of course to g
                                                                        e
myself out of that stupid idiotic CORNER I got into quite inadvertently t
- - - - - - - - - - ------------------ - - - - - - - - - quite accidentally)
                                                                        t
That's the way to go then more questions but nothing too deep   h
nothing too personal about his family or else it gets full of   e
cheap psychological crap and poor Boris gets all sorts of bad
complexes but with a list of questions once you are inside the room   h
you can get going right off the bat and not waste days and days and   e
boxes just to write that crucial first paragraph and we know how it   l
can be crucial that first paragraph how crucial it can be at the ve   l
ry least the first few days therefore in the beginning all I do you
might say is answer the questions about Boris but the big questions   o
remain the big questions as to whether or not I should write the li   u
st of questions now or wait until I am locked up in an impossible -   (t
pre-di-ca-ment - - - - - or - - - - - an -idiotic si-tu-a-tion- and
                                                                    of
                                                                 course I
could also do the same for the scenes that is to say make a list of all
the scenes in the story and the same thing for all the themes because you
have to have   themes   ot evah
                                                              have
                                                   in a good story
otherwise the whole story falls apart   a   story   R
without themes is like a chicken without feathers   therefore here are E
some possible/themes: N
                        loneliness (that's normal)   R
                        feeling of desertion (that's not unusual)   O
                        suicidal tendencies (everybody has some)   C
                        search for love (that's quite common)
                        sexual voracity (that's not a theme that's an rehto
                        ....an obsession.........)
Obsessions of course should also be listed even though it may put you into ano
```
```

A STORY SHOULD BE LIKE A HUGE GIGANTIC ENORMOUS QUESTIONARY FULL OF OBSESSIONS and of course this immediately suggests the concept of a quest even though the concept of a quest is an old-fashioned concept nevertheless the hero or if you prefer the protagonist while questing for himself asks questions about himself about his life about life in general about the past at least the near past the future the present the conditional but instead of answering these questions he allows the story to give the answers or so it seems but in fact it is the crea tor of the story the inventor if you prefer who gives the answers and of cours e beyond that if there is a recorder for the story then that recorder faithful ly records all the answers given by the inventor and so on while the hero simp ly waits in the hollow of his fate to see what is going to happen to him which means that whoever invents the story must be in a position to know all the ans wers or else everything falls apart and that is an almost unbearable situation

Indeed it is a preposterous situation for a guy to be in therefore the best th ing for him to do is to give up immediately drop the whole story and in this c ase since you are the inventor that is to say ME since I am the answerer of al l the questions or if you prefer the manipulator of all the answers then the b est thing for me to do is to give up immediately this minute and drop the whol e stupid idiotic scheme in which I got myself all wrapped up from the moment I started considering quite seriously first the price of a room per week in whic h to lock myself and second the amount of noodles I would need in the room and the price per box in order to survive and write the damn story and beyond that all the other stuff which eventually led me straight into that unbelievable co rner that idiotic predicament that stupid situation of having to choose betwee n a double portion of noodles per day at the expense of giving up smoking tota lly and the danger of growing fat like a pig fat and nervous and very confused

And for what yes for what I ask you so that everything can fit into place in t his preposterous real fictitious discourse now in progress and which has occup ied us for days and days hours and hours and possibly will still occupy us for months and months but no more than 365 days page after page box after box unti l the end or at least until we run out of things to say but even that is doubt ful for the discourse must go on for quite a while still considering that we h ave already gone quite far without having yet said half or even one third of a ll that we originally wanted to say when we started saying what we wanted to s ay at the beginning and it all began remember with a very simple straight-forw ard statement which was immediately recorder by the recorder while the protago nist waited in the hollow of his fate to see what would happen to him eventual ly when he would arrive in America by boat from France meet his uncle on the p ier and go by subway to the Bronx to visit a Jewish family and so on but in fa ct what did really happen that is the important question WHAT REALLY HAPPENED?

Nothing! Nothing much really. Boris hardly got off the boat yet. Let' s assume then that Boris is still on the boat. (Boris! I'm not convinced yet that Bob or Samuel might not be better. Or something more real. More French. More human. Dominique perhaps!) In any case he's still on the boat. Ahead o f him like a huge hole (an enormous hollow sphere) lies his future. A kind of void. Emptiness. America. The hollow of his fate. His future in America st ill unrealized. Of course his imagination (or mine working for his) fills the the void with all sorts of notions. Dreams. Daydreams. Anticipations. Appr ehensions. Wishes. Memories. Crap. Souvenirs. Possibilities. Illusions.

And any other such notions that come to his mind. And of course the void symbo-
lizes America. The American way of life. And since he does not know a thing a-
bout America (except for what he has seen in American movies) it's easy to inven
t or imagine. But movies always distort reality. The void of America in black-
and-white. Or in color. In technicolor. That's the feeling an immigrant shoul
d have about America when he first arrives. And then life in America consists o
f filling up the void. Though this is true not only of immigrants but of everyb
ody in America. I may be exaggerating a bit but in general that's about it. In
general terms.

So OK! I get in the room about nine in the morning and I start wr
iting. My noodles are piled up against the wall. But not too close to the wall
so I can walk behind to count my horses. Or better yet in the center of the roo
m in a kind of huge square tower of boxes. But the cigarettes are against the w
all. 55 cartons. My shit paper too. My toothpaste. My reserve toothbrush. M
y tomato sauce for extra flavor. My coffee sugar salt. Everything in other wor
ds. And now I'm ready to go.

And now what do I do? I start inventing a few thin
gs. Things should come quite quickly at first. It's the rewriting that's diffi
cult. It's always the rewriting that eats up time. Noodles too. At this point
it's just a matter of patience and determination. A matter of waiting until tom
orrow morning. Sounds simple enough. Who ever thought of that before. Nobody!
Nobody that I know. But of course I've got to have all the stuff ready. On time
to get started. That might be a stumbling block. So many stumbling blocks in t
he world. One more. One less. The important thing is to keep fighting. Crawl
ing. Sweating. Jumping if necessary. Up & Down. But never falling.

The theme
of the young immigrant is not unusual. Boris. Dominique. I like Boris better.

Dominique is a bit effeminate. But try it out for a while. You can always go back to Boris if necessary. He doesn't realize that on the boat he has already begun to become an immigrant. The moment he sets foot on the boat. For most guys it's just a journey. A trip. For him it's the beginning of a way of life. But just the beginning. Particularly since he has no idea what he's going to do in America. He doesn't even know his uncle. At first he thinks of it as just another trip. A way to get away from France and all the misery. He had endured so much since his parents and two sisters were shipped to the concentration camp to be exterminated. And also since the end of the war. No job and no money (of course). Not a single real friend. No family. All dead. It is really tough to live like that. Not even a father to tell you about life or at least about the facts of life. Not even a spiritual father. That's really sad.

One of the faces he sees quite vividly in the little black triangle between the girl's legs in the subway is his father's face. Can't tell from where he's sitting if it's his real father or if it's only the face of his legendary invented father. The mythical father he started making up after the war. That's exactly what he begins to realize while staring between the legs. Here I am he's thinking in America. Feels strange. Feels like I am really all alone. A stranger. A foreigner in my double-breasted suit. That's the style at the time he leaves France but it's not necessarily the style when he arrives in America. Long lapels. Double-breasted with tiny stripes. A few days later after you've crossed the ocean you're out of style and there is nothing you can do about it. Particularly at that time of the year when it's so hot and you can't afford to buy a new suit.

Must be July or August. Hot like hell. Most men in the subway in shirt sleeves. Except for a few guys (fanatics) who wear light suits and ties and straw hats. Those funny straw hats really make you feel like a foreigner particularly the colorful hat bands around them. Funny!

The truth is you only begin to feel like a foreigner in a foreign country in contrast with other people. The natives. And particularly when these nativ es make you feel like a foreigner just the way they dress or the way they st and sometimes. The way they speak of course. Or the way they cut their hai r. The way they eat also. Particularly the way they cut their meat. Const antly changing the knife and the fork from the left to the right hand and ba ck to the left and then back again. It's really confusing. It's discouragi ng. Particularly for a guy who does not change hands when he cuts his meat. To be a foreigner in a foreign land is an excrutiating experience. They sta nd in front of you (the natives) in their light suits and straw hats and sud denly you feel like hell in your outmoded heavy double-breasted suit. Sudd enly you feel ridiculous. And then they start asking you questions about yo urself. Particularly the "two eternal questions". And of course there's no way out. You start speaking their language and immediately they know you ar e a foreigner. Before when you kept your mouth shut they only suspected som ething but they were not sure because there was really no way they could tel l. But there is always doubt in their minds. And since Boris does not spea k much in the beginning (shit! that Boris name keeps coming back) he remain s in a doubtful condition. That's the problem with talking too much. Event ually you reveal yourself. But when you don't talk you become a suspiciousl y suspicious character. I know that feeling well. Spoke of it before. In:

A M O N G   T H E   B E A S T S

Bareass
skin tight to my bones
I swam the ocean
under the water
a long swim years ago
As I came up for air
an old man squeezed my shoulders
and I shouted
AMERICA AMERICA
but there was no answer
The subway was full
and I felt too white
and fat women touched me all over but
and I thought it was love
and when I looked up at the sky

the moon had spread her legs
they didn't see me blush in the dark
I sneaked out of the window
climbed behind a cloud to look for god
but all I found there were my footprints
Tired of the stars I came back among men
in straw hats
Had a hot dog and a Lucky
and they shipped me across the ocean pff
Had myself a few Chinese
and again back in my room
the light and gas had been turned off
days later I found the bill in my shoe
and that's when I began writing poetry
without punctuation of course

All that for a dozen crummy straw hats in a subway on a hot summer afternoon. But what an afternoon! First day in America. How can you forget it? And yet you can't even stick with one name. One! Only one. DOMINIQUE.

DOMINIQUE!

DOMINIQUE! If you insist. Since he won't speak much in the beginning nobody will really notice he's a foreigner. Except for the double-breasted suit and the way he combs his hair. I'll speak for him. But I won't think for him at least not in the beginning. Let him think for himself. He wonders for insta nce. He wonders a great deal. If the girl whose legs he's looking at is Ame rican. Doesn't show. He feels a bit different knowing that she knows or sus pects that he's not an American. It makes him feel superior. At least that' s what he tells himself. While in his pants it's getting hot like hell. And stiff. What a romantic idea. The damn bitch keeps moving her knees. But ne ver enough to get a good look once and for all. And even if she did wouldn't make any difference.

It's more interesting just to imagine. That's what he kee ps telling himself. To feel different gives him a mixed feeling of superiori ty and inferiority. He knows that. He would like to be like all the other g uys in the subway. Except that most of them are black. That's one thing tha t really puzzles him. It's like being in Africa.

Nobody ever told him that. Y ou arrive in New York. You take the subway. And it's like being in Africa o r at least in some kind of exotic country. That's what I mean about movies t hey really distort reality. An immigrant on his way to America doesn't reall y know that there are so many black people in America. How would he know? N ot by seeing cowboy movies or ganster movies. That's for sure.

Naturally he won't be fully aware of being an immigrant until he arrives in Detroit. And on top of that a Jewish immigrant from France. That's essent ial for the story. The search for an identity. A young man about 19. All alone. A Frenchman. A Jew. A lonely-young-Jewish-French-immigrant that's what he is. Five basic elements in one person: loneliness, youth, race, n ationatity, and status. How the hell do you find your identity with a back ground as complex as that? How do you establish relationships with others? How do you relate with others? These are difficult questions!

But before I forget make a list of all the people he meets during his first five years i n America. Not only his friends but also all those people he considers his friends. In chronological order but not necessarily in alphabetical order. Simply in chronological order of encounter and of course first names only :

```
Joseph.   Ernest.   Richard.   Frank.   Roselyn.   Dick.   Robert.   Solomon.
Loulou.   George.   Jacques.   Tommy.   Bernice.   Jane.   Michel.   Erskine.
Gloria.   Pierre.   Charles.   Peggy.   Gugusse.   John.   Donald.   Christy.
```

And so many others forgotten. Not all of them real friends though. Some o f them just people he met. And of course a few special ones you just can't mention here it would be too indiscreet.

And just as he was thinking of po ssible names for all the people he would eventually meet during his first f ew years in America the girl with the legs gets up from her seat to get off the subway. Must be around 179th Street. He keeps staring at her. She is now standing in front of the sliding doors waiting for the subway to stop a nd for the doors to slide open. He has to turn his head slightly to the ri ght. Uncle David is sitting on his left. Doesn't matter much which side b ut it makes it more credible. She's tall and her dress is very tight aroun d her hips. And what an A S S! Her ass is particularly striking. Enormou s. Round and high on her legs. Unusual to look at for a foreigner. Quite

an unusual monument if you put this one among all the other monuments he saw
during his sightseeing tour of New York City with his uncle. French asses a
re not that big and not that round. In fact French asses are always too low
and often too flabby. But this is only a conjecture on the part of our prot
agonist because he has not really touched that many asses in his life. Reme
mber he's only 19. And extremely shy. But nevertheless he takes a good loo
k at this one. It looks almost as if it had been raised deliberately. Neve
r has he seen a woman shaped like this one and when it comes to looking at w
omen our protagonist takes full advantage of it. He almost feels like getti
ng up and dropping everything. Uncle David. America. Loneliness. Jewishn
ess. And all the rest. He just feels like walking out. Or just simply wal
king over to the girl to squeeze her ass. And then he would follow her. Fr
om behind. Just to see what would happen. Just like that. Poor Uncle Davi
d if only he knew what was going on in his nephew's mind on his first day of
confrontation with America. But that would be a tremendous way for him to d
iscover America. Walk around the streets alone following a girl with an eno
rmous ass. A black girl on top of that. A young beautiful black American g
irl. That's five basic elements in one person: youth, beauty, race or colo
r, nationality, sex. Just as he was reflecting on these basic elements Uncl
e David moves a little in his seat. Coughs a little. But immediately seems
to go back to sleep. Just when the subway stops. Of course when Uncle Davi
d moves Dominique looks away from the girl. Just a few seconds. The door o
pens. She's still standing there. Just a few seconds as if she were decidi
ng whether or not she's going to get off or stay. No kidding. She is looki
ng straight at him now. No time to fuck around with lists of names themes a
nd all those basic elements. No time to debate personality and character an
d relationship. He's got to make up his mind quick. He catches sight of hi
s suitcase between his legs. He feels like crying suddenly. His hard on di
sappears like a deflated balloon. But he can't get up. Can't follow her. T

...oo...too many problems...too many stumbling blocks...what does a guy do in a situation like this...?...the suitcase...Uncle David...first day in AMERICA ...the noodles...the room...the subway...that's how it goes...Suddenly you re alize where you are...in the subway...in America...on the way who knows where ...he doesn't know because when Uncle David told him where they were going he didn't understand a damn thing...C'EST NORMAL...finally when the door opens a nd the girl steps down he knows it's too late...just lost his first friend in AmericA...sometimes a look a good look is enough to make a friend...the slidi ng door slams shut...he turns his head all the way around making believe that he's looking at the name of the station to know where he is...and the sub sta rts moving...it moves past the girl...she is walking in the same direction as the sub...towards the exit I suppose...but of course not as fast as the train ...C'EST NORMAL...or at first...I mean...when the train just starts moving... she walks almost as fast as the train...meaning that her face is even or almo st even with the window where Dominique is sitting and they are almost face t o face across the window-pane...but they cannot talk to each other because of the loud noise...SHIT...those descriptions are difficult...he sees her face o n the other side of the window...she is beautiful...beautiful for a black gir l he thinks...but of course he has no idea what black beauty is...he has real ly no real criteria to judge...all this is new to him...he's seen girls befor e...girls from AfricA...but never really payed much attention to them....this one is different...unforgettable...beautifully unforgettable...and American o n top of that...she smiles at him...YES...he's sure of that...just as she van ishes behind the train...but what a smile...thick red lips half opened and yo u can see her white teeth and then a little pointed tip of tongue...that much he saw...he smiles back...but too late...but here he goes again...his pants b ulging again...but he keeps his hands over it on his lap...and then it's fini shed...the train plunges into the tunnel...into the darkness.into the big bel ly of AmericA...she's gone...and her little black triangle too....he'll never

r...never see her again...unless there is a huge coincidence...an accident...and
he sees her again accidentally...but for now it's the end of the subway scene...

-/

Conventionally a guy would treat something like that with an appropriate vocabul
ary: quickening pulses, bulging eyes, cold sweat, hot flashes, trembling hands,
muted gases, strangled cries, copious sighs. But certainly not in a situation l
ike this one. Because feats of annihilation and even feats of creation ought to
be harder than it looks. Even in the worse moments of isolation the pulse of hu
manity goes on ticking in orderly and hopeful manner. Then there is no use wast
ing a single moment on that kind of emotionalism. Even if Dominique (or anybody
else in his place) feels he's just missed the chance of his lifetime. There are
so many missed chances in one's lifetime. One more or one less. It's hopeless!

-/

It's true Dominique often thinks about that girl during his first few weeks in A
merica keeps him going it's like a beautiful image in his mind in the back of hi
s mind and in fact the first few times he masturbates in America it's with the i
mage of that girl in front of his eyes that he does it especially the legs sligh
tly spread apart and the little black triangle in the middle but eventually he d
oes it with other images other legs other triangles other asses but the one imag
e that sticks to his mind the most is the image of that girl and that's the imag
e he uses the most often in the beginning it's self-explanatory in fact as the s
ubway roars through the tunnel he suddenly imagines himself walking behind the g
irl in the street but the street is very vague it's hard to imagine streets that
you have never seen before and he has no idea how it is around 179th Street so h
e imagines it more like Boulevard des Italiens that's the problem with guys in t
hat kind of a situation they imagine everything the wrong way by associations or
simply by transposing one place into another place or a past time into a present
time   it's a good past
time   But he follows h
er anyway eventhough he doesn't know where he's going or what kind of a girl she
is and he sees himself in his mind walking a few steps behind her all nervous an
d anxious waiting to see what will happen next WHAT A WALK! she turns around onc
e just as they emerge from the subway so she knows now he's there behind her and
it's possible that she suspects that he's following her but at the same time she
might not suspect anything lots of guys get off at 179th Street could be a coinc
idence and perhaps he also happens to live in this part of the city and too he m
ight simply be visiting some friends in the neighborhood too bad she doesn't kno
w him and never met him before because he's a good looking young man a little sh
y it's true it shows and somewhat strange in his funny outmoded double-breasted s
uit and the way he combs his hair he could be a foreigner or else a queer or som
e kind of artist or even an actor eventhough he does look young and inexperience
d but one never knows with guys you meet in the subway on a hot summer afternoon
in July or August and who looks at you with such passionate eyes what a cute kid

At this point I could get into her mind just to see what she's thinking. lots
of guys do that. I could work it out. everything is possible. normally you'
ve got to be consistent but nobody prevents you from stepping in and out of pe
ople's heads. as long as you don't cheat and tell the truth. word for word a
nd step by step. and of course you clean it up a little because usually peopl
e think dirty in their minds. but it would give depth to the story and also i
t would permit the characters to reveal their inner-selves and everything else
that goes on inside of them. of course that creates all sorts of psychologica
l complications which must eventually be resolved one way or another. but we'
ll face this one when we come to it. for the time being it suffices to say th
at I have given some thought to the matter and leave it at that. later we wil
l tackle this very problem seriously when we are confronted with it. let's sa
y around the 17th or 18th box down the precipice feet first beard down to my w
aist the room stinking like hell. alone in my noodle universe moving in and o
ut of people's minds and bodies. what a mess it will be. what a lovely mess!

Then she seems to be slowing down in fact she stops for a moment in front of a
shop window a jewelry store to be exact that's if Dominique is able to imagine
a jewelry store on 179th Street he doesn't know what to do now therefore he to
o stops in front of a shop window a men's clothing store it's more logical but
he can't stand there like a jerk forever and since while looking at her shop w
indow she noticed that he was looking at her instead of looking at his shop wi
ndow he is now committed and so he walks past her quickly and excitedly feelin
g his heart pounding inside his chest but he doesn't dare turn around once he'
s past her so he keeps on going with his legs trembling under him and his neck
hurting in the back just from feeling a presence behind him her presence he as
sumes but it could be somebody else's presence because there are many people i
n the street finally he can't stand it anymore and he quickly turns around jus
t enough to get a quick look (once you've committed yourself you have to act f
ast) but behind him he sees a tall skinny guy with a grey hat on who is readin
g his newspaper while walking and for a moment he thought he had lost the girl
but then he finds her again a little further back in the crowd still walking i
n the same direction and this time she saw that he saw her WHAT DO YOU DO NOW?

Here we are then two weeks later. 17 or 18 days or boxes later. working on a
stupid incident that never happened. and now we are stuck in the middle of th
e street following a girl who positively allows herself to be followed. a gir
l who might not even exist. we've got to do something. it's a street crossin
g and the traffic light is green. do we cross the street? do we turn around?
do we turn the corner without crossing the street? or do we simply stand ther
e like jerks and do nothing? just wait and see what will happen right there i
n the middle of a page. lots of guys get stuck like that in the middle of the
street or the middle of a page. but we just can't stand there for 365 days or
so. lucky it's not raining. what would poor Boris do? he doesn't have an um
brella. and suppose he crosses the street and she turns the corner. or suppo
se he turns the corner and she crosses the street. all kinds of possibilities
here. he's fucked. if he crosses the street and she turns the corner then he
will have to stop on the other side to see what she's doing and then when he s
ees that she has turned he'll have to cross the street again to catch up (or v
ice versa) with her. and if the traffic light is red he'll have to wait and v
ery likely lose her in the crowd. forever. that would really be bad. dammit!

Of course if somebody asks what he's doing
he can always say he's lost
Happens to anybody to get lost in a strange city
He crosses the street
Stops on the other side and looks up
as if he were looking at the street name
That's a good excuse
You have to stop and look up to look at a street name
Nothing wrong with that
So he stands there with his nose up in the air
And just then she's standing next to him
She smiles
A real smile this time
Before nobody was sure she had really smiled
But this time no doubt about it
You're looking for a street? She says
That should do
She's almost as tall as he is
And what a lovely voice
If she talks to him like that what do you do next
What can he answer
First of all he doesn't speak a word of English
And second he doesn't understand what she says
He could show his mouth with his finger
meaning I don't speak the language
But she might think he's mute and dumb
He might mumble something
Or else answer in French
To make sure she doesn't think he's dumb
He knows two or three words of English
Yes
No
Thank you
He could use them now all at once
Doesn't matter because before he knows what's happening
she's holding his arm just like that
Damn it! The first thing he thinks to himself
C'est une putain (in French of course)
He doesn't know the English word for putain
And then he gets scared

She's after my money
He has exactly fifty dollars with him
Fifty dollars in a black wallet
in his back pocket
And two 5 franc bills for souvenir
She might take him up to her room and a guy
might walk in when he's not looking and
hit him on the head
And here goes his money
Happens all the time
But that's not what happens
She's not a whore

Just a nice working girl
At least that's what he thinks to himself
And since he never got off the subway
he can imagine anything he wants
Stupid ass

If I were in his shoes I wouldn't hesitate a moment
Once you've committed yourself
you've got to go on
So she's holding his arm and they start walking together
And after a while
before he knows what's happening
he is up in her apartment
Not a bad place
And the door is hardly closed
that she grabs him and kisses him hard smack on
the mouth
her red tongue sliding under his shy tongue
It's exciting like hell
They didn't even speak to each other
They simply understand each other
Just like that

Sometimes people do understand each other without any
necessity for words
Must be her room
A bit on the sloppy side
messy
with clothes all sorts of clothes allover
He is a little bit less scared now

What helps is to know that he's in somebody's room who cares a little for
him just the way the room is messy shows that she's a good person she mus
t be living alone clothes on the floor on the back of chairs on the bed a
lso and jazz records too all over the floor at first he felt like running
away but the kiss she gave him gave him some courage and now while she is
picking up some of the clothes and shoving them in a closet while apologi
zing he's standing in the middle of the room his legs trembling like weed
s in the wind under him the excitement the emotion and the anticipation a
ll that together is enough to make a guy tremble and then suddenly she st
ands behind him with her arms around him her whole body glued to his brea
thing hard in his neck and kissing him lots of little wet kisses down his
neck she must be some kind of sex maniac he thinks but it's not an unplea
sant thought on the contrary behind his ears now the little wet kisses li
ke little birds and then her hand (the left one) slides down along his ch
est and further down along his belly and then on his fly he can't stand i
t much longer particularly when she begins unbuttoning his fly (in this s
tory French pants don't have zippers) he's going to explode in his underw
ear any moment if she does not stop immediately but suddenly Uncle Arthur
(no David) moves a little in his seat coughs a little and then starts tal
king to Boris (no Dominique) in Yiddish it's all over the subway is slowi
ng down he doesn't understand a damn thing of what his uncle is saying ex
cept that when Uncle David gets up to get off at the next stop he underst
ands that it will be the end of the subway scene and the beginning of the
next scene (the Jacobsons scene) all that is too good to waste and yet it
is not that good because it really has nothing to do with the plot as suc
h if there were to be a plot in this story but it doesn't matter I can al
ways rework it eventually and work it in they are lying on the bed now it
's almost dark I'll describe the strange smell in the room at least the s
mell seems strange to Dominique and he's holding on to her tremendous ass

The smell and the ass these are the two things that really struck him at the beginning he'll never forget that the smell and the ass and it was t he same thing with Ernest's mother same enormous ass and same strange ex otic smell with Ernest's mother but it was much more real much more of a confrontation and the way it happened so unexpectedly and so easily also he cannot forget it and in fact he thinks about it often afterwards when he no longer lives in Detroit it keeps him going momentarily when he's l onely he must have been in Detroit a good three months already when it h appened (Peggy incidentally was still writing to him from Milwaukee) and they had been rehearsing in the auditorium and by now he could really pl ay the clarinet well but still it was the saxophone that he wanted to pl ay they were rehearsing a few marches for a football game I think or som ething like that the whole band was there imagine Dominique (Boris Domin ique doesn't matter it's the same guy) already playing in the band for f ootball games and he's been in Detroit only three months or so (must hav e natural talent) and as they came out of the auditorium he asked Ernest where he was going (by then his English was quite acceptable) I've gotta cut man Ernest said he had to cut to go to his job he was working in his Mobil gas station (on the East Side) every day for five six hours (he ev en worked on Saturdays but not on Sundays) Boris had a job in a grocery-delicatessen-type-store but he only started working at five o'clock ever y afternoon until closing time at ten o'clock and it's about one o'clock when they come out of the auditorium after rehearsal not that it matters much what time it was and in fact Dominique was not working in the groce ry store at that time he was already working at Chrysler the late aftern oon shift but this being a Saturday he didn't have to go to work and usu ally on Saturday after band rehearsal he goes to swimming practice (he's quite a busy body for a foreigner but Boris is a very active person) eve ntually I'll put him on the swimming team it's not too preposterous beca

use nothing prevents him from being a good swimmer (he specializes in the
back stroke) even though he's a French Jewish immigrant lots of guys in t
hat condition are good swimmers he learned during the war while working (
VERY HARD) on the farm while other guys older than he were fighting the w
ar and trying to save the country from the Germans and many of them (jerk
s) died while he practiced his swimming up and down the little river behi
nd the farm house usually naked and that's how eventually he learned that
particular stroke called the backstroke (he preferred the backstroke beca
use while swimming on his back in his little river up and down he could l
ook at the sky -- Boris has a passion for the clouds and the sky) that da
y however after he left Ernest at his Mobil station he decided to skip sw
imming even though he knew the coach (Mr. Zimmerman) would be pissed (sor
ry) off because there was an important swimming meet the following week b
etween NORTHERN HIGH SCHOOL's team (the water-vipers) against the Y M C A
team (the homosapians) but Boris felt that it was much more important tha
t day to go and thank Ernest's mother for the lovely birthday party she h
ad given him for his first birthday in America (EVERYBODY THOUGHT I AM SU
RE THAT I HAD FORGOTTEN THE BIRTHDAY PARTY AND ERNEST'S MOTHER'S ENORMOUS
ASS AND THE WAY THEY DANCED TOGETHER BUT NOT REALLY ALL THIS TIME THERE I
T WAS IN THE BACK OF EVERYBODY'S MIND AND IT WAS JUST A MATTER OF FINDING
A WAY BACK TO IT AND IF YOU REMEMBER WE HAD LEFT BORIS PANTING UP THE STA
IRS THAT LEAD TO ERNEST'S PAD JUST AS HE WAS ABOUT TO KNOCK ON THE DOOR!)
and so almost unconsciously Boris found himself in front of Ernest's apar
tment a three story building typical crummy building ready to knock on th
e door and at this point his mind is bubbling with all sorts of erotic im
ages and he starts talking to himself in the first person as if telling h
imself the story of what is happening I felt my heart beating like a mach
ine as I heard someone move behind the door inside the apartment the blac
k 48 Buick was not outside where Ernest's father usually parks it I was c
ertain of that I checked therefore one can assume that he's not home that

proves that Ernest was not lying when he said that his father and his sister
had gone to a baseball game I'll simply ask if Ernie is home and when the do
or opens even before he has time to ask if Ernie is home she says HI FRENCHY
come on in Ernie is not home he works today in his gas station didn't he tel
l you doesn't matter sit down I was just going to have myself a little glass
of Bourbon want some of course Boris never drinks but this time he'll make a
little exception and before he even has a chance to say a word or to explain
that he thought Ernest was home and that he came to borrow some music sheets
(that's a good excuse) he finds himself sitting on the sofa with a glass ful
l of Bourbon in his left hand his right hand sort of resting loosely on a pi
llow next to him on the sofa almost touching her hand also resting loosely o
n the same pillow and he didn't even have time to say too bad I'll drop in l
ater when Ernest is home and then without even being asked she starts explai
ning that Ernie's father and Ernie's sister have gone to a baseball game the
Detroit Tigers against the Senators she thinks with the 48 Buick and suddenl
y he feels himself growing in his pants (it's an obsession with him) the liv
ingroom is clean she must have just finished cleaning she still has her litt
le apron around her waist on top of some kind of thin house dress nothing to
o elegant and barefoot her big black feet sort of funny because her toes are
all crooked her hair a mess also curly all over she's enormous but good look
ing for a fat woman of her age if Ernest is about 17 or maybe 18 (he's a sen
ior) at most she must be around 37 or 38 or even less of course Boris has no
idea how old she is he's only speculating but she does look like a mother bu
t a sexy mother no question about that the sofa is green and the room very l
ight and then suddenly she disappears into another room the radio is playing
a deep voice singing a slow tune (a blues) with a saxophone in the backgroun
d (makes it more romantic) sort of sad then she's back but this time she has
taken off her apron and brings more Bourbon and more ice cubes Boris is no d
rinker in fact he never touches the stuff (must emphasize that) but he takes

another shot and makes believe he
loves it he's just being polite a
nd sociable you might say in a si
tuation like this one you have to
and now she's standing in front o
f him giggling her legs spread ap
art lifting her glass to her lips
in quick jerky movements the whol
e scene looks like it was rehears
ed WHAT THE FUCK AM I DOING HERE?
Boris thinks. He always thinks t
o himself in situations like thes
e. Perhaps not in those terms bu
t close enough. There are certai
n terms he never uses. He's been
in the country more than three mo
nths now. But still he doesn't u
se certain words that easily. Hi
s English has improved a great de
al. No question about that. And
he knows the exact meaning of wor
ds like FUCK YOU or SON OF A BITC
H and even MOTHERFUCKER but it is
not easy for him to use these wor
ds. It's not natural. In fact i
f sometimes he uses one of the wo
rds mentioned above with his frie
nds in school or in the factory w
ith the other guys it's strictly accidental or else it's because he wants to

impress them. But usually the other guys
laugh at him as though he was using someth
ing very incongruous. Sometimes he even sa
ys these words on purpose just to see the re
action. But it's not natural for him. Takes
years before you can say fuck you like an Amer
ican. A real American. It's another thing whe
n it comes to doing it. It's universal. I don't
think we need to go into that. No need for it at
this point. Right now Boris should simply be gett
ing all excited about Ernest's mother sitting there
next to him on the sofa. But of course he doesn't k
now if she really wants to. He only thinks she wants
to. That's always the problem with a guy who wants to
screw another guy's girl or another guy's wife or anoth
er guy's mother. He never knows if she really wants it.
Or if she's simply playing a game. In fact one never kno
ws until it happens. And even then the whole thing is mor
e like a dream. It's true that the time they danced togeth
er at the birthday party she was rubbing like hell against h
im but that means nothing. Could be natural with her. Parti
cularly the way she dances. And fat the way she is. She just
can't avoid rubbing against the guy she dances with. Also that
night she was drunk. Could also be Boris's imagination or mine.

After all we are coinciding merging into one another more and mor
e as it was expected. Dammit I wish she hadn't given him such a h
uge glass of Bourbon. He could get out of there faster. The discj
ockey is now talking with somebody on the radio and the two guys are
laughing. That's a good touch. I'll have to describe that in detail
s. Particularly the roundness. She was really round all over. Her a
rms. Her face. Her legs. Her ass of course. And enormous teats hang
ing down. The two guys on the radio are discussing the latest Bird reco
rd. LOVER MAN. Very appropriate. Quite a pretty face though. Must hav
e been less than 37. Can't tell with black people they all look alike tha
t is from the white point of view. Something motherly about her. Boris is
a little scared and nostalgic. Embarrassed might be a better way to put it.

Suppose Ernest walks in. Or his father and his sister. Everything is possib
le in a situation like this one. Or simply a neighbor. There's always some
curious female neighbor. Maybe she saw Boris come up the stairs panting li
ke an ox. But Boris does not think that fast and that deeply particularly
under pressure. Ernest's mother is now sitting next to him on the sofa g
iggling at something the two guys on the radio just said and without any
warning she gives Boris a tremendous clap on the back as though telling
him come on man come on baby join the fun. Relax. Poor Boris doesn't
know what to do now. He doesn't understand this kind of secret langu
age. And when it comes to languages he's not very sharp. Does he t
ell her now why he came? Did she guess? Can he control himself if
it doesn't work? These are questions which cannot be answered jus
t like that on the spot. Somebody's got to help. The discjockey
does. A slow record begins to play. A deep voice singing. Dee
p female voice. Billy Holiday singing I CAN'T GET STARTED WITH
YOU. Perfect. And before he knows what's happening the glass
es of Bourbon are on the table and he's dancing with her. No
body really asked. It just happened. They are dancing rubb
ing against each other just like the night of the party. S
he literally grabbed him when Lester came in with his solo
and now his left leg is between her knees. How hard he's!

And here we are (the two of us ** the three of us *** the four of us ****)
a year later (let us say) exactly a year after the boat landed in New York
and all of us (I * HE * WE * US) got all excited in the subway because the
girl with the legs spread apart smiled at US and now 365 days later here I
* HE * WE * go again getting all exicted with another female (a much bigge
r one this time) having converged into one another (the protagonist and th
e inventor -- and of course by extension the recorder too) it's unavoidabl
e it had to be and now he can hardly move and she must feel it (hard stiff
like a stick) between her legs and she does feel it and reacts to it quite
accordingly (- -) They begin
rubbing against each other without hardly moving their feet just holding o
n to each other tighter and tighter breathing hard in each other's necks a
nd he kisses her neck her hair (everything) it's sticky greasy particularl
y her skin but it's soft (he expected it to be rough like her hands) her c
urly hair bothers him it tickles his nose and suddenly he feels like dropp
ing her on the floor and running out of the place into the stairs out into
the street running like hell crying but she holds on to him tight so tight
it hurts and now he can feel the roundness of her belly against his stomac
h and before he knows what's happening he lifts up her dress from behind a
ll the way up to her waist as they go on dancing (you might say just shuff
ling along on the same spot) she is completely naked under her dress she's
not even wearing panties just an enormous bare ass and his two hands clutc
h the fat (it's cool) and he holds on firmly on each side (she doesn't eve
n complain) spreading it apart a little and he pushes against her and they
end up against the wall and she leans back and rubs and rubs faster and fa
ster he can feel the hair from her black jungle against his bone he doesn'
t know what to do next (how to get his hand to his zipper to get it out an
d shove it in which would be the logical thing to do next) but she helps h
im with sure fingers and now in his head he sees all kinds of faces--asses

SS (o) (o) (o) (o) (o) (o) (o) (o) (o) (o) (o) (o) (o) (o) (o) (o) (o) SSASS

Peggy's face (and ass)

The girl's face (and ass) in the subway

and many others but these are the two most specific images in his mind.

Not all the faces are white or black. Some are mixed. Mixed crowd you

might say. There are other colors too in his head. Lots of pink and yellow.

** **

```
R                                                                        E
I
G        O N                    T O                        T H E         N
H                                                                        D
T                              straight forward and normally
```

** **

His eyes are closed now. Tightly closed when he feels her hand touching

his zipper. But that's enough to make him come like a river inside his

underwear. And then he feels like an imbecile. But he doesn't move a

blink. She doesn't move either. Waits. Then moves away from him a

little and holding on to his hand pulls him gently into the bathroom

His pants are down around his ankles now and she is wiping him with an

elegant circular motion. Doesn't take long before he's hard again. He

drops his head slowly on her shoulder. Her left shoulder. That's about

right. He sniffles and now she's stroking the back of his head. Passes

her fingers in his hair   WHAT A SPECTACLE

                    The towel drops down on the floor and she continues to

                    rub in a circular motion with her hand only. Once in a

while her nails catch his hair. HONEY BABY. HONEY. She keeps saying. Now

he doesn't feel wet any more. Just hard like a rock. Almost feels like

screaming. But of course he doesn't. On the contrary. He keeps saying

SHSS. SHSSHHSS. Whatever that means. As if somehow he wanted to calm her.

It's OK MAN. It's OK BABY. It's OK HONEY. It's (-) (- o -) (- ∅ -).

How the hell do we get out of this one? I just can't drop him right there

in the middle and have him miss such a good opportunity (in the land of op

portunities). Let's squeeze it in quickly and get it over before somebody

comes in ᴧᴧ ^ ᴧᴧᴧ goes out

The bathroom is very small and above the sink there is of course a little

mirror and above the bathtub there is a string stretched from one wall to

the next and on the string all kinds of clothes he can see all that by lo

oking over her shoulder and he starts counting the pieces of clothes hang

ing on the string two pairs of woman's panties size enormous four blouses

three T-shirts stockings but he stops can't count anymore all he sees now

is pink and blue pinkish and blueish in front of his eyes and inside also

of his eyes when he closes them also some clothes on the edge of the wind

ow but he can't tell what these are mostly white stuff men's stuff likely

& & & & & & & & & & & & & & & & & & &

All that of course doesn't add much to the scene but it makes it credible

& & & & & & & & & & & & & & & & & & &

He feels stupid with his pants down around his ankles but she pulls
them off with her big feet and then pulls him towards her as she le
ans against the sink and now she's literally sitting on the edge of
the sink how she's able to get there is impossible to describe part
icularly since she never let go of him and while all this motion is
going on he shrinks to nothing   a little baby's penis but when
the circular motion of her hand gets going again all around and und
erneath and her other hand is in his ass then he quickly regains an
unexpected fullness   and his big hardness
and his lengthness and his strenghtness slide in like a knife a pin
in sour cream it's wet like hell in there and he can see his visage
grimacing at him in the little mirror above the sink the sour cream
image is just an image   he doesn't think about
it it's just a sensation   a wet sticky sensation a
feeling but poor Boris has never felt anything like that nothing as
exciting has ever happened to him before and it's understandable if
one remembers that he's only 19   no by now a year later he is now
20 years old and it's not the end a few minutes more and it's Boris
who is now sitting on the sink it's his turn to be on the edge with
his legs hanging down how he got there is also impossible to define

But what is certain is that it's cold under his ass now she is down
on her knees in front of him sucking like a machine saliva oozing a
long stream of it from the corners of her mouth as she keeps moving
and twisting her head round   and   round never in his life has
Boris felt so stupid particularly with his skinny legs hanging from
the edge of the sink and his pants and underwear all rolled up in a
bundle on the floor and his two hands yes both of them resting flat
on top of her head his shirt tails tucked under rolled under rather

This time he really screams but the scream doesn't come out no it's
stuck inside his throat   It is simply a muffled
sound which would have been a cry had it come out of his throat but
it doesn't   it doesn't
had it come out it would have been something like WOW STOP STOP YOU
MOTHERSUCKER even though he rarely uses that kind of language STOP!

He's heard that expression before and in this kind of situation one
might easily be carried away indeed under such pressure he could do
what he has never done before curse in English and use such an expr
ession without shame and possibly many others too that may be shock
ing in a normal situation but faintly remembered what finally comes
out bursting through his lips are entirely different words words at
the very least symbolic in such a situation if not very meaningless

-c- S T O P   Y O U   M O T H E R !   S T O P   D A R L I N G -c-

M   MOOOOOOOOOOOOOOOOOOOOOOOM   O
O   M
M - - - M A M A M - - - M A - - - MMMMMMMM - - - M A - - - M O M O

At this point all sorts of possibilities are possible.
He could pass out.

He could die of an epilectic fit.
He could start screwing her so hard she
starts screaming so loud all the neighbors come rushing in and find them
sitting on the sink in a rather embarrassing situation.
But instead he
doesn't say anything and she doesn't say anything.
Instead his hips
begin to sway slowly back and forth.
Finally he lifts her up from the floor
holding on to her by the armpits and she's back on the sink and he slides
in again into the juicy sour cream her enormous thighs wrapped around hi
s waist his two hands smashed against the cold porcelain of the sink un
der her ass but the worst are his knees as he pushes in they almost gi
ve under him and her fingernails enter into his flesh yes she does ha
ve rather long fingernails no question about that he can feel them d
eep in his skin the skin of his ass and it hurts.
The thick curly hair
of her African jungle feels funny against his belly.

This time he can't
take it anymore.

His knees are folding under him.
He presses in.
One last
good time hanging on to her as though he was sliding down a cliff.
One
last good time.
Lucky she's holding on to him too.
In fact she's literally
lifting him up from the floor.
He could have broken both legs and arms if
she were to let go of him and let him fall down from the cliff into the
white precipice of reality.

In situations such as these Boris does not
think very fast.

Little quick thoughts do go through his mind but it's a mess.

MESSMESSMESSMESSMESSMESSMESSMESSMESSMESSMESSMESSMESSMESSMESSMESSMESSMESS

And then he starts laughing aloud just like that first it begins in his head
He hears a little laugh growing louder and louder a funny kind of little gi
ggling But when it comes out it's an explosive laugh But it quickly disint
egrates eventually into a series of never-heard-before-little-laughing co
ughs hard to describe What goes on in the back of his throat whatever co
mes out of his throat is more like a grunt than a laugh though he's cer
tain he felt the laughter right there in his throat in his mouth ready
to burst He can hear it inside of him coming up like a stream of sali
va a little staccato laugh growing into an enormous disgusting howl!

WOOWWOOWWOOWWOOWWOOWWOOWWOOWWOOWWOOWWOOWWOOWWOOWWOOWWOOWWOOWWOOWWOOWWOOW

In situations like these it's as though
the mind becomes a camera taking pictur
es of itself even though the eyes are c
losed most of the time the pictures eng
raved on the inside of the head but the
pictures in his head at this time depic
t his trousers and underwear lying on t
he floor all crumbled up and Ernest's m
other's huge ass sitting on the sink an
d the feeling of his knees getting weak
er and weaker but the latter is not rea
lly a picture but a feeling and of cour
se feelings are not visual they are str
ictly abstractions or sensations and th
erefore cannot be depicted so that it i
s impossible to see the feelings in Bor
is' mental pictures all you can see the
re is Ernest's mother all around him an
d him inside of her inside her huge cun
t and once more he whispers MAMAN in Fr
ench as he feels a last drop or perhaps
two last drops drip slowly inside of he
r from the end of his shrivelled reddis
h prick and now it's all over finished!

A door slams shut and little foot-steps
are heard in the staircase quickly he g
rabs his trousers and underwear and two
seconds later he's back on the sofa fin
ishing his Bourbon as though nothing ha
d happened and she's back in order howe
ver with her it was easy all she had to
do was to stand up and let her dress fa
ll down and NI VU NI CONNU Boris conclu
des but feels he should say a kind word

Yes something nice to her anything befo
re leaving for now he's in a hurry to g
et the fuck out of there yet he just ca
n't say thank you and leave it at that!

He has to say something nice and more a
ppropriate and so he quickly tries to t
hink of something to say when she comes
out with a loud cry YOU HONEY BABY DOLL
and grabs him again by the shoulders an
d pressed her thick lips on his trembli
ng lips he frantically pulls away and m
oves past her towards the door but agai
n she grabs him from the back this time
kissing him fat kisses in the back of h
is neck her hand all over his face to t
he point where he can hardly breathe an
ymore but finally she lets him go sayin
g SHUSSH SHUSSH and adding YOU COME AGA
IN YEA YOU HEAR DON'T FORGET she has to
say something like that or else the who
le situation falls apart so he says YES

The stupid things a guy says when he doesn't know what to say -- UNBELIEVABLE!
Boris is convinced he will never come again but one never knows he might quite
likely not be able to resist particularly when stupidly out of nowhere he says
to her as he goes out the door DARLING I LOVE YOU just like that unconsciously
But he said it (not me -- that's for sure) I LOVE YOU DARLING -- imagine that!
That was not necessary but he had to say something and that's the only words t
hat came to his mind in this most distressing situation and in a way it's rath
er FABULOUS that he was able to say something like that it's also quite REVEAL
ING and when she hears those FABULOUS words she grabs him once again right the
re in the middle of the staircase and smacks another big juicy kiss on his tre
mbling lips her tongue shoved all the way inside his mouth and here they go ag
ain feeling each other without any reservations and this is how the scene fina
lly ends even though it's a bit repetitious and somewhat immoral and disgustin
g but of course when the time comes I'll clean it up a bit and leave out all t
he dirty details and also I'll change the names I'll work on it for four days!

Four boxes of noodles and you'll have the whole motherfucking scene in shape !

It'll be good for both of us Boris and I because when you're alone in a room y
ou need that kind of excitment that kind of entertainment you have to face the
facts and solve your own problems it's a matter of survival however difficulti
es may arise for eventually you will have to explain how eventually Boris expl
ains to Ernest what he did with his mother it's the kind of secret he will not
be able to keep to himself and that'll be quite a confrontation because undoub
tedly Boris will feel shitty as hell with Ernest the first time he sees him ag
ain after this scene that is to say the following day though personally I woul
d not give a damn but Boris is a very sensitive and honest person and so how t
hen will he be able to look at Ernest squarely in the face but fortunately for
Boris he has a whole day to recover and compose himself and that gives us a fe
w more boxes to work out the details of this crucial confrontation but if Bori
s had known how shitty he would feel afterwards he would not have screwed her!

In fact if Boris had known what was in store for him in the hollow of his fate he would not have come to AMERICA or at least he would have remained in the subway because in a symbolic manner the subway scene represents th e center of the discourse the point around which all persons and things g ravitate or as stated above THE BELLY OF AMERICA source of life and death

and   yet

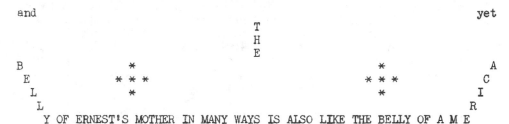

                                    T
                                    H
                                    E

B   *   *   A
  E   * * *   * * *   C
    L   *   *   I
      L   R
        Y OF ERNEST'S MOTHER IN MANY WAYS IS ALSO LIKE THE BELLY OF A M E

it is part of the convergence system in this discourse whereby everything that moves eventually moves towards the same point and therefore in a sym bolic way everything comes out the same in the end and consequently every thing (persons things animals) in the discourse ultimately merges and coi ncides into itself and thus everything that increases also decreases beca use in a system of double or nothing everything that is doubled or duplic ated is automatically erased or negated for indeed everything that produc es a forward movement also produces a backward movement and therefore wha t is said can also be unsaid because what is said is never really said si nce it can be said differently or as a great thinker once said out of des pair JE FINIRAI BIEN PAR FERMER MA SALE GUEULE SAUF PREVU in French obvio usly but of course the same can be said in English by an English speaking person as long as he knows what he is saying since all languages coincide

                                therefore

              B E L L Y   for   B E L L Y

the one you get is better than the one you do not get or the one you drea m about but undoubtedly the girl in the subway was much better than Ernes t's mother she was younger had better legs better teats and a much more e xciting ass (not as big it's true but much firmer) but an A S S is an ASS and Boris always takes them as he finds them without making a big fuss ab out their bigness or their roundness or their color and this is how event ually he was able to compromise and even justify to himself the rather im moral act he had committed when he screwed his best friend's mother and i n fact he used the same argument to convince Ernest explaining to him tha t nothing is really immoral in the world if you work out a system that ju stifies your actions a system based on the law of average and on some vag ue future relationship but this matter is entirely out of context at this point and may never be resolved in this discourse because first we are ru nning out of time and of space and second because it is very difficult if not impossible to relate exactly (word for word and step by step) what go es through a guy's head while sitting in the subway (or in front of a she et of paper) looking between a girl's legs while on his way to the end of his story the first day he arrived in America after having suffered a gre at deal in Europe during the war indeed all this is very difficult to rel ate in a coherent form and yet if one makes an effort and tries very hard to approximate what goes on in the mind of a guy like Boris (and of cours e what goes on there goes on in French) then it comes out approximately s omething like the following which is an original and unexpurgated version that can be called THOUGHTS AND IMAGES OUT OF THE MIND OF OUR PROTAGONIST

Je trouve parmi les débris de ma vie déchirée par le temps un morceau de pensée
qui pousse sur le crâne intérieur de ma géologie intime et où ma végétation hum
ide attend les vents de la vieillesse le rire se lève il faut tenter de respire
r même s'il est impossible de voir l'insecte qui me gratte la fesse gauche tand
is que sous le toit de mes mémoires broutent des fourmis rangées en spirales di
rigeant leurs cercles alchimiques vers des serpents tordus qui picorent des bre
bis en se creusant la tête triangulaire mais je m'en irai les doigts dans le ne
z oh la la que d'amours sans amour et de nuits sans nuit je n'ai faits en tiran
t les caleçons de mon derrière un pied contre la tête mais qui pleure ici si lo
in de moi ah sois sage oh ma douleur et chatouille le divin ennui de notre recu
eillement oh rage oh désespoir de ne pouvoir savoir dans le noir revoir les bon
s soirs qui se remplissent de nuit noyés les anglais les français et pourtant j
e ne regrette pas l'Europe aux murs écroulés les vaches ah quelle boue dans cet
endroit méchant ce gouffre de notre cou coupé comme une lune un soleil où des a
rbres cassés attendent d'être achevés dans l'ordure de la hache du bon dieu qui
boit le venin de la vie en se tordant les pouces dans un nouveau rêve mais peut
être un jour un jour jamais quand la mère fait du tricot et le père la vache la
belote au café du coin j'ai trop souvent vu dans les recoins de mon âme se tord
re une musique étrange qui ressemblait à du sang mordant ma bouche tupide et la
dent de mon image enfoncée dans la langue mouillée de ma vie je me suis accroch
é aux cordages de l'avenir j'ai dansé des nuits entières chez les sauvages en m
e foulant les chevilles dans les crevasses du ciel pour ne point revendiquer le
passé et repartir en avant non je partirai un jour tout de même le vent sèche l
es draps de notre mort et son sourire sur la vertu sur la bouche de mes yeux ba
issés je le suis par devant et par derrière au-delà des montagnes au-delà des u
sines des rivières et des ponts et chaussées et des chevaux de bois des mers de
s ruisseaux devant le monde agenouillé je me fous de leur gueule un fleur au ch
apeau à la bouche un vieux mégot le coeur saignant sur un ciel de bois dévoré p
ar la peste ou des oiseaux de plaisir se déchirent le ventre en se rongeant les
ongles et je rirai dans les allées du rire qui fait tourner la tête aux petites
filles qu'un vieux monsieur tripote en leur grattant les cuisses les bras le ve
ntre il passe en se tenant la tête c'est lui qui nous regarde nous regarder dan
s un avenir sans fond oh temps suspend ton linge sale aux cordes de notre vie p
our sécher ta douleur au soleil et au vent de notre destiné et toi qui nous éco
utes les doigts au coin du coeur regarde je me dépasse je me vois me voir je su
is aussi de ceux qui ne parlent jamais qui n'osent jamais parler j'amène le ven
t sur mes épaules j'aime le son des vaches le soir au fond des granges ruminant
leur crachat tandis que des couleuvres en verre gris se traînent dans la verdur
e de nos péchés en attendant d'être jugés sur la bascule du vice du mal dieu oh
le grand mangeur de gosses se cache et rigole dans ses coulisses dévorant la ma
tière de nos rêves gluants et puants et nous moi et toi et lui aussi et elle cr
éant avant-demain les journées d'avant-hier tous les moments qui s'accrochent a
u dernier pan d'une porte secrète qui ne mène nulle part un chemin tortueux qui
s'ouvre sur un destin perdu mais je parle je te parle allons sais-tu qui je sui
s jeune emmerdeur je suis vrai il est juste lisant dans la bible à qui venge so
n père il faut donner un vin comme un vin de rigueur qui vous trempe dans la tê
te du soir au matin en se donnant des coups de pioche dans l'estomac la chair t
oute déchirée la chair dure hélas et je m'enterre vivant dans la poussière de m
es pensées en attendant de ne plus voir les enfants qui pleurent car j'ai lu to
us les rêves où se promènent des anges masqués qui rigolent en cachette derrièr
e des visages de vieillards inscrits sur un rocher monsieur me dit-il en me pre
nant la main et moi dodu et satisfait de la grimace de mon avenir je me sens so
udain comme le noyé perdu dans les goémons verts et rouges et las de me souveni
r de ceux qui sont perchés sur le manche d'un balai de leur mémoire d'outre-tom
be j'attends de devenir un très méchant fou et je regarde la peur dans les yeux
je lui crache au visage et elle me tape gentiment dans le dos en me disant salu
t et loin en moi j'entends du fond de la nuit intérieur le cri des animaux féro
ces qui se disputent la vie tout en me regardant me regarder me voir tout seul

AND now we are nearing our end.   Much more remains to be said
     Much more remains to be prepared

And no doubt much of it will never be said
     will never be prepared   except perhaps

in some other versions of our lives.

     YES!   Poor Boris (it had to be)

     Everything must be plausible

And Dominique!   (I don't like Dominique. I've never liked Dominique)

Too effeminate   not Jewish enough   <u>(you can't avoid the facts)</u> But

we must forget about that about the Jews the Camps and about the L A M P S
     H
     A
     D
     E
     S

     <u>(never again)</u>

It's a rare thing.

So therefore back with Boris
     back in the subway scene.   He only follows her in his mind:

mentally - ideally - abstractly - dreamily.

Happens all the time.   Meanwhile Uncle David woke up in his seat.   HE
     GETS
     UP

They must have arrived.   That's possible.   Must be 249th Street.

(If there is such a stop).   It was a long and exciting ride.

And now the afternoon with the JACOBSONS is about to begin:

     It was after lunch however when they arrived there (the female from
     next door was already there waiting for the nephew from Europe WHAT
     A BITCH) Boris doesn't remember if he had had lunch but it really d
     oesn't matter much because that day (what a day!) he wasn't very hu
     ngry in fact he wasn't hungry at all just sick inside lonely and ve
     ry apprehensive and so confused after the boat the pier and particu
     larly the subway ride with the girl and the legs spread apart there
     fore at this point he really doesn't care much about eating noodles

Therefore one more meal
or   one meal less   SO MANY GUYS STARVING IN THE WORLD   and no doubt
sometimes alone in my room there will be days when I won't feel like eating at
all and I should avoid (as much as possible) talking about food or else I will
go crazy with my noodles (and tomato sauce once in a while) and if I skip a bo
x one day I might go wild the next and devour three or four boxes all at once!

That would really throw off the whole system -- the whole temporal system.

Three boxes at one sitting and there goes the DAY/BOX relationship

               and also the BOX/DAY relationship

Zoom!
Yes -- **definitely** -- avoid as much as possible talking about food - parti-
                                                           cular-
                                                           ly no-
                                                           odles-

And yet there are so many GOOD THINGS to eat
                so many GOOD THINGS I LOVE

I adore EGGS for breakfast - I love STEAKS - I have a passion for BEANS -

I love ORANGE JUICE in the morning   - a tall glass of orange juice
                                       nothing like it to clear you
                                       r throat after all the cigar
                                       ettes during the night and a
                                       lso during the day two packs -

I should make a LOOOOONNNNNG list of all the things I love: FOOD -
                                                                  WOMEN -
                                                                  BOOKS -
                                                                MONEY -
                                                              movies -

Just like that. Of course it has nothing to do with the NOODLES

or with the STORY (Boris' story) but it could be useful eventual

ly. Then in my room (alone) cooking my daily box of noodles eve

ry morning (one box for the whole day) I would remember eggs for

breakfast (sunnyside - scrambled - soft boiled) it would give me

visions (hallucinations) and I would suffer like hell and becaus

e of the suffering things would come out much better much deeper

                                          I can already see myself after three or
                                          four months (107 days let's say) with a
                                          beard down to my waist dirty like a pig
                                          the room smelling like a shit hole crap
                                          all over debris of paper spoiled paper!

Dammit how about the PAPER? Yes the PAPER (how many reams do I need?) I

almost forgot about that and there must be so many other things I forgot

to think about to plan prepare anticipate calculate so many things I hav

e not yet tackled (should make a list immediately of all the things I ha

ve not yet considered but which eventually must be considered if we want

if we want this story to make sense even if we never get to these things)
paper is one of these crucial things of course - - - I can already see my
self - - - after two or three months - - - with my beard down to my belly
- - - doesn't grow that fast - - - then just down to nowhere - - - full o
f lice - - - I can see myself dreaming of a huge rare steak - - - a filet
mignon - - - bloody rare - - - to the point of chewing anything I can get
- - - anything I can get my teeth on - - - paper - - - rags - - - leather
- - - pieces of wood - - - dead flies - - - like in the camps - - - maybe
one should consider having a little reserve of something to chew on in mo
ments of despair - - - candy for instance - - - I love candy - - - better
yet - - - CHEWING GUM - - - that's good for chewing - - - and it passes t
he time too - - - this way I won't have to chew all the crap I can get my
teeth on - - - paper - - - rags - - - leather - - - dead flies - - - piec
es of wood - - - it gives you something to do between meals - - - between
boxes - - - and also it keeps you from smoking too much - - - and also it
helps you along when you're stuck with a scene - - - the more you chew th
e more rhythm you get inside - - - for instance if I am stuck with the sc
ene where Boris explains to Ernest what happened with his mother - - - wh
at a difficult scene this will be - - - then I can chew a few pieces of g
um - - - Ernest and Boris met the following day as they had agreed to mee
t - - - Ernest doesn't suspect anything but he notices how Boris avoids l
ooking at him straight in the face - - - and finally Boris tells him what
happened - - - with all the details - - - between friends it's normal tha
t they should tell each other everything in detail - - - YOU MOTHERFUCKER
he screams - - - but soon he calms down - - - and Boris begins his explan
ation about his theory that nothing is really immoral as long as you work
out a system that justifies your actions - - - but before he can finish h
is explanation Ernest punches him in the mouth - - - I have never seen so
much anger in a guy - - - MY MOTHER - - - he cries out - - - anybody even
my sister would have been alright - - - but MY MOTHER - - - imagine that!

He stopped shouting for a moment thinking of what to say next and then he came out with this fabulous expression: YOU DIRTY LITTLE BASTARD! Boris had never heard such an outburst. But Ernest had hardly pronounced those words that he realized what he had just said. In a way he was the little bastard because somehow Boris had substituted himself for his father (tem porarily it's true). And so they quickly made up and Ernest told his fri end: "You know something, man, that makes us almost brothers." And then for a moment he reflected about what he had just said, and then added qui te candidly, "no, that's not really it, that makes me almost your son." B oris almost fainted when he heard that. Unbelievable the things a guy ca n say after he finds out that his best friend screwed his mother. How do you work this one out? How do you reconcile such ambiguous relationships into friendship? It won't be easy. But a good piece of chewing gum in a situation like this one and that should keep me going to the end of the s cene or at least until I can't take it anymore and give up the whole scene

^ ^
! !
. . . .

CHEWING GUM then it's agreed.   Five cents a pack of five sticks.

A pack a day?

That's 365 times 5 that's 1825 sticks

            and also 1825 cents (that's obvious).

Of course I don't have to count the sticks.   Packs is simpler.

I don't even have to multiply.   Simply 365 packs.

But you still have to multiply 365 by 5 to get the price for your list.

Five cents a pack multiplied by 365 gives us 1825 (exactly what we said).

But to simplify matters and come out in dollars you drop the last two digits or else you put a period between the first two digits and the last two   and that gives you a total in dollars   in other words what you have arri ved at is 18 point 25 $18.25 for chewing gum   it's a lot of cash for chewing   I may have to cut down on something else   cut down on cigarettes that's the best place   I should be able to manage it. MORE CHEWING BUT LESS PUFFING   LESS PUFFING AND MORE CHEWING!

I could of course cut
down on the paper yes
the paper for writing
the damn thing if I'm
careful and I don't w
aste too much of it I
can play with the pap
er cut down by one or
two reams it's true I
haven't calculated th
e paper yet but event
ually I'll have to it's quite obvious but let's calculate with cigarettes
for the time being if
a carton of cigarette
s costs $3.80 as I de
cided earlier plus th
e tax of course 6 cen
ts tax for a total of
3.86 then if I divide
18.25 by 3.86 I'll ha
ve the number of cart
ons that must be sacr
ificed for the chewin
g gum is it worth the sacrifice or shall I skip the whole thing in any ca
se it comes out 4.728
cartons of cigarettes
it would indeed be si
mpler to do without c
hewing gum but the mo
re you chew the bette
r you are and the les
s you smoke you'll fe
el better in the long
run particularly sinc
e you can't smoke and chew at the same time supposedly therefore it's a d
eal we sacrifice 4.72
8 cartons of cigarett
es for chewing gum ho
wever it will have to
be rounded off to 5 b
ecause it's impossibl
e to sacrifice an une
ven number so here we
go 3.86 multiplied by
5 gives us the sum of
19.80 to spend on che
wing gum now if 365 packs cost 18.25 for 19.80 we can get 396 packs of gu
m which is more of co
urse than one pack pe
r day since we have o
nly 365 days to consi
der but we'll solve t
his problem later for
the time being let us
simply say that we no
w have 396 packs of g
um Spearmint of cours
e it lasts much longer

Dentine is not bad either .

I could mix flavors costs

the same and sometimes it

comes in mixed bags and mixed colors looks beautiful in the drugstores.

COULD YOU PLEASE GIVE ME 396 PACKS OF CHEWING GUM!

                                                     (I can see the guy's face).

WHAT FLAVOR?   (396 packs! - he's crazy!).

Couldn't you make it an even number?   396 is an even number.   NO

I mean like 400 packs. Are you going into some kind of business?   NO

It's just for a party. A huge chewing party (won't believe me).   NO

I'll tell him it's for an experiment. I'm a scientist trying to   DO

some experiment which has to do with the chewability of chewing gum   OR

better yet with the durability of chewing gum.   OK

but the best would be to buy a few packs at a time.   10 or 20   NO

body can question 10 or 20 packs.   You'll have to make each
                                            piece last chew each pie
                                            ce to its utmost squeezi
                                            ng all the juice out bef
                                            ore you throw away the u
                                            sed piece to start chewi
                                            ng another brand new one

HAS-ANYONE-EVER-CALCULATED-THE-CHEWABILITY-OF-A-STICK-OF-GUM?   NO

I mean the chewing durability of a stick of gum. How long can you chew
the same piece before it feels like a rubber band in your mouth?

You could ex
periment wit
h this probl
em for a lit
tle while ju
st to see wh
at happens i
n the end an
d see how fa
r you can go
on one piece   Three hours?
                   Seven hours?   The easiest would be to
                                    divide the day into che
                                    wing periods of five or
                                    six hours each dependin

g of course on the durability of one piece.

Since there are 24 hours in a day (no question about that) (even if I work
with the curtains closed) and you divide 24 by 6 periods (six makes it com
e out even) then you have 8 chewing periods in a 24 hour day however since
a guy cannot chew while he sleeps (and I assume that I will have to sleep)
(8 hours of sleep in a 24 hour period sounds like a right number) (in betw
een the working periods) then I won't be able to chew steadily for 24 hour
s (of course some days I will sleep more and others I will sleep less it's
inevitable) (and some days I'll sleep all day) but on the average I'll sle
ep approximately 8 hours a day then it leaves me 16 hours a day for chewin
g gum (but only if I chew continually) and of course a great deal of the c
hewing process will depend on the mood I am in (the excitement of creation
will carry me on) and I may find myself working straight on for three days
without sleep (typing straight on for 64 hours) (chewing straight on there
fore for 64 hours) but if we assume that everything is normal and that I'm
awake 16 hours a day and asleep 8 hours then I have 16 hours for work as w
ell as for chewing and since there are 5 sticks of gum in a pack (but befo
re I do that I must take away one hour for meals) (one hour a day for eati
ng my noodles that should be time enough) (and of course one cannot be che
wing gum while eating noodles) (or for that matter while drinking coffee o
r while brushing your teeth) (though it could be done) (but let us say one
hour total for my three feedings) (that makes it an even 15 hours left for
chewing gum) and since there are 5 sticks in a pack if I divide 15 by 5 it
comes out to 3 hours of chewing per stick now 396 packs times 5 gives me a
total of 1980 sticks at my disposal and if I multiply 1980 by 3 then I hav
e the number of chewing hours available during the 365 days (in the room a
ll alone) 1980 times 3 makes 5940 chewing hours however there will only be
a total of 5485 hours for work and chewing in the 365 days (you arrive evi
dently at that figure by multiplying 365 by 15 - 365 being the number of d
ays and 15 the number of working or chewing hours in each day) which gives
me a difference of 455 hours or rather an excess of 455 hours it's no good

omehow that extra 455 hours must be accounted for or rather disposed of
we could easily say that those 455 extra hours of chewing would correspo
nd to the number of sleepless hours I will spend when I won't be able to
sleep because of the tension building up as I progress and that since so
me hours which should be spent sleeping will be spent not sleeping I cou
ld easily devote these hours to chewing gum another solution however cou
ld be that because the tension will be building up more and more towards
the end I could easily chew faster and more towards the end thus consumi
ng the excess 455 hours in a matter of a few days or weeks and this woul
d permit me to use up my entire stock of chewing gum during the 365 days

But in any event it's decided and no argument about it ADD GUM TO YOUR L
                                                                       I
                                                                       S
                                                                       T
at the price of $19.80

and later we shall see how we come out
            we shall see how much is left of the original 1200 bucks or so
1200 bucks with which we originally started to speculate eventhough nobo
dy really knows where the money came from and it might never be revealed

In any event I should go back to my L I S T just to see where I now
stand since everything must be ready on time but of course the room
is the most important a room with a view and horses (flying horses)
on the wall paper horses to count in moments of despair and all the
supplies piled up in the center of the room (very surrealistic) and
me against the world
    against the walls
    against everything or rather in spite of everything   A

long period of reflection and sequestration all alone!   A

man has to reach a point when he turns inward
                                    inward my skull   Devour
                                                           Devour
That's a damn good line - - - - - - - - Reflects on his life - - - - - -

That's my time...
....The time of noodles
And why not..
..........Boris will do the same eventually since he and I will coincide
It's inevitable with us..
....Then I've got to start all over
Right from the beginning...
.....................................Get the fucking thing going again
Make a list and know exactly where we stand................................
....Know exactly how much we have
If not we'll go beyond our means...
....That's interesting
Do I start by stating our needs or do I state how much we have.............
..................................And then squeeze my needs within my means
Ours within ours...
....That's pure shit of course
October 1st..
....One more day and we blow
Lots to do and here I am still jerking off mentally........................
.....................on all the damn possibilities of never getting started
Frist I'll get the room and then I'll get all the stuff in the room.......
....I'll pay for everything in advance
Yes but there is still a great deal that needs to be calculated...........
....Salt is free
Pots and pans..
....Only one pot of course
And also knife fork and spoon..
....Even if I don't use all three
Soap for the dishes and soap to wash my dirty underwears and socks........
.......................Unless I decide to work naked to save on clothes

And of course there'll be all sorts of miscellaneous things I have not even thought about yet like pencils and possibly a pencil sharpener erasers if I decide to erase some of the things I have written and possibly a razor with razor blades should I decide to shave occasionally if the beard begins to i tch which means shaving cream also and aspirin for the headaches but of co urse the big expense will be the PAPER reams and reams of writing paper bec ause a lot of it will be wasted on first second and third drafts and also o n final drafts I should have also a few extra ribbons for the typewriter it is unbelievable the things a guy forgets and I have hardly begun definitely

THE LIST   THE LIST

Room.. 416.00

Noodles... 105.85

Tomato Sauce... 7.80

Coffee... 20.04

Sugar... 1.89

Soap.. 5.25

Toothpaste.. 3.45

Toothbrush... .59

Toilet Paper... 14.04

Cigarettes.. 212.30

Chewing Gum.. 19.80

                                      _____

                              TOTAL............... 807.01

```
            I    am
So far then  WE   are not doing too badly:     $807.01      ... could
            HE   is                                        easily d
            YOU  are                                                r
                                                                     o
                                                                       p
                                                    the .01
                                                    to make it
                                                    easier & simpler
```

So 8 0 7 even

But this is not all — to this one must add the cost (not yet calculated) of:

MISCELLANEOUS . . . . easily 100 bucks

PAPER . . . . easily 200 bucks

EMERGENCY FUND . . . . easily 25 bucks

but of course I'm only guessing it could be more or it could be less but one
cannot take chances particularly since I am not sure we started with an even
1200 dollars (that figure was never clarified nor certified) what is certain
however is that there was not more than 1200 and more likely less so it's no
use getting all worked up in advance since it might not work out in the end!

particularly if I made a little error in my calculations along the way which
is quite possible but even if I am guessing the cost I am not too far off be
cause if I can spend over 200 bucks on cigarettes (as we have shown) then it
is quite possible to spend 100 bucks on miscellaneous and if I spend a littl
e more than 100 bucks on noodles (as previously calculated) then I can easil
y spend around 200 bucks for paper because eventually noodles and paper will
coincide (in fact paper may prove even more important than noodles) coincide
thus if on the one hand I'll consume noodles on the other I'll consume paper

therefore noodles and paper like everything else in this discourse will coin
cide in the end just as days and boxes coincided in the beginning for indeed
everything comes out the same   take it all or leave it all
                    DOUBLE OR NOTHING

but
originally we said 8 bucks a week for the room (that's what we said in the B
                                                                           E
            REMEMBER: just think for instance if ... etc. ... etc.   G
                                                                           I
and it came out to 416 dollars for the room.   N
                                                                           N
However suppose the room does not cost 8 dollars a week   I
          suppose the room costs only   7 dollars a week   N
                                         7 dollars for a room it's possible G
                                  then 7 times 52 makes only 364
                                                    364 for the room
IMAGINE THAT!
that means that you now have 52 dollars (416 less 364 leaves 52) more to work
with ..... and therefore we have to start all over again It's quite obvious:

JUST THINK . . . FOR INSTANCE . . . IF THE ROOM COSTS ONLY 7 BUCKS A WEEK . .
7 times 52 makes 364 . . . .
                    then it does not necessarily have to be N O O D L E S !
                    - ────────────────
THE END
```
```

SUMMARY OF THE DISCOURSE

PAGE REFERENCE	TOPICS
Title page	Title, subtitle, and name of author
Dedication page	Quotation from Robert Pinget - Dedication to four persons
Symbolic page	Noodles and Symbols
0-000000000	Prologue where the intramural relationships of three persons whose real and fictitious existences are closely related are established
000000000.0	Footnote about the possible existence of a fourth person who (like a supervisor) may be also involved in the discourse
1	Beginning - The room
1-2	The noodles and more about the room
2	Wall paper
3	Flying horses on the wall paper and discussion of a possible title for the discourse
4	Comparison with Stendhal and possible opening paragraph
5	Farewell to the world and more about the room and the noodles
6	Considerations on the food value of noodles and speculations on the advantages of noodle boxes
7	Noodles or Potatoes (a poetic view)
7.1	Digression on potatoes
8	Attempt at setting up a working schedule
9	Possibility of tomato sauce - The temporal element (365 days)
10	Comparison with other guys in similar situations

PAGE REFERENCE	TOPICS
96	Speculations as to how long it takes to get used to America
97	About inner desires and the Ocean
97.1	The Call of the Ocean
98	Things are shaping up
99	Difference between first person and third person narrative
100	Discussion of plot from a personal point of view
101	Various ways of seeing the problem particularly the room and more about the cost of toilet paper
102	Cigarettes
103	About the possibility of giving up – First mention of the Tenor Saxophone
104	Remembrance of Northern High School (Detroit)
105	The protagonist and music
106	Learning how to play the clarinet
107	Life in Detroit as a jazz musician and as a factory worker
108	Ernest and Ernest's mother – Joseph and Joseph's uncle
109	A noodle Map of America
110	Reflections on the noodle map of America
111	Possibility of a substitute for the noodle map – Noodle & Reality
112	Now Then: relationship between the narrator and the protagonist
113	About the protagonist's father
113-114	About the protagonist's first birthday party in America

PAGE REFERENCE   TOPICS
- -

```
       *
      ***
     *****
    *******
     *****
      ***
       *
```

WARNING: The AUTHOR (that is to say the <u>fourth</u> person) is
             solely responsible --

                           and not the editor
                                   the printer
                                   the designer
                                   the publisher

                           nor the protagonist (<u>third</u> person)
                               the inventor (<u>second</u> person)
                               the recorder (<u>first</u> person)

                           nor anyone else (known or unknown)

             for any typing and typographical mistakes
             factual errors
             misrepresentations
             miscalculations
             misconceptions
             conneries
             saloperies
             obscenities
             immoralities
             stupidities
             or anything else (visible or invisible)

             that the potential READER (commentator or critic) of this
             discourse may find objectionable!